Arabian Nights

Paper Mill Press Illustrated Classics
is an imprint of Book Depot Inc.
67 Front Street North, Thorold, L2V 1X3 Canada
Printed in China
www.bookdepot.com
Selection, design, arrangement, typesetting, and image reproduction all copyright.
©2022 North Parade Publishing
All rights reserved

ISBN: 978-1-77402-218-4

25 24 23 22 • 5 4 3 2 1

Arabian Nights

An Illustrated Classic

by Anonymous

with color illustrations by Alida Massari

Contents

Color Illustrations

Introduction

Treacherous enchanters, exquisite maidens, intrepid adventurers and exotic lands—the tales of the Arabian Nights have them all. A collection of Middle Eastern folk tales which probably date back to between the tenth and fourteenth centuries, the stories offer a fascinating portrayal of Oriental life, full of Eastern richness and splendor.

They were first brought to us at the start of the 18th century by a French professor named Antoine Galland, who was fascinated by the Orient and who translated into French stories from an Arabic book which he had come across. Since then multiple translations and multiple collections of the stories have been published, and the tales have gained popularity across the world.

Over time the stories have become woven together within the framework of one tale—that of the beautiful maiden Scheherazade who spins yarns each night in the hope that her new husband, a great sultan, will postpone her execution because of his curiosity about how the stories will end. For this reason the stories were originally titled "The Book of a Thousand Nights and a Night" (or "A Thousand and One Nights").

This edition brings together some of the best known of the stories, and one or two less familiar tales, and combines them with some of the earliest line art illustrations by renowned artists such as George Soper, Réné Bull, John Betten and H. J. Ford, along with enchanting new coloured illustrations by Alida Massari.

Let the magic and adventure begin …

THE SULTAN AND HIS VOW

It is written in the chronicles of the Sassanian monarchs that there once lived an illustrious prince, beloved by his own subjects for his wisdom and his prudence, and feared by his enemies for his courage and for the hardy and well-disciplined army of which he was the leader. This prince had two sons, the elder called Schahriar, and the younger Schahzenan, both equally good and deserving of praise.

When the old king died at the end of a long and glorious reign, Schahriar, his eldest son, ascended the throne and reigned in his stead. Schahzenan, however, was not in the least envious, and a friendly contest soon arose between the two brothers as to which could best promote the happiness of the other. Schahzenan did all he could to show his loyalty and affection, while the new sultan loaded his brother with all possible honors, and in order that he might in some degree share the sultan's power and wealth, bestowed on him the kingdom of Great Tartary. Schahzenan immediately went to take possession of the empire allotted him, and fixed his residence at Samarcand, the chief city.

After a separation of ten years Schahriar so ardently desired to see his brother, that he sent his first vizier, with a splendid embassy, to invite him to revisit his court. As soon as Schahzenan was informed of the approach of the vizier, he went out to meet him, with all his ministers, in most magnificent dress, and inquired after the health of the sultan, his brother. Having replied to these affectionate inquiries, the vizier told the purpose of his coming. Schahzenan, who was much affected at the kindness and recollection of his brother, then addressed the vizier in these words: "Sage vizier, the sultan, my brother, does me too much honor. It is impossible that his wish to see me can exceed my desire of again beholding him. You have come at a happy moment. My kingdom is tranquil, and in ten days' time I will be ready to depart with you. Meanwhile pitch your tents on this spot, and I will order every refreshment and accommodation for you and your whole train."

At the end of ten days everything was ready, and Schahzenan took a tender leave of the queen, his consort. Accompanied by such officers as he had appointed to attend him, he left Samarcand in the evening and camped near the tents of his brother's ambassador, that they might proceed on their journey early the following morning. Wishing, however, once more to see his queen, whom he tenderly loved, he returned privately to the palace, and went directly to her apartment. There, to his extreme grief, he found her in the company of a slave whom she plainly loved better than himself. Yielding to the first outburst of his indignation, the unfortunate monarch drew his scimitar, and with one rapid stroke slew them both.

He then went from the city as privately as he had entered it, and returned to his pavilion. Not a word did he say to any one of what had happened. At dawn he ordered the tents to be struck, and the party set forth on their journey to the sound of drums and other musical instruments. The whole train was filled with joy, except the king, who could think of nothing but his queen, and he was a prey to the deepest grief and melancholy during the whole journey.

When he approached the capital of Persia he perceived the Sultan Schahriar and all his court coming out to greet him. As soon as the parties met the two brothers alighted and embraced each other; and after a thousand expressions of regard, remounted and entered the city amid the shouts of the multitude. The sultan there conducted the king his brother to a palace which had been prepared for him. This palace communicated by a garden with the sultan's own and was even more magnificent, as it was the spot where all the fêtes and splendid entertainments of the court were given.

Schahriar left the King of Tartary in order that he might bathe and change his dress; but immediately on his return from the bath went to him again. They seated themselves on a sofa, and conversed till supper time. After so long a separation they seemed even more united by affection than by blood. They ate supper together, and then continued their conversation till Schahriar, perceiving the night far advanced, left his brother to repose.

The unfortunate Schahzenan retired to his couch; but if in the presence of the sultan he had for a while forgotten his grief, it now returned with doubled force. Every circumstance of the queen's death arose to his mind and kept him awake, and left such a look of sorrow on his face that next morning the sultan could not fail to notice it. He did all in his power to show his continued love and affection, and sought to amuse his brother with the most splendid entertainments, but the gayest fêtes served only to increase Schahzenan's melancholy.

One morning when Schahriar had given orders for a grand hunting party at the distance of two days' journey from the city, Schahzenan requested permission to remain in his palace on account of a slight illness. The sultan, wishing to please him, consented, but he himself went with all his court to partake of the sport.

The King of Tartary was no sooner alone than he shut himself up in his apartment, and gave way to his sorrow. But as he sat thus grieving at the open window, looking out upon the beautiful garden of the palace, he suddenly saw the sultana, the beloved wife of his brother, meet a man in the garden with whom she held an affectionate conversation. Upon witnessing this interview, Schahzenan determined that he would no longer give way to such inconsolable grief for a misfortune which came to other husbands as well as to himself. He ordered supper to be brought, and ate with a better appetite than he had before done since leaving Samarcand. He even enjoyed the fine concert performed while he sat at table.

Schahriar returned from the hunt at the close of the second day, and was delighted at the change which he soon found had taken place in his brother. He urged him to explain the cause of his former depression and of his present joy. The King of Tartary, feeling it his duty to obey his suzerain lord, related the story of his wife's misconduct, and of the severe punishment which he had visited on her. Schahriar expressed his full approval of his brother's conduct.

"I own," he said, "had I been in your place I should have been less easily satisfied. I should not have been contented to take away the life of one woman, but should have sacrificed a thousand to my resentment. Your fate, surely, is most singular. Since, however, it has pleased God to afford you consolation, which, I am sure, is as well founded as was your grief, inform me, I beg, of that also."

Schahzenan was very reluctant to relate what he had seen, but at last yielded to the urgent commands and entreaties of his brother, and told him of the faithlessness of his own queen.

At this unexpected news, the rage and grief of Schahriar knew no bounds. He far exceeded his brother in his invectives and indignation. Not only did he sentence to death his unhappy sultana but bound himself by a solemn vow that, immediately on the departure of the king his brother, he would marry a new wife every night, and command her to be strangled in the morning. Schahzenan soon after had a solemn audience of leave, and returned to his own kingdom, laden with the most magnificent presents.

When Schahzenan was gone the sultan began to carry out his unhappy oath. Every night he married the daughter of some one of his subjects, and the next morning she was ordered out and put to death. It was the duty of the grand vizier to execute these commands of the sultan's, and revolting as they were to him, he was obliged to submit or lose his own head.

The report of this unexampled inhumanity spread a panic of consternation throughout the city. Instead of the praises and blessings with which, until now, they had loaded their monarch, all his subjects poured out curses on his head.

The grand vizier had two daughters, the elder of whom was called Scheherazade, and the younger Dinarzade. Scheherazade was possessed of a remarkable degree of courage. She had read much, and had so good a memory that she never forgot anything she had once read or heard. Her beauty was equaled only by her virtuous disposition. The vizier was passionately fond of her.

One day as they were talking together, she made the astonishing request that she might have the honor of becoming the sultan's bride. The grand vizier was horrified, and tried to dissuade her. He pointed out the fearful penalty attached to the favor she sought. Scheherazade, however, persisted, telling her father she had in mind a plan which she thought might put a stop to the sultan's dreadful cruelty.

"I am aware of the danger I run, my father," she said, "but it does not deter me from my purpose. If I die, my death will be glorious; if I succeed, I shall render my country an important service."

Still the vizier was most reluctant to allow his beloved child to enter on so dangerous an enterprise, and attempted to turn her from her purpose by telling her the following story:

THE FABLE OF THE ASS, THE OX, AND THE LABORER

A very rich merchant had several farmhouses in the country, where he bred every kind of cattle.

This merchant understood the language of beasts. He obtained this privilege on the condition of not imparting to any one what he heard, under penalty of death.

By chance he had put an ox and an ass into the same stall; and being seated near them, he heard the ox say to the ass: "How happy do I think your lot. A servant looks after you with great care, washes you, feeds you with fine sifted barley, and gives you fresh and clean water; your greatest task is to carry the merchant, our master. My condition is as unfortunate as yours is pleasant. They yoke me to a plow the whole day, while the laborer urges me on with his goad. The weight and force of the plow, too, chafes all the skin from my neck. When I have worked from morning till night, they give me unwholesome and uninviting food. Have I not, then, reason to envy your lot?"

When he had finished, the ass replied in these words: "Believe me, they would not treat you thus if you possessed as much courage as strength. When they come to tie you to the manger, what resistance, pray, do you ever make? Do you ever push them with your horns? Do you ever show your anger by stamping on the ground with your feet? Why don't you terrify them with your bellowing? Nature has given you the means of making yourself respected, and yet you neglect to use them. They bring you bad beans and chaff. Well, do not eat them; smell at them only and leave them. Thus, if you follow my plans, you will soon perceive a change, which you will thank me for."

The ox took the advice of the ass very kindly, and declared himself much obliged to him.

Early the next

morning the laborer came for the ox, and yoked him to the plow, and set him to work as usual. The latter, who had not forgotten the advice he had received, was very unruly the whole day; and at night, when the laborer attempted to fasten him to the stall, he ran bellowing back, and put down his horns to strike him; in short, he did exactly as the ass had advised him.

On the next morning, when the man came, he found the manger still full of beans and chaff, and the ox lying on the ground with his legs stretched out, and making a strange groaning. The laborer thought him very ill, and that it would be useless to take him to work; he, therefore, immediately went and informed the merchant.

The latter perceived that the bad advice of the ass had been followed; and he told the laborer to go and take the ass instead of the ox, and not fail to give him plenty of exercise. The man obeyed; and the ass was obliged to drag the plow the whole day, which tired him the more because he was unaccustomed  to it; besides which, he was so beaten that he could scarcely support himself when he came back, and fell down in his stall half dead.

Here the grand vizier said to Scheherazade: "You are, my child, just like this ass, and would expose yourself to destruction."

"Sir," replied Scheherazade, "the example which you have brought does not alter my resolution, and I shall not cease importuning you till I have obtained from you the favor of presenting me to the sultan as his consort."

The vizier, finding her persistent in her request, said, "Well then, since you will remain thus obstinate, I shall be obliged to treat you as the rich merchant I mentioned did his wife."

Being told in what a miserable state the ass was, he was curious to know what passed between him and the ox. After supper, therefore, he went out by moonlight, accompanied by his wife, and sat down near them; on his arrival, he heard the ass say to the ox, "Tell me, brother, what you mean to do when the laborer brings you food to-morrow!"

"Mean to do!" replied the ox. "Why, what you taught me, to be sure."

"Take care," interrupted the ass, "what you are about, lest you destroy yourself; for in coming home yesterday evening, I heard our master say these sad words: 'Since the ox can neither eat nor support himself, I wish him to be killed to-morrow; do not, therefore, fail to send for the butcher.' This is what I heard; and the interest I take in your safety, and the friendship I have for you, induces me to mention it. When they bring you beans and chaff, get up, and begin eating directly. Our master, by this, will suppose that you have recovered, and will, without doubt, revoke the sentence for your death; in my opinion, if you act otherwise, it is all over with you."

This speech produced the intended effect; the ox was much troubled, and lowed with fear. The merchant, who had listened to everything with great attention, burst into a fit of laughter that quite surprised his wife.

"Tell me," said she, "what you laugh at, that I may join in it. I wish to know the cause."

"That satisfaction," replied the husband, "I cannot afford you. I can only tell you that I laughed at what the ass said to the ox; the rest is a secret, which I must not reveal."

"And why not?" asked his wife.

"Because, if I tell you, it will cost me my life."

"You trifle with me," added she; "this can never be true; and if you do not immediately inform me what you laughed at, I swear by Allah that we will live together no longer."

In saying this, she went back to the house in a pet, shut herself up, and cried the whole night. Her husband, finding that she continued in the same state all the next day, said, "How foolish it is to afflict yourself in this way! Do I not seriously tell you, that if I were to yield to your foolish importunities, it would cost me my life?"

"Whatever happens rests with Allah," said she; "but I shall not alter my mind."

"I see very plainly," answered the merchant, "it is not possible to make you submit to reason, and that your obstinacy will kill you."

He then sent for the parents and other relations of his wife; when they were all assembled, he explained to them his motives for calling them together, and requested them to use all their influence with his wife, and endeavor to convince her of the folly of her conduct. She rejected them all, and said she had rather die than give up this point to her husband. When her children saw that nothing could alter her resolution, they began to lament most bitterly—the merchant himself knew not what to do.

A little while afterward he was sitting by chance at the door of his house, considering whether he should not even sacrifice himself in order to save his wife, whom he so tenderly loved, when he saw his favorite dog run up to the cock in the farmyard, and tell him all the circumstances of the painful situation in which he was placed. Upon which the cock said, "How foolish must our master be. He has but one wife, and cannot gain his point, while I have fifty, and do just as I please. Let him take a good-sized stick, and not scruple to use it, and she will soon know better, and not worry him to reveal what he ought to keep secret." The merchant at once did as he suggested, on which his wife quickly repented of her ill-timed curiosity, and all her family came in, heartily glad at finding her more rational and submissive to her husband.

"You deserve, my daughter," added the grand vizier, "to be treated like the merchant's wife."

"Do not, sir," answered Scheherazade, "think ill of me if I still persist in my sentiments. The history of this woman does not shake my resolution. I could recount, on the other hand, many good reasons which ought to persuade you not to oppose my design. Pardon me, too, if I add that your opposition will be useless; for if your paternal tenderness should refuse the request I make, I will present myself to the sultan."

At length the vizier, overcome by his daughter's firmness, yielded to her entreaties; and although he was very sorry at not being able to conquer her resolution, he immediately went to Schahriar, and announced to him that Scheherazade herself would be his bride on the following night.

The sultan was much astonished at the sacrifice of the grand vizier. "Is it possible," said he, "that you can give up your own child?"

"Sire," replied the vizier, "she has herself made the offer. The dreadful fate that hangs over her does not alarm her; and she resigns her life for the honor of being the consort of your majesty, though it be but for one night."

"Vizier," said the sultan, "do not deceive yourself with any hopes; for be assured that, in delivering Scheherazade into your charge to-morrow, it will be with an order for her death; and if you disobey, your own head will be the forfeit."

"Although," answered the vizier, "I am her father, I will answer for the fidelity of this arm in fulfilling your commands."

When the grand vizier returned to Scheherazade, she thanked her father; and observing him to be much afflicted, consoled him by saying that she hoped he would be so far from repenting her marriage with the sultan that it would become a subject of joy to him for the remainder of his life.

Before Scheherazade went to the palace, she called her sister, Dinarzade, aside, and said, "As soon as I shall have presented myself before the sultan, I shall entreat him to suffer you to sleep in the bridal chamber, that I may enjoy for the last time your company. If I obtain this favor, as I expect, remember to awaken me to-morrow morning an hour before daybreak, and say, 'If you are not asleep, my sister, I beg of you, till the morning appears, to recount to me one of those delightful stories you know.' I will immediately begin to tell one; and I flatter myself that by these means I shall free the kingdom from the consternation in which it is."

Dinarzade promised to do with pleasure what she required.

Within a short time Scheherazade was conducted by her father to the palace, and was admitted to the presence of the sultan. They were no sooner alone than the sultan ordered her to take off her veil. He was charmed with her beauty; but perceiving her tears, he demanded the cause of them.

"Sire," answered Scheherazade, "I have a sister whom I tenderly love—I earnestly wish that she might be permitted to pass the night in this apartment, that we may again see each other, and once more take a tender farewell. Will you allow me the consolation of giving her this last proof of my affection?"

Schahriar having agreed to it, they sent for Dinarzade, who came directly. The sultan passed the night with Scheherazade on an elevated couch, as was the custom among the eastern monarchs, and Dinarzade slept at the foot of it on a mattress prepared for the purpose.

Dinarzade, having awakened about an hour before day, did what her sister had ordered her. "My dear sister," she said, "if you are not asleep, I entreat you, as it will soon be light, to relate to me one of those delightful tales you know. It will, alas, be the last time I shall receive that pleasure."

Instead of returning any answer to her sister, Scheherazade addressed these words to the sultan: "Will your majesty permit me to indulge my sister in her request?"

"Freely," replied he.

Scheherazade then desired her sister to attend, and, addressing herself to the sultan, began as follows:

"Will your majesty permit me to indulge my sister in her request?"

THE STORY OF THE MERCHANT
AND THE GENIE

There was formerly, sire, a merchant, who was possessed of great wealth, in land, merchandise, and ready money. Having one day an affair of great importance to settle at a considerable distance from home, he mounted his horse, and with only a sort of cloak-bag behind him, in which he had put a few biscuits and dates, he began his journey. He arrived without any accident at the place of his destination; and having finished his business, set out on his return.

On the fourth day of his journey he felt himself so incommoded by the heat of the sun that he turned out of his road, in order to rest under some trees by which there was a fountain. He alighted, and tying his horse to a branch of the tree, sat down on its bank to eat some biscuits and dates from his little store. When he had satisfied his hunger he amused himself with throwing about the stones of the fruit with considerable velocity. When he had finished his frugal repast he washed his hands, his face, and his feet, and repeated a prayer, like a good Mussulman.

He was still on his knees, when he saw a genie, white with age and of an enormous stature, advancing toward him, with a scimitar in his hand. As soon as he was close to him he said in a most terrible tone: "Get up, that I may kill thee with this scimitar, as thou hast caused the death of my son." He accompanied these words with a dreadful yell.

The merchant, alarmed by the horrible figure of this giant, as well as by the words he heard, replied in trembling accents: "How can I have slain him? I do not know him, nor have I ever seen him."

"Didst thou not," replied the giant, "on thine arrival here, sit down, and take some dates from thy wallet; and after eating them, didst thou not throw the stones about on all sides?"

"This is all true," replied the merchant; "I do not deny it."

"Well, then," said the other, "I tell thee thou hast killed my son; for while thou wast throwing about the stones, my son passed by; one of them struck him in the eye, and caused his death, and thus hast thou slain my son."

"Ah, sire, forgive me," cried the merchant.

"I have neither forgiveness nor mercy," replied the giant; "and is it not just that he who has inflicted death should suffer it?"

"I grant this; yet surely I have not done so: and even if I have, I have done so innocently, and therefore I entreat you to pardon me, and suffer me to live."

"No, no," cried the genie, still persisting in his resolution, "I must destroy thee, as thou hast killed my son."

At these words, he took the merchant in his arms, and having thrown him with his face on the ground, he lifted up his saber, in order to strike off his head.

Scheherazade, at this instant perceiving it was day, and knowing that the sultan rose early to his prayers, and then to hold a council, broke off.

"What a wonderful story," said Dinarzade, "have you chosen!"

"The conclusion," observed Scheherazade, "is still more surprising, as you would confess if the sultan would suffer me to live another day, and in the morning permit me to continue the relation."

Schahriar, who had listened with much pleasure to the narration, determined to wait till to-morrow, intending to order her execution after she had finished her story.

He arose, and having prayed, went to the council.

The grand vizier, in the meantime, was in a state of cruel suspense. Unable to sleep, he passed the night in lamenting the approaching fate of his daughter, whose executioner he was compelled to be. Dreading, therefore, in this melancholy situation, to meet the sultan, how great was his surprise in seeing him enter the council chamber without giving him the horrible order he expected!

The sultan spent the day, as usual, in regulating the affairs of his kingdom, and on the approach of night, retired with Scheherazade to his apartment.

On the next morning, the sultan did not wait for Scheherazade to ask permission to continue her story, but said, "Finish the tale of the genie and the merchant. I am curious to hear the end of it." Scheherazade immediately went on as follows:

When the merchant, sire, perceived that the genie was about to execute his purpose, he cried aloud: "One word more, I entreat you; have the goodness to grant me a little delay; give me only one year to go and take leave of my dear wife and children, and I promise to return to this spot, and submit myself entirely to your pleasure."

"Take Allah to witness of the promise thou hast made me," said the other.

"Again I swear," replied he, "and you may rely on my oath." On this the genie left him near the fountain, and immediately disappeared.

The merchant, on his reaching home, related faithfully all that had happened to him. On hearing the sad news, his wife uttered the most lamentable groans, tearing her hair and beating her breast; and his children made the house resound with their grief. The father, overcome by affection, mingled his tears with theirs.

The year quickly passed. The good merchant having settled his affairs, paid his just debts, given alms to the poor, and made provision to the best of his ability for his wife and family, tore himself away amid the most frantic expressions of grief; and mindful of his oath, he arrived at the destined spot on the very day he had promised.

While he was waiting for the arrival of the genie, there suddenly appeared an old man leading a hind, who, after a respectful salutation, inquired what brought him to that desert place. The merchant satisfied the old man's curiosity, and related his adventure, on which he expressed a wish to witness his interview with the genie. He had scarcely finished his speech when another old man, accompanied by two black dogs, came in sight, and having heard the tale of the merchant, he also determined to remain to see the event.

Soon they perceived, toward the plain, a thick vapor or smoke, like a column of dust raised by the wind. This vapor approached them, and then suddenly disappearing, they saw the genie, who, without noticing the others, went toward the merchant, scimitar in hand. Taking him by the arm, "Get up," said he, "that I may kill thee, as thou hast slain my son."

Both the merchant and the two old men, struck with terror, began to weep and fill the air with their lamentations.

When the old man who conducted the hind saw the genie lay hold of the merchant, and about to murder him without mercy, he threw himself at the monster's feet, and, kissing them, said, "Lord Genie, I humbly entreat you to suspend your rage, and hear my history, and that of the hind, which you see; and if you find it more wonderful and surprising than the adventure of this merchant, whose life you wish to take, may I not hope that you will at least grant me one half part the blood of this unfortunate man?"

After meditating some time, the genie answered, "Well then, I agree to it."

THE HISTORY OF THE FIRST OLD MAN AND THE HIND

The hind, whom you, Lord Genie, see here, is my wife. I married her when she was twelve years old, and we lived together thirty years, without having any children. At the end of that time I adopted into my family a son, whom a slave had borne. This act of mine excited against the mother and her child the hatred and jealousy of my wife. During my absence on a journey she availed herself of her knowledge of magic

to change the slave and my adopted son into a cow and a calf, and sent them to my farm to be fed and taken care of by the steward.

Immediately on my return I inquired after my child and his mother.

"Your slave is dead," said she, "and it is now more than two months since I have beheld your son; nor do I know what has become of him."

I was sensibly affected at the death of the slave; but as my son had only disappeared, I flattered myself that he would soon be found. Eight months, however, passed, and he did not return; nor could I learn any tidings of him. In order to celebrate the festival of the great Bairam, which was approaching, I ordered my bailiff to bring me the fattest cow I possessed, for a sacrifice. He obeyed my commands. Having bound the cow, I was about to make the sacrifice, when at the very instant she lowed most sorrowfully, and the tears even fell from her eyes. This seemed to me so extraordinary that I could not but feel compassion for her, and was unable to give the fatal blow. I therefore ordered her to be taken away, and another brought.

My wife, who was present, seemed very angry at my compassion, and opposed my order.

I then said to my steward, "Make the sacrifice yourself; the lamentations and tears of the animal have overcome me."

The steward was less compassionate, and sacrificed her. On taking off the skin we found hardly anything but bones, though she appeared very fat.

"Take her away," said I to the steward, truly chagrined, "and if you have a very fat calf, bring it in her place."

He returned with a remarkably fine calf, who, as soon as he perceived me, made so great an effort to come to me that he broke his cord. He lay down at my feet, with his head on the ground, as if he endeavored to excite my compassion, and to entreat me not to have the cruelty to take away his life.

"Wife," said I, "I will not sacrifice this calf, I wish to favor him. Do not you, therefore, oppose it."

She, however, did not agree to my proposal; and continued to demand his sacrifice so obstinately that I was compelled to yield. I bound the calf, and took the fatal knife to bury it in his throat, when he turned his eyes, filled with tears, so persuasively upon me, that I had no power to execute my intention. The knife fell from my hand, and I told my wife I was determined to have another calf. She tried every means to induce me to alter my mind; I continued firm, however, in my resolution, in spite of all she could say; promising, for the sake of appeasing her, to sacrifice this calf at the feast of Bairam on the following year.

The next morning my steward desired to speak with me in private. He informed me that his daughter, who had some knowledge of magic, wished to speak with me. On being admitted to my presence, she informed me that during my absence my wife had turned the slave and my son into a cow and calf, that I had already sacrificed the cow, but that she could restore my son to life if I would give him to her for her husband, and allow her to visit my wife with the punishment her cruelty had deserved. To these proposals I gave my consent.

The damsel then took a vessel full of water, and pronouncing over it some words I did not understand, she threw the water over the calf, and he instantly regained his own form.

"My son! My son!" I exclaimed, and embraced him with transport. "This damsel has destroyed the horrible charm with which you were surrounded. I am sure your gratitude will induce you to marry her, as I have already promised for you."

He joyfully consented; but before they were united the damsel changed my wife into this hind, which you see here.

Since this, my son has become a widower, and is now traveling. Many years have passed since I have heard anything of him. I have, therefore, now set out with a view to gain some information; and as I did not like to trust my wife to the care of any one during my search, I thought proper to carry her along with me. This is the history of myself and this hind. Can anything be more wonderful?

"I agree with you," said the genie, "and in consequence, I grant to you a half of the blood of this merchant."

As soon as the first old man had finished, the second, who led the two black dogs, made the same request to the genie for a half of the merchant's blood, on the condition that his tale exceeded in interest the one that had just been related. On the genie signifying his assent, the old man began.

THE HISTORY OF THE SECOND OLD MAN AND THE TWO BLACK DOGS

Great Prince of the genies, you must know that these two black dogs, which you see here, and myself, are three brothers. Our father, when he died, left us one thousand sequins each. With this sum we all embarked in business as merchants. My two brothers determined to travel, that they might trade in foreign parts. They were both unfortunate, and returned at the end of two years in a state of abject poverty, having lost their all. I had in the meanwhile prospered. I gladly received them, and gave them one thousand sequins each, and again set them up as merchants.

My brothers frequently proposed to me that I should make a voyage with them for the purpose of traffic. Knowing their former want of success, I refused to join them, until at the end of five years I at length yielded to their repeated solicitations. On consulting on the merchandise to be

*"Great Prince of the genies, you must know that these two black dogs,
which you see here, and myself, are three brothers."*

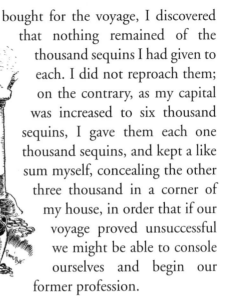

bought for the voyage, I discovered that nothing remained of the thousand sequins I had given to each. I did not reproach them; on the contrary, as my capital was increased to six thousand sequins, I gave them each one thousand sequins, and kept a like sum myself, concealing the other three thousand in a corner of my house, in order that if our voyage proved unsuccessful we might be able to console ourselves and begin our former profession.

We purchased our goods, embarked in a vessel, which we ourselves freighted, and set sail with a favorable wind. After sailing about a month, we arrived, without any accident, at a port, where we landed, and had a most advantageous sale for our merchandise. I, in particular, sold mine so well that I gained ten for one.

About the time that we were ready to embark on our return, I accidentally met on the seashore a female of great beauty, but very poorly dressed. She accosted me by kissing my hand, and entreated me most earnestly to permit her to be my wife. I stated many difficulties to such a plan; but at length she said so much to persuade me that I ought not to regard her poverty, and that I should be well satisfied with her conduct, I was quite overcome. I directly procured proper dresses for her, and after marrying her in due form, she embarked with me, and we set sail.

During our voyage I found my wife possessed of so many good qualities that I loved her every day more and more. In the meantime my two brothers, who had not traded so advantageously as myself, and who were jealous of my prosperity, began to feel exceedingly envious. They even went so far as to conspire against my life; for one night, while my wife and I were asleep, they threw us into the sea. I had hardly, however, fallen into the water, before my wife took me up and transported me to an island. As soon as it was day she thus addressed me:

"You must know that I am a fairy, and being upon the shore when you were about to sail, I wished to try the goodness of your heart, and for this purpose I presented myself before you in the disguise you saw. You acted most generously, and I am therefore delighted in finding an occasion of showing my gratitude, and I trust, my husband, that in saving your life I have not ill rewarded the good you have done me. But I am enraged against your brothers, nor shall I be satisfied till I have taken their lives."

I listened with astonishment to the discourse of the fairy, and thanked her, as well as I was able, for the great obligation she had conferred on me.

"But, madam," said I to her, "I must entreat you to pardon my brothers."

I related to her what I had done for each of them, but my account only increased her anger.

"I must instantly fly after these ungrateful wretches," cried she, "and bring them to a just punishment; I will sink their vessel, and precipitate them to the bottom of the sea."

"No, beautiful lady," replied I, "for heaven's sake moderate your indignation, and do not execute so dreadful an intention; remember, they are still my brothers, and that we are bound to return good for evil."

No sooner had I pronounced these words, than I was transported in an instant from the island, where we were, to the top of my own house. I descended, opened the doors, and dug up the three thousand sequins which I had hidden. I afterward repaired to my shop, opened it, and received the congratulations of the merchants in the neighborhood on my arrival. When I returned home I perceived these two black dogs, which came toward me with a submissive air. I could not imagine what this meant, but the fairy, who soon appeared, satisfied my curiosity.

"My dear husband," said she, "be not surprised at seeing these two dogs in your house; they are your brothers."

My blood ran cold on hearing this, and I inquired by what power they had been transformed into that state.

"It is I," replied the fairy, "who have done it, and I have sunk their ship; for the loss of the merchandise it contained I shall recompense you. As to your brothers, I have condemned them to remain under this form for ten years, as a punishment for their perfidy."

Then informing me where I might hear of her, she disappeared.

The ten years are now completed, and I am traveling in search of her. This, O Lord Genie, is my history; does it not appear to you of a most extraordinary nature?

"Yes," replied the genie, "I confess it is most wonderful, and therefore I grant you the other half of this merchant's blood," and having said this, the genie disappeared, to the great joy of the merchant and of the two old men.

The merchant did not omit to bestow many thanks upon his liberators, who, bidding him adieu, proceeded on their travels. He remounted his horse, returned home to his wife and children, and spent the remainder of his days with them in tranquillity.

THE THREE CALENDERS, SONS OF KINGS, AND THE FIVE LADIES OF BAGDAD

In the reign of Caliph Haroun al Raschid there was at Bagdad a porter, who was a fellow of infinite wit and humor. One morning as he was at the place where he usually waited for employment, with a great basket before him, a handsome lady, covered with a great muslin veil, accosted him, and said with a pleasant air, "Hark you, porter, take your basket and follow me."

The delighted porter took his basket immediately, set it on his head, and followed the lady, exclaiming, "Oh, happy day! Oh, day of good luck!"

In a short time the lady stopped before a gate and knocked: a Christian, with a venerable long white beard, opened it, and she put money into his hand without speaking; but the Christian, who knew what she wanted, went in, and shortly after brought out a large jar of excellent wine.

"Take this jar," said the lady to the porter, "and put it into the basket."

This being done, she desired him to follow her, and walked on; the porter still exclaiming, "Oh, day of happiness! Oh, day of agreeable surprise and joy!"

The lady stopped at a fruit shop, where she bought some apples, apricots, peaches, lemons, citrons, oranges, myrtles, sweet basil, lilies, jasmine, and some other plants. She told the porter to put all those things into his basket and follow her. Passing by a butcher's shop, she ordered five and twenty pounds of his finest meat to be weighed, which was also put into the porter's basket.

At another shop she bought capers, small cucumbers, parsley, and other herbs; at another, some pistachios, walnuts, hazelnuts, almonds, kernels of the pine, and other similar fruits; at a third, she purchased all sorts of almond patties.

The porter, in putting all these things into his basket, said, "My good lady, you should have told me that you intended buying so many things, and I would have provided a camel to carry them, for if you buy ever so little more, I shall not be able to bear it."

The lady laughed at the fellow's pleasant humor, and ordered him still to follow her.

She then went to a druggist's, where she furnished herself with all manner of sweet-scented waters, cloves, musk, pepper, ginger, and a great piece of ambergris, and several other Indian spices; this quite filled the porter's basket and she ordered him to follow her. They walked till they came

to a magnificent house, whose front was adorned with fine columns, and had a gate of ivory. There they stopped, and the lady knocked softly. Another lady soon came to open the gate, and all three, after passing through a handsome vestibule, crossed a spacious court, surrounded by an open gallery which communicated with many magnificent apartments, all on the same floor. At the end of this court there was a dais richly furnished, with a couch in the middle, supported by four columns of ebony, enriched with diamonds and pearls of an extraordinary size, and covered with red satin, relieved by a bordering of Indian gold. In the middle of the court there was a large basin lined with white marble, and full of the finest transparent water, which rushed from the mouth of a lion of gilt bronze.

But what principally attracted the attention of the porter, was a third most beautiful lady, who was seated on the couch before mentioned. This lady was called Zobeide, she who opened the door was called Safie, and the name of the one who had been for the provisions was Amina. Then said Zobeide, accosting the other two, "Sisters, do you not see that this honest man is ready to sink under his burden? Why do you not ease him of it?"

Then Amina and Safie took the basket, the one before and the other behind; Zobeide also assisted, and all three together set it on the ground, and then emptied it. When they had done, the beautiful Amina took out money and paid the porter liberally.

The porter was well satisfied, but when he ought to have departed he was chained to the spot by the pleasure of beholding three such beauties, who appeared to him equally charming; for Amina, having now laid aside her veil, proved to be as handsome as either of the others. What surprised him most was that he saw no man about the house, yet most of the provisions he had brought in, as the dry fruits and the several sorts of cakes and confections, were adapted chiefly for those who could drink and make merry.

"Madam," said he, addressing Zobeide, "I am sensible that I act rudely in staying longer than I ought, but I hope you will have the goodness to pardon me, when I tell you that I am astonished not to see a man with three ladies of such extraordinary beauty; and you know that a company of women without men is as melancholy as a company of men without women."

To this he added some pleasantries in proof of what he advanced; and did not forget the Bagdad proverb, "That the table is not completely furnished, except there be four in company"; so concluded, that since they were but three, they wanted another.

The ladies fell a-laughing at the porter's reasoning; after which Zobeide gravely addressed him, "Friend, you presume rather too much; and though you do not deserve it, I have no objection to inform you that we are three sisters, who transact our affairs with so much secrecy that no one knows anything of them. A good author says, 'Keep thy own secret, and do not reveal it to any one. He that maketh his secret known is no longer its master. If thy own breast cannot keep thy counsel, how canst thou expect the breast of another to be more faithful?'"

"Permit me, I entreat thee, to say, that I also have read in another a maxim, which I have always happily practiced: 'Conceal thy secret,' he says, 'only from such as are known to be indiscreet, and who will abuse thy confidence; but make no difficulty in discovering it to prudent men, because they know how to keep it.' The secret, then, with me, is as safe as if locked up in a cabinet, the key of which is lost and the door sealed."

The porter, notwithstanding his rhetoric, must, in all probability, have retired in confusion if Amina had not taken his part, and said to Zobeide and Safie, "My dear sisters, I conjure you to let him remain; he will afford us some diversion. Were I to repeat to you all the amusing things he addressed to me by the way, you would not feel surprised at my taking his part."

At these words of Amina the porter fell on his knees, kissed the ground at her feet, and raising himself up, said, "Most beautiful lady, you began my good fortune to-day, and now you complete it by this generous conduct. I cannot adequately express my acknowledgments. As to the rest, ladies," said he, addressing himself to all the three sisters, "since you do me so great an honor, I shall always look upon myself as one of your most humble slaves."

When he had spoken these words he would have returned the money he had received, but Zobeide ordered him to keep it.

"What we have once given," said she, "we never take back. We are willing, too, to allow you to stay on one condition, that you keep secret and do not ask the reason for anything you may see us do. To show you," said Zobeide, with a serious countenance, "that what we demand of you is not a new thing among us, read what is written over our gate on the inside."

The porter read these words, written in large characters of gold: "He who speaks of things that do not concern him, shall hear things that will not please him."

"Ladies," said he, "I swear to you that you shall never hear me utter a word respecting what does not relate to me, or wherein you may have any concern."

These preliminaries being settled, Amina brought in supper, and after she had lighted up the room with tapers made of aloewood and ambergris, which yield a most agreeable perfume as well as a delicate light, she sat down with her sisters and the porter. They began again to eat and drink, to sing, and repeat verses. The ladies diverted themselves by intoxicating the porter, under pretext of making him drink their healths, and the repast was enlivened by reciprocal sallies of wit. When they were all as merry as possible, they suddenly heard a knocking at the gate.

Safie, whose office it was, went to the porch, and quickly returning, told them thus: "There are three calenders at the door, all blind of the right eye, and have their heads, beards, and eyebrows shaved. They say that they are only just arrived at Bagdad, where they have never been before; and, as it is dark, and they know not where to lodge, they knocked at our door by chance and pray us to show compassion, and to take them in. They care not where we put them, provided they obtain shelter. They are young and handsome; but I cannot, without laughing, think of their amusing and exact likeness to each other. My dear sisters, pray permit them to come in; they will afford us diversion enough, and put us to little charge, because they desire shelter only for this night, and resolve to leave us as soon as day appears."

"Go, then," said Zobeide, "and bring them in, but make them read what is written over the gate." Safie ran out with joy, and in a little time after returned with the three calenders.

At their entrance they made a profound obeisance to the ladies, who rose up to receive them and told them courteously that they were welcome, that they were glad of the opportunity to oblige them and to contribute toward relieving the fatigues of their journey, and at last invited them to sit down with them.

The magnificence of the place, and the civility they received, inspired the calenders with high respect for the ladies; but before they sat down, having by chance cast their eyes upon the porter, whom they saw clad almost like those devotees with whom they have continual disputes respecting several points of discipline, because they never shave their beards nor eyebrows, one of them said, "I believe we have got here one of our revolted Arabian brethren."

The porter, having his head warm with wine, took offense at these words, and with a fierce look, without stirring from his place, answered, "Sit you down, and do not meddle with what does not concern you. Have you not read the inscription over the gate? Do not pretend to make people live after your fashion, but follow ours."

"Honest man," said the calender, "do not put yourself in a passion. We should be sorry to give you the least occasion. On the contrary, we are ready to receive your commands." Upon which, to put an end to the dispute, the ladies interposed, and pacified them. When the calenders were seated, the ladies served them with meat; and Safie, being highly pleased with them, did not let them want for wine.

When the calenders had finished their repast, they signified to the ladies that they wished to entertain them with a concert of music, if they had any instruments in the house, and would cause them to be brought. The ladies willingly accepted the proposal, and Safie went to fetch the instruments. Each man took the instrument he liked, and all three together began to play a tune. The ladies, who knew the words of a merry song that suited the air, joined the concert with their voices; but the words of the song made them now and then stop, and fall into excessive laughter. While their amusement was at its height, there was a knock of unwonted loudness at their gate.

Now, it was the custom of the sultan Haroun al Raschid sometimes during the night to go through the city in disguise, in order to discover whether everything was quiet. On this evening he set out from his palace accompanied by Giafar, his grand vizier, and Mesrour, chief of the household, all three disguised as merchants. He it was, who, in passing through the street, was attracted by the noise of the music and of the peals of loud laughter, and had desired his grand vizier to knock at the gate, and to demand shelter and admittance as for three strangers who knew not where to seek shelter for the night. Safie, who had opened the door, came back and obtained permission of her sisters to admit the newly arrived strangers.

The caliph and his attendants, upon their entrance, most courteously made obeisance to the ladies and to the calenders. The ladies returned their salutations, supposing them to be merchants. Zobeide, as the chief, addressed them with a grave and serious countenance and said, "You are welcome. But while you are here you must have eyes but no tongues; you must not ask the reason of anything you may see, nor speak of anything that does not concern you, lest you hear and see what will by no means please you."

"Madam," replied the vizier, "you shall be obeyed. It is enough for us to attend to our own business, without meddling with what does not concern us." After this, each seated himself, and the conversation became general, and they drank to the health of the new guests.

While the vizier Giafar entertained them, the caliph ceased not from admiring the beauty, elegance, and lively disposition of the ladies; while the appearance of the three calenders, all blind of the right eye, surprised him very much. He anxiously wished to learn the cause of this singularity, but the conditions they had imposed upon him and his companions prevented any inquiry. Besides all this, when he reflected upon the richness of the services and furniture, with the regularity and arrangement everywhere apparent, he could hardly persuade himself it was not the effect of enchantment.

The guests continued their conversation, when, after an interval, Zobeide rose up, and taking Amina by the hand, said to her, "Come, sister, the company shall not prevent us from doing as we have always been accustomed."

Amina, who perfectly understood what her sister meant, got up, and took away the dishes, tables, bottles, glasses, and also the instruments on which the calenders had played. Nor did Safie remain idle; she snuffed the candles, and added more aloewood and ambergris. Having done this, she requested the three calenders to sit on a sofa on one side, and the caliph and his company on the other.

"Get up," said she then to the porter, looking at him, "and be ready to assist in whatever we want of you."

A little while after, Amina came in with a sort of seat, which she placed in the middle of the room. She then went to the door of a closet, and having opened it, she made a sign to the porter to approach.

"Come and assist me," she cried. He did so, and went in with her, and returned a moment after, followed by two black dogs, each of them secured by a collar and chain. They appeared as if they had been severely whipped with rods, and he brought them into the middle of the apartment.

Zobeide, rising from her seat between the calenders and the caliph, moved very gravely toward the porter.

"Come," said she, heaving a deep sigh, "let us perform our duty."

She then tucked up her sleeves above her elbows, and receiving a rod from Safie, "Porter," said she, "deliver one of the dogs to my sister Amina, and bring the other to me."

The porter did as he was commanded. Upon this, the dog that he held in his hand began to howl, and, turning toward Zobeide, held

her head up in a supplicating posture; but Zobeide, having no regard to the sad countenance of the animal, which would have moved any one else to pity, nor to its cries that resounded through the house, whipped her with the rod till she was out of breath; and having spent her strength, threw down the rod, and taking the chain from the porter, lifted up the dog by her paws, and looking upon her with a sad and pitiful countenance, they both wept. After this Zobeide, with her handkerchief, wiped the tears from the dog's eyes, kissed her, returned the chain to the porter, and desired him to carry the dog to the place whence he took her, and to bring the other. Then taking the whip, she served this in the same manner; she then wept with it, dried its tears, kissed it, and returned it to the porter.

The three calenders, with the caliph and his companions, were extremely surprised at this exhibition, and could not comprehend why Zobeide, after having so furiously beaten those two dogs, that by the Mussulman religion are reckoned unclean animals, should weep with them, wipe off their tears, and kiss them. They muttered among themselves; and the caliph, who, being more impatient than the rest, longed exceedingly to be informed of the cause of so strange a proceeding, could not forbear making signs to the vizier to ask the question. The vizier turned his head another way; but being pressed by repeated signs, he answered by others, that it was not yet time for the caliph to satisfy his curiosity.

Zobeide sat still some time in the middle of the room, where she had whipped the two dogs, to recover herself of her fatigue; and Safie called to her, "Dear sister, will you not be pleased to return to your place, that I may also act my part?"

"Yes, sister," replied Zobeide, and then went and sat down upon the sofa, having the caliph, Giafar, and Mesrour on her right hand, and the three calenders, with the porter, on her left.

The whole company remained silent for some time. At last Safie, sitting on a chair in the middle of the room, spoke to her sister Amina: "Dear sister, I conjure you to rise; you know what I would say." Amina rose, and went into another closet near to that where the dogs were, and brought out a case covered with yellow satin, richly embroidered with gold and green silk. She went toward Safie and opened the case, from whence she took a lute, and presented it to her; and after some time spent in tuning it, Safie began to play, and, accompanying the instrument with her voice, sang a song about the torments that absence creates to lovers.

Having sung with much passion and action, she said to Amina, "Pray take it, sister, for my voice fails me; oblige the company with a tune and a song in my stead."

"Very willingly," replied Amina, who, taking the lute from her sister Safie, sat down in her place. Having sung most delightfully, the caliph expressed his admiration. While he was doing so, Amina fainted away; and on opening her robe to give her air, they discovered that her breast was covered with fearful scars.

While Zobeide and Safie ran to assist their sister, the caliph inquired of the calender, "Cannot you inform me about these two black dogs, and this lady, who appears to have been so ill-treated?"

"Sir," said the calender, "we never were in this house before now, and entered it only a few minutes sooner than you did."

This increased the astonishment of the caliph.

"Perhaps," said he, "the man who is with you can give you some information?"

The calender made signs to the porter to draw near, and asked him if he knew why the black dogs had been beaten, and why the bosom of Amina was so scarred.

"Sir," replied the porter, "if you know nothing of the matter, I know as little as you do. I never was in the house until now; and if you are surprised to see me here, I am as much so to find myself in your company."

The caliph, more and more perplexed at all he heard, determined that he would have the information he required for the explaining these mysterious proceedings. But the question was, who should first make the inquiry? The caliph endeavored to persuade the calenders to speak first, but they excused themselves. At last they all agreed that the porter should be the man.

While they were consulting how to put the question, Zobeide herself, as Amina had recovered from her fainting, approached them, and inquired, "What are you talking of? What is your contest about?"

The porter then addressed her as follows: "These gentlemen, madam, entreat you to explain why you wept with those dogs, after having treated them so ill, and how it has happened that the lady who fainted has her bosom covered with scars."

At these words Zobeide put on a stern look, and turning toward the caliph and the rest of the company: "Is it true, gentlemen," said she, "that you desired him to ask me these questions?"

All of them, except the vizier Giafar, who spoke not a word, answered "Yes." She thereupon exclaimed, in a tone of resentment: "Before we granted you the favor of receiving you into our house, and to prevent all occasion of inquiry from you, we imposed the condition that you should not speak of anything that did not concern you, lest you might hear that which would not please you; and yet, after having received our entertainment, you make no scruple to break your promise. Our easy compliance with your wishes may have occasioned this, but that shall not excuse your rudeness."

As she spoke these words, she gave three stamps with her foot, and clapping her hands as often together, cried, "Come quickly!"

Upon this a door flew open, and seven black slaves rushed in; each one seized a man, threw him to the ground, and dragged him into the middle of the room, brandishing a scimitar over his head.

We can easily conceive the alarm of the caliph. He repented, but too late, that he had not taken the advice of his vizier, who, with Mesrour, the calenders, and porter, were, from his ill-timed curiosity, on the point of forfeiting their lives.

Before they gave the fatal stroke, one of the slaves said to Zobeide and her sisters, "Would it not be right to interrogate them first?" On which Zobeide, with a grave voice, said: "Answer me, and say who you are, otherwise you shall not live one moment longer. I cannot believe you to be honest men, or persons of authority or distinction in your own countries; for, if you were, you would have been more modest and more respectful to us."

The caliph, naturally warm, was infinitely more indignant than the rest, to find his life depending upon the command of a woman: but he began to conceive some hopes, when he found she wished to know who they all were; for he imagined that she would by no means take away his life when she should be informed of his rank. He whispered to his vizier, who was near him, instantly to declare who he was. But this wise vizier, being more prudent, resolved to save his master's honor, and not let the world know the affront he had brought upon himself by his own imprudence; and therefore answered, "We have what we deserve."

But if he had intended to speak as the caliph commanded him, Zobeide would not have allowed him time: for having turned to the calenders, and seeing them all blind with one eye, she asked if they were brothers.

One of them answered, "No, madam, no otherwise than as we are calenders; that is to say, as we observe the same rules."

"Were you born blind of the right eye?" continued she.

"No, madam," answered he; "I lost my eye in such a surprising adventure, that it would be instructive to every one to hear it."

Zobeide put the same question to the others in their turn, when the last she addressed replied, "Pray, madam, show some pity on us, for we are all the sons of kings. Although we have never seen each other before this evening, we have had sufficient time to become acquainted with this circumstance; and I can assure you that the kings who have given us birth have made some noise in the world!"

During this speech Zobeide became less angry, and said to the slaves, "Give them their liberty a while, but remain where you are. Those who tell us their history, and the occasion of their coming, do them not hurt, let them go where they please; but do not spare those who refuse to give us that satisfaction."

The three calenders, the caliph, the grand vizier Giafar, the captain of his guards, and the porter were all in the middle of the hall, seated upon a carpet in the presence of the three ladies, who reclined upon a sofa, and the slaves stood ready to do whatever their mistresses should command.

The porter spoke first, and briefly related the adventures of the morning with Amina, and the kind favors to him of herself and her fair sisters in the evening, which he declared to be the whole of his history.

When the porter had concluded, Zobeide said, "Save thyself and begone, nor ever let us see thee again."

"I beg of you, madam," replied he, "to let me remain a little longer. It would be unfair that I should not hear their histories, after they have had the pleasure of hearing mine."

Saying this, he took his place at the end of the sofa, truly delighted at finding himself free from the danger which so much alarmed him.

One of the calenders, addressing himself to Zobeide, next spoke.

The three calenders, the caliph, the grand vizier Giafar, the captain of his guards, and the three sisters.

THE HISTORY OF THE FIRST CALENDER

Madam, I am the son of a sultan. My father had a brother, who reigned over a neighboring kingdom. His son, my cousin, and I were nearly of the same age. I went regularly every year to see my uncle, at whose court I amused myself for a month or two, and then returned home.

On one occasion I arrived at my father's capital, where, contrary to custom, I found a numerous guard at the gate of the palace. They surrounded me as I entered. The commanding officer said, "Prince, the army has proclaimed the grand vizier sultan, instead of your father, who is dead, and I take you prisoner in the name of the new sultan."

This rebel vizier had long entertained a mortal hatred toward me. When I was a boy I loved to shoot with a crossbow. Being one day upon the terrace of the palace, and a bird happening to come by, I shot but missed him, and the ball by misfortune hit the vizier, who was taking the air upon the terrace of his own house, and put out one of his eyes. He never forgave me, and, as opportunity offered, made me sensible of his resentment. But now that he had me in his power he came to me like a madman, and thrusting his finger into my right eye, pulled it out, and thus I became blind of one eye.

His cruelty did not stop here; he commanded the executioner to cut off my head, and leave me to be devoured by birds of prey. The executioner conveyed me to the place of execution to complete this barbarous sentence, but by my prayers and tears, I moved the man's compassion: "Go," said he to me, "get you speedily out of the kingdom, and never return, or you will destroy yourself and me."

I thanked him, and as soon as I was left alone, comforted myself for the loss of my eye by considering that I had very narrowly escaped a much greater evil.

Being thus surrounded with sorrows and persecuted by fortune, I had recourse to a stratagem, which was the only means left me to save my

life: I caused my beard and eyebrows to be shaved, and putting on a calender's habit, I passed, unknown by any, out of the city. I avoided the towns till I arrived in the empire of the commander of the faithful, the renowned caliph Haroun al Raschid, when I ceased to fear. I resolved to come to Bagdad and throw myself at the feet of this great monarch. I shall move him to compassion, said I to myself, by the relation of my uncommon misfortunes, and without doubt he will take pity on a persecuted prince, and not suffer me to implore his assistance in vain.

In short, after a journey of several months, I arrived to-day at the gate of this city, into which I entered at dusk: and as I entered, another calender came up. He saluted me, and I him.

"You appear," said I, "to be a stranger, as I am."

"You are not mistaken," replied he.

He had no sooner returned this answer, than a third calender overtook us. He saluted us, and told us he was a stranger newly come to Bagdad; so that as brethren we joined together, resolving not to separate from one another.

It was now late, and we knew not where to seek a lodging in the city, where we had never been before. But good fortune having brought us to your gate, we made bold to knock, when you received us with so much kindness that we are incapable of rendering suitable thanks. This, madam, is, in obedience to your commands, the account I was to give how I lost my right eye, wherefore my beard and eyebrows are shaved, and how I came to be with you at this time.

"It is enough," said Zobeide; "you may retire to what place you think fit."

The calender begged the ladies' permission to stay till he had heard the relations of his two comrades, "whom I cannot," said he, "leave with honor"; and that he might also hear those of the three other persons in company.

The history of the first calender appeared very surprising to the whole company, and particularly to the caliph. The presence of the slaves, armed with their scimitars, did not prevent him from saying in a whisper to the vizier, "As long as I can remember, I never heard anything to compare with this history of the calender, though I have been all my life in the habit of hearing similar narratives."

He had no sooner finished than the second calender began, and addressing himself to Zobeide, spoke as follows:

THE HISTORY OF THE SECOND CALENDER

Madam, to obey your commands, and to show you by what strange accident I became blind of the right eye, I must give you the account of my life. I was yet a youth when the sultan, my father (for you must know I am a prince by birth), perceived that I was endowed with good natural ability, and spared nothing proper for improving it. No sooner was I able to read and write than I learned the Koran from beginning to end by heart, all the traditions collected from the mouth of our prophet, and the works of poets. I applied myself to geography, chronology, and to speak the Arabian language in its purity; not forgetting in the meantime all such exercises as were proper for a prince to understand. But one thing which I was fond of, and succeeded in, was penmanship. In this I surpassed all the celebrated scribes of our kingdom.

The fame of my learning reached the Emperor of Hindustan, who sent an embassy with rich presents to my father and invited me to his court. I returned with the ambassador.

We had been about a month on our journey when we saw in the distance an immense cloud of dust, and soon after we discovered fifty fierce horsemen, sons of the desert, well armed.

Not being able to repel force by force, we told them we were the ambassadors of the sultan of India; but the sons of the desert insolently answered, "Why do you wish us to respect the sultan, your master? We are not his subjects, nor even within his realm." They attacked us on all sides.

I defended myself as long as I could, but finding that I was wounded, and that the ambassador and all our attendants were overthrown, I took advantage of the remaining strength of my horse, and escaped. My horse was wounded and suddenly fell dead under me. Alone, wounded, and a stranger, I bound up my own wound and walked on the rest of the day, and arrived at the foot of a mountain, where I perceived, as the sun set, a cave; I went in, and stayed there that night, after I had eaten some fruits that I gathered by the way. I continued my journey for several successive days without finding any place of abode; but after a month's time I came to a large town, well inhabited. It was surrounded by several streams, so that it seemed to enjoy perpetual spring.

My face, hands, and feet were black and sunburnt; and by my long journey, my boots were quite worn out, so that I was forced to walk barefooted; and my clothes were all in rags. I entered the town to inform myself where I was, and addressed myself to a tailor that was at work in his shop. He made me sit down by him, and asked me who I was, from whence I came, and what had brought me thither. I did not conceal anything that had befallen me, nor made I any scruple to reveal to him my rank. The tailor listened to me with attention; then he brought me something to eat, and offered me an apartment at his house, which I accepted.

Some days after my arrival the tailor asked me if I knew anything by which I could acquire a livelihood. I told him that I was well versed in the science of laws, both human and divine; that I was a grammarian, a poet, and, above all, that I wrote remarkably well.

"None of these things will avail you here. If you will follow my advice," he added, "you will procure a short jacket, and as you are strong and in good health, you may go into the neighboring forest and cut wood for fuel. You may then go and expose it for sale in the market. By these means you will be enabled to wait till the cloud which hangs over you, and obliges you to conceal your birth, shall have blown over. I will furnish you with a cord and hatchet."

The next day the tailor brought me a rope, a hatchet, and a short jacket, and recommended me to some poor people who gained their bread after the same manner, that they might take me into their company. They conducted me to the wood, and the first day I brought in as much upon my head as procured me half a piece of gold of the money of that country; for though the wood was not far distant from the town, yet it was very scarce, by reason that few would be at the trouble of fetching it for themselves. I gained a good sum of money in a short time, and repaid my tailor what he had loaned me.

I continued this way of living for a whole year. One day, having by chance penetrated farther into the wood than usual, I happened to light on a pleasant spot, where I began to cut. In pulling up the root of a tree I espied an iron ring, fastened to a trap door of the same metal. I took away the earth that covered it, and having lifted it up, discovered a flight of stairs, which I descended with my ax in my hand.

When I had reached the bottom I found myself in a palace, which was as well lighted as if it had been above ground in the open air. I was going forward along a gallery supported by pillars of jasper, the base and capitals being of massy gold, when I saw a lady of a noble and graceful air, and extremely beautiful, coming toward me.

I hastened to meet her; and as I was making a low obeisance she asked me, "Are you a man, or a genie?"

"A man, madam," said I.

"By what adventure," said she, fetching a deep sigh, "are you come hither? I have lived here for twenty-five years, and you are the first man I have beheld in that time."

Her great beauty, and the sweetness and civility wherewith she received me, emboldened me to say, "Madam, before I satisfy your curiosity, give me leave to say that I am infinitely gratified with this unexpected meeting, which offers me an occasion of consolation in the midst of my affliction; and perhaps it may give me an opportunity of making you also more happy than you are."

I then related my story to her from beginning to end.

"Alas! prince," she replied, sighing, "the most enchanting spots cannot afford delight when we are there against our will. But hear now my history. I am a princess, the daughter of a sultan, the king of the Ebony Island, to which the precious wood found in it has given its name.

"The king, my father, had chosen for my husband a prince, who was my cousin; but on the very night of the bridal festivities, in the midst of the rejoicings of the court, a genie took me away. I fainted with alarm, and when I recovered I found myself in this place. I was long inconsolable; but time and necessity have reconciled me to see the genie. Twenty-five years I have passed in this place, in which I have everything necessary for life and splendor.

"Every ten days," continued the princess, "the genie visits me. In the meantime, if I have any occasion for him, I have only to touch a talisman, and he appears. It is now four days since he was here, and I have therefore to wait six days more before he again makes his appearance.

You, therefore, may remain five with me, if it be agreeable to you, in order to keep me company; and I will endeavor to regale and entertain you equal to your merit and dignity."

The princess then conducted me to a bath, the most commodious, and the most sumptuous imaginable; and when I came forth, instead of my own clothes I found a costly robe, which I did not esteem so much for its richness as because it made me appear worthy to be in her company. We sat down on a sofa covered with rich tapestry, with cushions of the rarest Indian brocade; and some time after she covered a table with several dishes of delicate meats. We ate, and passed the remaining part of the day, as also the evening, together very pleasantly.

The next day I said to her, "Fair princess, you have been too long buried alive in this subterranean palace; pray rise—follow me and enjoy the light of day, of which you have been deprived so many years."

"Prince," replied she, with a smile, "if you out of ten days will grant me nine, and resign the tenth to the genie, the light of day would be nothing to me."

"Princess," said I, "the fear of the genie makes you speak thus. For my part, I regard him so little that I will break in pieces his talisman, with the spell that is written about it. Let him come; and how brave or powerful he be, I will defy him." On saying this I gave the talisman a kick with my foot, and broke it in pieces.

The talisman was no sooner broken than the whole palace shook as if ready to fall to atoms, and the walls opened to afford a passage to the genie. I had no sooner felt the shock than, at the earnest request of the princess, I took to flight. Having hastily put on my own robe, I ascended the stairs leading to the forest, and reached the town in safety. My landlord, the tailor, was very glad to see me.

In my haste, however, I had left my hatchet and cord in the princess's chamber.

Shortly after my return, while brooding over this loss and lamenting the cruel treatment to which the princess would be exposed, the tailor came in and said, "An old man, whom I do not know, brings your hatchet and cords, and wishes to speak to you, for he will deliver them to none but yourself."

At these words I changed color, and fell a-trembling. While the tailor was asking me the reason, my chamber door opened, and the old man, having no patience to stay, appeared with my hatchet and cords.

"I am a genie," said he, speaking to me, "a grandson of Eblis, prince of genies. Is not this your hatchet and are not these your cords?"

After the genie had put these questions to me he gave me no time to answer. He grasped me by the middle, dragged me out of the chamber, and mounting into the air carried me up to the skies with extraordinary swiftness. He descended again in like manner to the earth, which on a sudden he caused to open with a stroke of his foot, when I found myself

in the enchanted palace, before the fair princess of the Isle of Ebony. But, alas! what a spectacle was there! I saw what pierced me to the heart; this poor princess was weltering in her blood, and lay upon the ground, more like one dead than alive, with her cheeks bathed in tears.

The genie, having loaded us both with many insults and reproaches, drew his scimitar and declared that he would give life and liberty to either of us who would with his scimitar cut off the head of the other.

We both resolutely declined to purchase freedom at such a price, and asserted our choice to be to die rather in the presence of each other.

"I see," said the genie, "that you both outbrave me, but both of you shall know by my treatment of you of what I am capable."

At these words the monster took up the scimitar and cut off one of her hands, which left her only so much life as to give me a token with the other that she bade me forever adieu; and then she died.

I fainted at the sight.

When I was come to myself again, I cried, "Strike, for I am ready to die, and await death as the greatest favor you can show me."

But instead of killing me, he said, "Behold how genies revenge themselves on those who offend them. Thou art the least to blame, and I will content myself with transforming thee into a dog, ape, lion, or bird; take thy choice of any of these. I will leave it to thyself."

These words gave me some hopes of being able to appease him.

"O genie," said I, "restrain your rage, and since you will not take away my life, pardon me freely, as a good dervish pardoned one who envied him."

"And how was that?" said he.

I answered as follows:

THE HISTORY OF THE ENVIOUS MAN
AND OF HIM WHO WAS ENVIED

In a certain town there were two men, neighbors, who lived next door to each other. One of them was so excessively envious of the other that the latter resolved to change his abode and go and reside at some distance from him. He therefore sold his house, and went to another city at no great distance, and bought a convenient house. It had a good garden and a moderate court, in which there was a deep well that was not now used.

The good man, having made this purchase, put on the habit of a dervish, and in a short time he established a numerous society of dervishes.

He soon came to be known by his virtues, through which he acquired the esteem of many people, as well of the commonalty as of the chief of the city. In short, he was much honored and courted by all ranks. People came from afar to recommend themselves to his prayers; and all who visited him, published what blessings they received through his means.

The great reputation of this honest man having spread to the town from whence he had come, it touched the envious man so much to the quick that he left his own house and affairs with a resolution to ruin him. With this intent he went to the new convent of dervishes, of which his former neighbor was the head, who received him with all imaginable tokens of friendship. The envious man told him that he was come to communicate a business of importance, which he could not do but in private; "and that nobody may hear us," he said, "let us take a walk in your court; and seeing night begins to draw on, command your dervishes to retire to their cells." The chief of the dervishes did as he was requested.

When the envious man saw that he was alone with this good man, he began to tell him his errand, walking side by side in the court, till he saw his opportunity; and getting the good man near the brink of the well, he gave him a thrust, and pushed him into it.

This old well was inhabited by peris and genies, which happened luckily for the relief of the head of the convent; for they received and supported him, and carried him to the bottom, so that he got no hurt. He perceived that there was something extraordinary in his fall, which must otherwise have cost him his life; but he neither saw nor felt anything.

He soon heard a voice, however, which said, "Do you know what honest man this is, to whom we have done this service?"

Another voice answered, "No." To which the first replied, "Then I will tell you. This man, out of charity, left the town he lived in, and has established himself in this place, in hopes to cure one of his neighbors of the envy he had conceived against him; he had acquired such a general esteem that the envious man, not able to endure it, came hither on purpose to ruin him; and he would have accomplished his design had it not been for the assistance we have given this honest man, whose reputation is so great that the sultan, who keeps his residence in the neighboring city, was to pay him a visit to-morrow, to recommend the princess his daughter to his prayers."

Another voice asked, "What need had the princess of the dervish's prayers?" To which the first answered, "You do not know, it seems, that she is possessed by a genie. But I well know how this good dervish may cure her. He has a black cat in his convent, with a white spot at the end of her tail, about the bigness of a small piece of Arabian money; let him only pull seven hairs out of the white spot, burn them, and smoke the princess's head with the fumes. She will not only be immediately cured, but be so safely delivered from the genie that he will never dare approach her again."

The head of the dervishes remembered every word of the conversation between the fairies and the genies, who remained silent the remainder of the night. The next morning, as soon as daylight appeared, and he could discern the nature of his situation, the well being broken down in several places, he saw a hole, by which he crept out with ease.

The other dervishes, who had been seeking for him, were rejoiced to see him. He gave them a brief account of the wickedness of the man to whom he had given so kind a reception the day before, and retired into his cell. Shortly after, the black cat, which the fairies and genies had mentioned the night before, came to fawn upon her master, as she was accustomed to do; he took her up, and pulled seven hairs from the white spot that was upon her tail, and laid them aside for his use when occasion should serve.

Soon after sunrise the sultan, who would leave no means untried that he thought likely to restore the princess to perfect health, arrived at the gate of the convent. He commanded his guards to halt, while he with his principal officers went in. The dervishes received him with profound respect.

The sultan called their chief aside, and said, "Good Sheik, you may probably be already acquainted with the cause of my visit."

"Yes, sir," replied he gravely, "if I do not mistake, it is the disease of the princess which procures me this unmerited honor."

"That is the real case," replied the sultan. "You will give me new life if your prayers, as I hope they may, restore my daughter's health."

"Sir," said the good man, "if your majesty will be pleased to let her come hither, I am in hopes, through God's assistance, that she will be effectually cured."

The prince, transported with joy, sent immediately for his daughter, who soon appeared with a numerous train of ladies and attendants, veiled, so that her face was not seen. The chief of the dervishes caused a carpet to be held over her head, and he had no sooner thrown the seven hairs upon the burning coals than the genie uttered a great cry and, without being seen, left the princess at liberty; upon which she took the veil from her face, and rose up to see where she was, saying, "Where am I, and who brought me hither?"

At these words, the sultan, overcome with excess of joy, embraced his daughter and kissed her eyes; he also kissed the sheik's hands, and said to his officers, "What reward does he deserve that has thus cured my daughter?"

They all cried, "He deserves her in marriage."

"That is what I had in my thoughts," said the sultan; "and I make him my son-in-law from this moment."

Some time after, the prime vizier died, and the sultan conferred the office on the dervish. Then the sultan himself died, without heirs male; upon which the religious orders and the army consulted together, and the good man was declared and acknowledged sultan by general consent.

The honest dervish ascended the throne of his father-in-law. One day as he was in the midst of his courtiers on a march, he espied the envious man among the crowd that stood as he passed along. Calling one of the viziers that attended him, he whispered in his ear, "Go bring me that man you see there; but take care you do not frighten him."

The vizier obeyed, and when the envious man was brought into his presence the sultan said, "Friend, I am extremely glad to see you."

Then he called an officer. "Go immediately," said he, "and cause to be paid to this man out of my treasury, one hundred pieces of gold. Let him have also twenty loads of the richest merchandise in my storehouses, and a sufficient guard to conduct him to his house."

After he had given this charge to the officer he bade the envious man farewell, and proceeded on his march.

When I had finished the recital of this story to the genie I employed all my eloquence to persuade him to imitate so good an example, and to grant me pardon; but it was impossible to move his compassion.

"All that I can do for thee," said he, "is to grant thee thy life, but I must place thee under enchantments." So saying, he seized me violently, and carried me through the arched roof of the subterranean palace, which opened to give him passage. He ascended with me into the air to such a height that the earth appeared like a little white cloud. He then descended again like lightning, and alighted upon the summit of a mountain.

Here he took up a handful of earth, and, muttering some words which I did not understand, threw it upon me. "Quit," said he, "the form of a man, and take that of an ape."

He instantly disappeared, and left me alone, transformed into an ape, and overwhelmed with sorrow, in a strange country, not knowing whether I was near or far from my father's dominions.

I descended the mountain, and entered a plain, level country, which took me a month to travel over, and then I came to the seaside. It happened at the time to be perfectly calm, and I espied a vessel about half a league from the shore. Unwilling to lose so good an opportunity, I broke off a large branch from a tree, carried it into the sea, and placed myself astride upon it, with a stick in each hand, to serve me for oars.

I launched out on this frail bark, and rowed toward the ship. When I had approached sufficiently near to be seen, the seamen and passengers on the deck regarded me with astonishment. In the meantime I got on board, and laying hold of a rope, jumped upon the deck, but having lost my speech, I found myself in great perplexity. And indeed the risk I ran was not less than when I was at the mercy of the genie.

The merchants, being both superstitious and scrupulous, thought if they received me on board I should be the occasion of some misfortune to them during their voyage. On this account they said, "Let us throw him into the sea." Some one of them would not have failed to carry this threat into execution had I not gone to the captain, thrown myself at his feet, and taken hold of his skirt in a supplicating posture. This action, together with the tears which he saw gush from my eyes, moved his compassion. He took me under his protection, and loaded me with a thousand caresses. On my part, though I had not power to speak, I showed by my gestures every mark of gratitude in my power.

The wind that succeeded the calm continued to blow in the same direction for fifty days, and brought us safe to the port of a city, well peopled, and of great trade, where we cast anchor.

Our vessel was instantly surrounded with multitudes of boats full of people. Among the rest, some officers of the sultan came on board, and said "Our master rejoices in your safe arrival, and he beseeches each of you to write a few lines upon this roll. The prime vizier, who, besides possessing great abilities for the management of public affairs, could write in the highest perfection, died a few days since, and the sultan has made a solemn vow not to give the place to any one who cannot write equally well. No one in the empire has been judged worthy to supply the vizier's place."

Those of the merchants who thought they could write well enough to aspire to this high dignity wrote one after another what they thought fit. After they had done, I advanced, and took the roll, but all the people cried out that I would tear it or throw it into the sea, till they saw how properly I held the roll, and made a sign that I would write in my turn.

Their apprehensions then changed into wonder. However, as they had never seen an ape that could write, and could not be persuaded that I was more ingenious than others of my kind, they wished to take the roll out of my hand; but the captain took my part once more.

"Let him alone," said he; "allow him to write."

Perceiving that no one opposed my design, I took the pen, and wrote six sorts of hands used among the Arabians, and each specimen contained an extemporary distich or quatrain (a stanza of four lines) in praise of the sultan. When I had done, the officers took the roll, and carried it to the sultan.

The sultan took little notice of any of the writings except mine, which pleased him so much that he said to the officers, "Take the finest horse in my stable, with the richest trappings, and a robe of the most sumptuous brocade to put on the person who wrote the six hands, and bring him hither."

At this command the officers could not forbear laughing. The sultan was incensed at their rudeness, and would have punished them, had they not explained.

"Sir," said they, "we humbly beg your majesty's pardon. These hands were not written by a man, but by an ape."

"What do you say?" exclaimed the sultan. "Those admirable characters, are they not written by the hands of a man?"

"No, sir," replied the officers; "we assure your majesty that it was an ape, who wrote them in our presence."

The sultan was too much surprised at this account not to desire a sight of me, and therefore said, "Do what I command you, and bring me speedily that wonderful ape."

The officers returned to the vessel, and showed the captain their order, who answered, "The sultan's command must be obeyed." Whereupon they clothed me with the rich brocade robe, and carried me ashore, where they set me on horseback, while the sultan waited for me at his palace with a great number of courtiers.

The procession commenced; the harbor, the streets, the public places, windows, terraces, palaces, and houses were filled with an infinite number of people of all ranks, who flocked from every part of the city to see me; for the rumor was spread in a moment that the sultan had chosen an ape to be his grand vizier; and after having served for a spectacle to the people, who could not forbear to express their surprise by redoubling their shouts and cries, I arrived at the sultan's palace.

I found the prince on his throne in the midst of the grandees; I made my obeisance three times very low, and at last kneeled and kissed the ground before him, and afterward took my seat in the posture of an ape. The whole assembly viewed me with admiration, and could not comprehend how it was possible that an ape should so well understand how to pay the sultan his due respect; and he himself was more astonished than any. In short, the usual ceremony of the audience would have been complete, could I have added speech to my behavior.

The sultan dismissed his courtiers, and none remained by him but the chief of the attendants of the palace, a little young slave, and myself. He went from his chamber of audience into his own apartment, where he ordered dinner to be brought. As he sat at table, he made me a sign to approach and eat with them. To show my obedience, I kissed the ground, arose, and placed myself at the table, and ate.

Before the table was cleared, I espied a standish, which I made a sign to have brought me; having got it, I wrote upon a large peach some verses expressive of my acknowledgment to the sultan; who, having read them, after I had presented the peach to him, was still more astonished. When the things were removed, they brought him a particular liquor, of which he caused them to give me a glass. I drank, and wrote upon the glass some new verses, which explained the state of happiness I was now in, after many sufferings. The sultan read these likewise, and said, "A man that was capable of composing such poetry would rank among the greatest of men."

The sultan caused to be brought to him a chessboard, and asked me

I kissed the ground, arose, and placed myself at the table, and ate.

by a sign if I understood that game, and would play with him. I kissed the ground; and laying my hand upon my head, signified that I was ready to receive that honor. He won the first game; but I won the second and third; and perceiving he was somewhat displeased at my success, I made a stanza to pacify him, in which I told him that two potent armies had been fighting furiously all day, but that they concluded a peace toward the evening, and passed the remaining part of the night very amicably together upon the field of battle.

So many circumstances appearing to the sultan beyond what had ever either been seen or known of apes, he determined not to be the only witness of these prodigies himself, but having a daughter, called the Lady of Beauty, sent for her, that she should share his pleasure.

The princess, who had her face unveiled, no sooner came into the room than she put on her veil, and said to the sultan, "Sir, I am surprised that you have sent for me to appear before a man. That seeming ape is a young prince, son of a powerful sultan, and has been metamorphosed into an ape by enchantment. When I was just out of the nursery, an old lady who waited on me was a most expert magician, and taught me seventy rules of magic. By this science I know all enchanted persons at first sight: I know who they are, and by whom they have been enchanted; therefore do not be surprised if I should forthwith restore this prince, in spite of the enchantments, to his own form."

"Do so, then," interrupted the sultan, "for you cannot give me greater pleasure, as I wish to have him for my grand vizier, and bestow you upon him for a wife."

"I am ready, sire," answered the princess, "to obey you in all things you please to command."

The princess, the Lady of Beauty, went into her apartment, and brought thence a knife, which had some Hebrew words engraved on the blade: she made the sultan, the little slave, and myself, descend into a private court of the palace, and there left us under a gallery that went round it. She placed herself in the middle of the court, where she made a great circle, and within it she wrote several words in ancient Arabian characters.

When she had finished and prepared the circle, she placed herself in the center of it, where she began incantations, and repeated verses of the Koran. The air grew insensibly dark, as if it had been night; we found ourselves struck with consternation, and our fear increased when we saw the genie appear suddenly in the shape of a lion of gigantic size.

"Thou shalt pay dearly," said the lion, "for the trouble thou hast given me in coming here." In saying this, he opened his horrible jaws, and advanced to devour her; but she, being on her guard, jumped back, and had just time to pluck out a hair; and pronouncing two or three words, she changed it into a sharp scythe, with which she immediately cut the lion in two pieces, through the middle.

The two parts of the lion directly disappeared, and the head changed into a large scorpion. The princess then took the form of a serpent, and fought the scorpion, which, finding itself defeated, changed into an eagle, and flew away. But the serpent then became another eagle, black, and very large, and went in pursuit of it. We now lost sight of them for some time.

Shortly after they had disappeared, the earth opened before us, and a black and white cat appeared, the hairs of which stood quite on end, and which made a most horrible mewing. A black wolf directly followed after her, and gave her no time to rest. The cat, being thus hard pressed, changed into a worm, and hid itself in a pomegranate which lay by accident on the ground; but the pomegranate swelled immediately, and became as big as a gourd, which, lifting itself up to the roof of the gallery, rolled there for some time backward and forward; it then fell down again into the court, and broke into several pieces.

The wolf had in the meanwhile transformed itself into a cock, and now fell to picking up the seeds of the pomegranate one after another; but finding no more, he came toward us with his wings spread, making a great noise, as if he would ask us whether there were any more seed. There was one lying on the brink of the canal, which the cock perceiving as he went back, ran speedily thither; but just as he was going to pick it up the seed rolled into a fountain and turned into a little fish.

The cock, flying toward the fountain, turned into a pike, and pursued the small fish; they both continued under water above two hours, and we knew not what was become of them; but suddenly we heard terrible cries, which made us tremble, and a little while after we saw the genie and princess all in flames. They threw ashes of fire out of their mouths at each other, till they came to close combat; then the two fires increased, with a thick, burning smoke, which mounted so high that we had reason to apprehend it would set the palace on fire. But we very soon had a more pressing occasion of fear, for the genie, having got loose from the princess, came to the gallery where we stood, and blew flames of fire upon us. We must all have perished had not the princess, running to our assistance, forced him to retire, and to defend himself against her; yet, notwithstanding all her exertions, she could not hinder the sultan's beard from being burned, and his face scorched, and a spark from entering my right eye, and making it blind. The sultan and I expected nothing but death, when we heard a cry of "Victory, victory!" and instantly the princess appeared in her natural shape; but the genie was reduced to a heap of ashes.

The princess approached us and hastily called for a cupful of water, which the young slave, who had received no hurt, brought her. She took it, and after pronouncing some words over it, threw it upon me, saying, "If thou art become an ape by enchantment, change thy shape, and take that of a man, which thou hadst before." These words were hardly uttered when I again became a man in every respect as I was before my transformation, excepting the loss of my eye.

I was preparing to return the princess my thanks, but she prevented me by addressing herself to her father: "Sire, I have gained the victory over the genie; but it is a victory that costs me dear. I have but a few minutes to live; the fire has pierced me during the terrible combat, and I find it is gradually consuming me. This would not have happened had I perceived the last of the pomegranate seeds, and swallowed it, as I did the others when I was changed into a cock; the genie had fled thither as to his last intrenchment, and upon that the success of the combat depended. This oversight obliged me to have recourse to fire, and to fight with those mighty arms as I did, between heaven and earth, in your presence; for in spite of all, I made the genie know that I understood more than he; I have conquered, and reduced him to ashes, but I cannot escape death, which is approaching."

Suddenly the princess exclaimed, "I burn, I burn!" She found that the fire had at last seized upon her vital parts, which made her still cry, "I burn!" until death had put an end to her intolerable pain. The effect of that fire was so extraordinary, that in a few moments she was wholly reduced to ashes, as the genie had been.

I cannot tell you, madam, how much I was grieved at so dismal a spectacle; I had rather all my life have continued an ape or a dog, than to have seen my benefactress thus miserably perish. The sultan cried piteously, and beat himself on his head and breast, until, being quite overcome with grief, he fainted away. In the meantime, the attendants and officers came running at the sultan's lamentations, and with much difficulty brought him to himself.

When the knowledge of the death of the princess had spread through the palace and the city, all the people greatly bewailed. Public mourning was observed for seven days, and many ceremonies were performed. The ashes of the genie were thrown into the air; but those of the princess were collected into a precious urn, to be preserved; and the urn was deposited in a superb mausoleum constructed for that purpose on the spot where the princess had been consumed.

The grief of the sultan for the loss of his daughter confined him to his chamber for a whole month. Before he had fully recovered his strength, he sent for me and said, "You are the cause of all these misfortunes; depart hence therefore in peace, without further delay, and take care never again to appear in my dominions on penalty of thy life."

I was obliged to quit the palace, again cast down to a low estate, and an outcast from the world. Before I left the city I went into a bagnio, where I caused my beard and eyebrows to be shaved, and put on a calender's robe.

I passed through many countries without making myself known; at last I resolved to visit Bagdad, in hopes of meeting with the Commander of the Faithful, to move his compassion by relating to him my unfortunate adventures. I arrived this evening; and the first man I met was this calender, our brother, who spoke before me.

You know the remaining part, madam, and the cause of my having the honor to be here.

When the second calender had concluded his story, Zobeide, to whom he had addressed his speech, said, "It is well; you are at liberty": but instead of departing he also petitioned the lady to show him the same favor vouchsafed to the first calender, and went and sat down by him.

Then the third calender, knowing it was his turn to speak, addressed himself, like the others, to Zobeide, and began his history as follows:

THE HISTORY OF THE THIRD CALENDER

My story, O honorable lady, differs from those you have already heard. The two princes who have spoken before me have each lost an eye by events beyond their own control; but I lost mine through my own fault.

My name is Agib. I am the son of a sultan. After his death I took possession of his dominions, and continued in the city where he had resided. My kingdom is composed of several fine provinces upon the mainland, besides a number of valuable islands. My first object was to visit the provinces. I afterward caused my whole fleet to be fitted out, and went to my islands to gain the hearts of my subjects by my presence, and to confirm them in their loyalty. These voyages gave me some taste for navigation, in which I took so much pleasure that I resolved to make some discoveries beyond my own territories; to which end I caused ten ships to be fitted out, embarked, and set sail.

Our voyage was very pleasant for forty days successively; but on the forty-first night the wind became contrary, and so boisterous that we were nearly lost. I gave orders to steer back to my own coast; but I perceived at the same time that my pilot knew not where we were. Upon the tenth day a seaman, being sent to look out for land from the masthead, gave notice that he could see nothing but sky and sea, but that right ahead he perceived a great blackness.

The pilot changed color at this account, and throwing his turban on the deck with one hand, and beating his breast with the other, cried, "O sir, we are all lost; not one of us can escape; and with all my skill it is not in my power to effect our deliverance."

I asked him what reason he had thus to despair.

He exclaimed, "The tempest has brought us so far out of our course that to-morrow about noon we shall be near the black mountain, or mine of adamant, which at this very minute draws all your fleet toward it by virtue of the iron in your ships; and when we approach within a certain distance the attraction of the adamant will have such force that all the nails will be drawn out of the sides and bottoms of the ships, and fasten to the mountain, so that your vessels will fall to pieces and sink. This mountain," continued the pilot, "is inaccessible. On the summit there is a dome of fine brass, supported by pillars of the same metal, and on the top of that dome stands a horse, likewise of brass, with a rider on his back, who has a plate of lead fixed to his breast, upon which some talismanic characters are engraved. Sir, the tradition is, that this statue is the chief cause why so many ships and men have been lost and sunk in this place, and that it will ever continue to be fatal to all those who have the misfortune to approach, until it shall be thrown down."

The pilot having finished his discourse, began to weep afresh, and all the rest of the ship's company did the same, and they took farewell of each other.

The next morning we distinctly perceived the black mountain. About noon we were so near that we found what the pilot had foretold to be true; for all the nails and iron in the ships flew toward the mountain, where they fixed, by the violence of the attraction, with a horrible noise; the ships split asunder, and their cargoes sank into the sea.

All my people were drowned, but God had mercy on me and permitted me to save myself by means of a plank, which the wind drove ashore just at the foot of the mountain. I did not receive the least hurt; and my good fortune brought me to a landing place where there were steps that led up to the summit of the mountain.

At last I reached the top, without accident. I went into the dome, and, kneeling on the ground, gave God thanks for His mercies.

I passed the night under the dome. In my sleep an old grave man appeared to me, and said, "Hearken, Agib; as soon as thou art awake dig up the ground under thy feet: thou wilt find a bow of brass, and three arrows of lead. Shoot the three arrows at the statue, and the rider and his horse will fall into the sea; this being done, the sea will swell and rise to the

foot of the dome. When it has come so high, thou wilt perceive a boat, with one man holding an oar in each hand; this man is also of metal, but different from that thou hast thrown down; step on board, but without mentioning the name of God, and let him conduct thee. He will in ten days' time bring thee into another sea, where thou shalt find an opportunity to return to thy country, provided, as I have told thee, thou dost not mention the name of God during the whole voyage."

When I awoke I felt

much comforted by the vision, and did not fail to observe everything that the old man had commanded me. I took the bow and arrows out of the ground, shot at the horseman, and with the third arrow I overthrew him and the horse. In the meantime the sea swelled and rose up by degrees. When it came as high as the foot of the dome upon the top of the mountain, I saw, afar off, a boat rowing toward me, and I returned God thanks.

When the boat made land I stepped aboard, and took great heed not to pronounce the name of God, neither spoke I one word. I sat down, and the man of metal began to row off from the mountain. He rowed without ceasing till the ninth day, when I saw some islands, which gave me hopes that I should escape all the danger that I feared. The excess of my joy made me forget what I was forbidden: "God is great! God be praised!" said I.

I had no sooner spoken than the boat and man sank, casting me upon the sea. I swam until night, when, as my strength began to fail, a wave vast as a mountain threw me on the land. The first thing I did was to strip, and to dry my clothes.

The next morning I went forward to discover what sort of country I was in. I had not walked far before I found I was upon a desert, though a very pleasant island, abounding with trees and wild shrubs bearing fruit. I recommended myself to God, and prayed Him to dispose of me according to His will.

Immediately after, I saw a vessel coming from the mainland, before the wind, directly toward the island. I got up into a very thick tree, from whence, though unseen, I might safely view them. The vessel came into a little creek, where ten slaves landed, carrying a spade and other instruments for digging up the ground. They went toward the middle of the island, where they dug for a considerable time, after which they lifted up a trapdoor. They returned again to the vessel, and unloaded several sorts of provisions and furniture, which they carried to the place where they had been digging; they then descended into a subterranean dwelling.

I saw them once more go to the ship, and return soon after with an old man, who led a handsome lad of about fifteen years of age. They all descended when the trapdoor had been opened. After they had again come up, they let down the trapdoor, covered it over with earth, and returned to the creek where the ship lay; but I saw not the young man in their company. This made me believe that he had stayed behind in the subterranean cavern.

The old man and the slaves went on board, and steered their course toward the mainland. When I perceived they had proceeded to such a distance that I could not be seen by them, I came down from the tree, and went directly to the place where I had seen the ground broken. I removed the earth by degrees, till I came to a stone two or three feet square. I lifted it up, and found that it covered the head of a flight of stairs, also of stone. I descended, and at the bottom found myself in a large room, brilliantly lighted, and furnished with a carpet, a couch covered with tapestry, and cushions of rich stuff, upon which the young man sat.

The young man, when he perceived me, was considerably alarmed; but I made a low obeisance, and said to him, "Sir, do not fear. I am a king, and I will do you no harm. On the contrary, it is probable that your good destiny may have brought me hither to deliver you out of this tomb, where it seems you have been buried alive. But what surprises me (for you must know that I have seen all that hath passed since your coming into this island) is, that you suffered yourself to be entombed in this place without any resistance."

The young man, much assured at these words, with a smiling countenance requested me to seat myself by him. As soon as I was seated he said: "Prince, my story will surprise you. My father is a jeweler. He has many slaves, and also agents at the several courts, which he furnishes with precious stones. He had been long married without having issue when he dreamed that he should have a son, though his life would be but short. Some time after, I was born, which occasioned great joy in the family. My father, who had observed the very moment of my birth, consulted astrologers about my nativity, and was answered, 'our son shall live happily till the age of fifteen, when his life will be exposed to a danger which he will hardly be able to escape. But if his good destiny preserve him beyond that time, he will live to a great age. It will be,' said they, 'when the statue of brass, that stands upon the summit of the mountain of adamant, shall be thrown into the sea by Prince Agib, and, as the stars prognosticate, your son will be killed fifty days afterward by that prince.'

"My father took all imaginable care of my education until this year, which is the fifteenth of my age. He had notice given him yesterday that the statue of brass had been thrown into the sea about ten days ago. This news alarmed him much; and, in consequence of the prediction of the astrologers, he took the precaution to form this subterranean habitation to hide me in during the fifty days after the throwing down of the statue; and therefore, as it is ten days since this happened, he came hastily hither to conceal me, and promised at the end of forty days to return and fetch me away. For my own part, I am sanguine in my hopes, and cannot believe that Prince Agib will seek for me in a place under ground, in the midst of a desert island."

He had scarcely done speaking when I said to him, with great joy: "Dear sir, trust in the goodness of God, and fear nothing. I will not leave you till the forty days have expired, of which the foolish astrologers have made you apprehensive; and in the meanwhile I will do you all the service in my power; after which, with leave of your father and yourself, I shall have the benefit of getting to the mainland in your vessel; and when I am returned into my kingdom, I will remember the obligations I owe you, and endeavor to demonstrate my gratitude by suitable acknowledgments."

This discourse encouraged the jeweler's son, and inspired him with confidence. I took care not to inform him I was the very Agib whom he dreaded, lest I should alarm his fears. I found the young man of ready wit, and partook with him of his provisions, of which he had enough to have lasted beyond the forty days though he had had more guests than myself. In short, madam, we spent thirty-nine days in this subterranean abode in the pleasantest manner possible.

The fortieth day appeared; and in the morning, when the young man awoke, he said to me, with a transport of joy that he could not restrain, "Prince, this is the fortieth day, and I am not dead, thanks to God and your good company. My father will not fail to make you, very shortly, every acknowledgment of his gratitude for your attentions, and will furnish you with every necessary for your return to your kingdom. But," continued he, "while we are waiting his arrival, dear prince, pray do me the favor to fetch me a melon and some sugar, that I may eat some to refresh me."

Out of several melons that remained I took the best, and laid it on a plate; and as I could not find a knife to cut it with, I asked the young man if he knew where there was one.

"There is one," said he, "upon this cornice over my head." I accordingly saw it there, and made so much haste to reach it that, while I had it in my hand, my foot being entangled in the carpet, I fell most unhappily upon the young man, and the knife pierced his heart.

At this spectacle I cried out with agony. I beat my head, my face, my breast; I tore my clothes; I threw myself on the ground with unspeakable sorrow and grief. I would have embraced death without any reluctance, had it presented itself to me. "But what we wish, whether it be good or evil, will not always happen according to our desire." Nevertheless, considering that all my tears and sorrows would not restore the young man to life, and, the forty days being expired, I might be surprised by his father, I quitted the subterranean dwelling, laid down the great stone upon the entrance, and covered it with earth. I again ascended into the tree which had previously sheltered me, when I saw the expected vessel approaching the shore.

The old man with his slaves landed immediately, and advanced toward the subterranean dwelling, with a countenance that showed some hope; but when they saw the earth had been newly removed, they changed color, particularly the old man. They lifted up the stone, and descended the stairs. They called the young man by his name, but no answer was returned. Their fears redoubled. They searched about, and at last found him stretched on his couch, with the knife through his heart, for I had not had the courage to draw it out. On seeing this, they uttered such lamentable cries that my tears flowed afresh. The unfortunate father continued a long while insensible, and made them more than once despair of his life; but at last he came to himself. The slaves then brought up his son's body, dressed in his best apparel, and when they had made a grave they buried it. The old man, supported by two slaves, and his face covered with tears, threw the first earth upon the body, after which the slaves filled up the grave.

This being done, all the furniture was brought up, and, with the remaining provisions, put on board the vessel. The old man, overcome with sorrow, was carried upon a litter to the ship, which stood out to sea, and in a short time was out of sight.

After the old man and his slaves were gone I was left alone upon the island. I lay that night in the subterranean dwelling, which they had shut up, and when the day came, I walked round the island.

I led this wearisome life for a whole month. At the expiration of this time I perceived that the sea had sunk so low that there remained between me and the continent but a small stream, which I crossed, and the water did not reach above the middle of my leg. At last I got upon more firm ground. When I had proceeded some distance from the sea I saw a good way before me something that resembled a great fire, which afforded me some comfort; for I said to myself, I shall here find some persons, it not being possible that this fire should kindle of itself. As I drew nearer, however, I found my error, and discovered that what I had taken for a fire was a castle of red copper, which the beams of the sun made to appear at a distance like flames. As I wondered at this magnificent building, I saw ten handsome young men coming along; but what surprised me was that they were all blind of the right eye. They were accompanied by an old man, very tall, and of a venerable aspect.

As I was conjecturing by what adventure these men could come together, they approached, and seemed glad to see me. After we had made our salutations, they inquired what had brought me thither. I told them my story, which filled them with great astonishment.

After I had concluded my account, the young men prayed me to accompany them into the palace, and brought me into a spacious hall, where there were ten small blue sofas set round, separate from one another. In the middle of this circle stood an eleventh sofa, not so high as the rest, but of the same color, upon which the old man before mentioned sat down, and the young men occupied the other ten. But as each sofa could only contain one man, one of the young men said to me, "Sit down, friend, upon that carpet in the middle of the room, and do not inquire into anything that concerns us, nor the reason why we are all blind of the right eye."

The old man, having sat a short time, arose, and went out; but he returned in a minute or two, brought in supper, distributed to each man separately his proportion, and likewise brought me mine, which I ate apart, as the rest did; and when supper was almost ended, he presented to each of us a cup of wine.

One of the young men observing that it was late, said to the old man, "You do not bring us that with which we may acquit ourselves of our duty." At these words the old man arose, and went into a closet, and brought out thence upon his head ten basins, one after another, all covered with black stuff; he placed one before every gentleman, together with a light.

They uncovered their basins, which contained ashes and powdered charcoal; they mixed all together, and rubbed and bedaubed their faces with it; and having thus blackened themselves, they wept and lamented, beating their heads and breasts, and crying continually, "This is the fruit of our idleness and curiosity."

They continued this strange employment nearly the whole of the night. I wished a thousand times to break the silence which had been imposed upon me, and to ask the reason of their strange proceedings. The next day, soon after we had arisen, we went out to walk, and then I said to them, "I cannot forbear asking why you bedaubed your faces with black—how it has happened that each of you has but one eye. I conjure you to satisfy my curiosity."

One of the young men answered on behalf of the rest, "Once more we advise you to restrain your curiosity; it will cost you the loss of your right eye."

"No matter," I replied; "be assured that if such a misfortune befall me, I will not impute it to you, but to myself."

He further represented to me that when I had lost an eye I must not hope to remain with them, if I were so disposed, because their number was complete, and no addition could be made to it. I begged them, let it cost what it would, to grant my request.

The ten young men, perceiving that I was so fixed in my resolution, took a sheep, killed it, and after they had taken off the skin, presented me with a knife, telling me it would be useful to me on an occasion, which they would soon explain. "We must sew you in this skin," said they, "and then leave you; upon which a bird of monstrous size, called a roc, will appear in the air, and, taking you for a sheep, will pounce upon you, and soar with you to the sky. But let not that alarm you; he will descend with you again, and lay you on the top of a mountain. When you find yourself on the ground, cut the skin with your knife, and throw it off. As soon as the roc sees you, he will fly away for fear, and leave you at liberty. Do not stay, but walk on till you come to a spacious palace, covered with plates of gold, large emeralds, and other precious stones. Go up to the gate, which always stands open, and walk in. We have each of us been in that castle, but will tell you nothing of what we saw, or what befell us there; you will learn by your own experience. All that we can inform you is, that it has cost each of us our right eye; and the penance which you have been witness to, is what we are obliged to observe in consequence of having been there; but we cannot explain ourselves further."

When the young man had thus spoken, I wrapped myself in the sheep's skin, holding fast to the knife which was given me; and after the young men had been at the trouble to sew the skin about me, they retired into the hall, and left me alone. The roc they spoke of soon arrived; he pounced upon me, took me in his talons like a sheep, and carried me up to the summit of the mountain.

When I found myself on the ground I cut the skin with the knife, and throwing it off, the roc at the sight of me flew away. This roc is a white bird of a monstrous size; his strength is such that he can lift up elephants from the plains, and carry them to the tops of mountains, where he feeds upon them.

Being impatient to reach the palace, I lost no time, but made so much haste that I got thither in half a day's journey; and I must say that I found it surpassed the description they had given me of its magnificence.

The gate being open, I entered a square court, so large that there were around it ninety-nine gates of sandalwood and wood of aloes, and one of gold, without reckoning those of several superb staircases that led to apartments above, besides many more which I could not see.

I saw a door standing open just before me, through which I entered into a large hall. Here I found forty young women, of such perfect beauty as imagination could not surpass; they were all most sumptuously appareled. As soon as they saw me they arose, and without waiting my salutations, said to me, with tones of joy, "Welcome! Welcome! We have long expected you. You are at present our lord, master, and judge, and we are your slaves, ready to obey your commands."

After these words were spoken, these ladies vied with each other in their eager solicitude to do me all possible service. One brought hot water to wash my feet; a second poured sweet-scented water on my hands; others brought me all kinds of necessaries and change of apparel; others again brought in a magnificent collation; and the rest came, with glasses in their hands, to pour me delicious wines, all in good order, and in the most charming manner possible. Some of the ladies brought in musical instruments, and sang most delightful songs; while others

danced before me, two and two, with admirable grace. In short, honored madam, I must tell you that I passed a whole year of most pleasurable life with these forty ladies. At the end of that time I was greatly surprised to see these ladies with great sorrow impressed upon their countenances, and to hear them all say, "Adieu, dear prince, adieu! For we must leave you."

After they had spoken these words, they began to weep bitterly.

"My dear ladies," said I, "have the kindness not to keep me any longer in suspense. Tell me the cause of your sorrow."

"Well," said one of them, "to satisfy you, we must acquaint you that we are all princesses, daughters of kings. We live here together in the manner you have seen; but at the end of every year we are obliged to be absent forty days, for reasons we are not permitted to reveal; and afterward we return again to this palace. Before we depart we will leave you the keys of everything, especially those of the hundred doors, where you will find enough to satisfy your curiosity, and to relieve your solitude during our absence. But we entreat you to forbear opening the golden door; for if you do, we shall never see you again; and the apprehension of this augments our grief."

We separated with much tenderness; and after I had embraced them all they departed, and I remained alone in the castle.

I determined not to forget the important advice they had given me, not to open the golden door; but as I was permitted to satisfy my curiosity in everything else, I took the first of the keys of the other doors, which were hung in regular order.

I opened the first door, and entered an orchard, which I believe the universe could not equal. I could not imagine anything to surpass it. The symmetry, the neatness, the admirable order of the trees, the abundance and diversity of unknown fruits, their freshness and beauty, delighted me. Nor must I neglect to inform you that this delightful garden was watered in a most singular manner; small channels, cut out with great art and regularity, and of different lengths, carried water in considerable quantities to the roots of such trees as required much moisture. Others conveyed it in smaller quantities to those whose fruits were already formed; some carried still less; to those whose fruits were swelling; and others carried only so much as was just requisite to water those which had their fruits come to perfection, and only wanted to be ripened. They far exceeded in size the ordinary fruits in our gardens. I shut the door, and opened the next.

Instead of an orchard, I found here a flower garden, which was no

I opened the first door, and entered an orchard, which I believe
the universe could not equal.

less extraordinary in its kind. The roses, jessamines, violets, daffodils, hyacinths, anemones, tulips, pinks, lilies, and an infinite number of flowers, which do not grow in other places except at certain times, were there flourishing all at once; and nothing could be more delicious than the fragrant smell which they emitted.

I opened the third door, and found a large aviary, paved with marble of several fine and uncommon colors. The trellis work was made of sandalwood and wood of aloes. It contained a vast number of nightingales, goldfinches, canary birds, larks, and other rare singing birds, and the vessels that held their seed were of the most sparkling jasper or agate. The sun went down, and I retired, charmed with the chirping notes of the multitude of birds, who then began to perch upon such places as suited them for repose during the night. I went to my chamber, resolving on the following days to open all the rest of the doors, excepting that of gold.

The next day I opened the fourth door. I entered a large court, surrounded with forty gates, all open, and through each of them was an entrance into a treasury.

The first was stored with heaps of pearls; and, what is almost incredible, the number of those stones which are most precious, and as large as pigeon's eggs, exceeded the number of those of the ordinary size. In the second treasury, there were diamonds, carbuncles, and rubies; in the third, emeralds; in the fourth, ingots of gold; in the fifth, money; in the sixth, ingots of silver; and in the two following, money. The rest contained amethysts, chrysolites, topazes, opals, turquoises, agate, jasper, cornelian, and coral, of which there was a storehouse filled, not only with branches, but whole trees.

Thus I went through, day by day, these various wonders. Thirty-nine days afforded me but just as much time as was necessary to open ninety-nine doors, and to admire all that presented itself to my view, so that there was only the hundredth door left, which I was forbidden to open.

The fortieth day after the departure of those charming princesses arrived, and had I but retained so much self-command as I ought to have had, I should have been this day the happiest of all mankind, whereas now I am the most unfortunate. But through my weakness, which I shall ever repent, and the temptations of an evil spirit, I opened that fatal door! But before I had moved my foot to enter, a smell, pleasant enough but too powerful for my senses, made me faint away. However, I soon recovered; but instead of taking warning from this incident to close the door and restrain my curiosity, I entered, and found myself in a spacious vaulted apartment, illuminated by several large tapers placed in candlesticks of solid gold.

Among the many objects that attracted my attention was a black horse, of the most perfect symmetry and beauty. I approached in order

the better to observe him, and found he had on a saddle and bridle of massive gold, curiously wrought. One part of his manger was filled with clean barley, and the other with rose water. I laid hold of his bridle, and led him out to view him by daylight. I mounted, and endeavored to make him move; but finding he did not stir, I struck him with a switch I had taken up in his magnificent stable. He had no sooner felt the whip than he began to neigh in a most horrible manner, and, extending wings, which I had not before perceived, flew up with me into the air. My thoughts were fully occupied in keeping my seat; and, considering the fear that had seized me, I sat well.

At length he directed his course toward the earth, and lighting upon the terrace of a palace, without giving me time to dismount, he shook me out of the saddle with such force as to throw me behind him, and with the end of his tail he struck out my eye.

Thus it was I became blind of one eye. I then recollected the predictions of the ten young gentlemen. The horse again took wing, and soon disappeared. I got up, much vexed at the misfortune I had brought upon myself. I walked upon the terrace, covering my eye with one of my hands, for it pained me exceedingly, and then descended, and entered into a hall. I soon discovered, by the ten sofas in a circle and the eleventh in the middle, lower than the rest, that I was in the castle whence I had been carried by the roc.

The ten young men seemed not at all surprised to see me, nor at the loss of my eye; but said, "We are sorry that we cannot congratulate you on your return, as we could wish; but we are not the cause of your misfortune."

"I should do you wrong," I replied, "to lay it to your charge; I have only myself to accuse."

"If," said they, "it be a subject of consolation to the afflicted to know that others share their sufferings, you have in us this alleviation of your misfortune. All that has happened to you we also have endured; we each of us tasted the same pleasures during a year; and we had still continued to enjoy them had we not opened the golden door when the princesses were absent. You have been no wiser than we, and have incurred the same punishment. We would gladly receive you into our company, to join with us in the penance to which we are bound, the duration of which we know not. But we have already stated to you the reasons that render this impossible; depart, therefore, and proceed to the court of Bagdad, where you will meet with the person who is to decide your destiny."

After they had explained to me the road I was to travel, I departed.

On the road I caused my beard and eyebrows to be shaven, and assumed a calender's habit. I have had a long journey, but at last I arrived this evening, and met these my brother calenders at the gate, being strangers as well as myself. We were mutually surprised at one another, to see that we were all blind of the same eye; but we had not leisure to converse long on the subject of our misfortunes. We have only had time enough to bring us hither, to implore those favors which you have been generously pleased to grant us.

The third calender having finished this relation of his adventures, Zobeide addressed him and his fellow-calenders thus: "Go wherever you think proper; you are at liberty."

But one of them answered, "Madam, we beg you to pardon our curiosity, and permit us to hear the stories of your other guests who have not yet spoken."

Then the lady turned to the caliph, the vizier Giafar, and Mesrour, and said to them, "It is now your turn to relate your adventures; therefore speak."

The grand vizier, who had all along been the spokesman, answered Zobeide: "Madam, in order to obey you, we need only repeat what we have already said to the fair lady who opened for us the door. We are merchants come to Bagdad to sell our merchandise, which lies in the khan where we lodge. We dined to-day with several other persons of our condition, at a merchant's house of this city; who, after he had treated us with choice dainties and excellent wines, sent for men and women dancers and musicians. The great noise we made brought in the watch, who arrested some of the company, but we had the good fortune to escape. But it being already late, and the door of our khan shut up, we knew not whither to retire. We chanced, as we passed along this street, to hear music at your house, which made us determine to knock at your gate. This is all the account that we can give you, in obedience to your commands."

"Well, then," said Zobeide, "you shall all be equally obliged to me; I pardon you all, provided you immediately depart!"

Zobeide having given this command, the caliph, the vizier, Mesrour, the three calenders, and the porter, departed; for the presence of the seven slaves with their weapons awed them into silence. As soon as they had quitted the house, and the gate was closed after them, the caliph said to the calenders, without making himself known, "You, gentlemen, who are newly come to town, which way do you design to go, since it is not yet day?"

"It is this," they replied, "that perplexes us."

"Follow us," resumed the caliph, "and we will convey you out of danger."

He then whispered to the vizier: "Take them along with you, and to-morrow morning bring them to me."

The vizier Giafar took the three calenders along with him; the porter went to his quarters, and the caliph and Mesrour returned to the palace.

On the following morning, as the day dawned, the sultan Haroun al Raschid arose and went to his council chamber, and sat upon his throne. The grand vizier entered soon after, and made his obeisance.

"Vizier," said the caliph, "go, bring those ladies and the calenders at the same time; make haste, and remember that I impatiently expect your return."

The vizier, who knew his master's quick and fiery temper, hastened to obey, and conducted them to the palace with so much expedition that the caliph was much pleased.

When the ladies had arrived the caliph turned toward them and said, "I was last night in your house, disguised in a merchant's habit; but I am at present Haroun al Raschid, the fifth caliph of the glorious house of Abbas, and hold the place of our great prophet. I have sent for you only to know who you are, and to ask for what reason one of you, after severely whipping the two black dogs, wept with them. And I am no less curious to know why another of you has her bosom so full of scars."

Upon hearing these words, Zobeide thus related her story:

THE STORY OF ZOBEIDE

Commander of the Faithful, my story is truly wonderful. The two black dogs and myself are sisters by the same father and mother. The two ladies who are now here are also my sisters, but by another mother. After our father's death, the property that he left was equally divided among us. My two half sisters left me, that they might live with their mother. My two sisters and myself resided with our own mother. At her death she left us three thousand sequins each. Shortly after my sisters had received their portions, they married; but their husbands, having spent all their fortunes, found some pretext for divorcing them, and put them away. I received them into my house, and gave them a share of all my goods.

At the end of a twelvemonth my sisters again resolved to marry, and did so. After some months were passed, they returned again in the same sad condition; and as they accused themselves a thousand times, I again forgave them, and admitted them to live with me as before, and we dwelt together for the space of a year. After this I determined to engage in a commercial speculation. For this purpose I went with my two sisters to Bussorah, where I bought a ship ready fitted for sea, and laded her with such merchandise as I had carried with me from Bagdad. We set sail with a fair wind, and soon cleared the Persian Gulf; when we had reached the open sea we steered our course to the Indies, and on the twentieth day saw land. It was a very high mountain, at the bottom of which we perceived a great town; having a fresh gale, we soon reached the harbor, and cast anchor.

I had not patience to wait till my sisters were dressed to go along with me, but went ashore alone in the boat. Making directly to the gate of the town, I saw there a great number of men upon guard, some sitting, and others standing with weapons in their hands; and they had all such dreadful countenances that I was greatly alarmed; but perceiving they remained stationary, and did not so much as move their eyes, I took courage and went nearer, when I found they were all turned into stone. I entered the town, and passed through several streets, where at different intervals stood men in various attitudes, but all motionless and petrified. In the quarter inhabited by the merchants I found most of the shops open; here I likewise found the people petrified.

Having reached a vast square, in the heart of the city, I perceived a large folding gate, covered with plates of gold, which stood open; a curtain of silk stuff seemed to be drawn before it; a lamp hung over the entrance. After I had surveyed the building, I made no doubt but it was the palace of the prince who reigned over that country; and being much astonished that I had not met with one living creature, I approached in hopes of finding some. I lifted up the curtain, and was surprised at beholding no one but the guards in the vestibule, all petrified.

I came to a large court. I went from thence into a room richly furnished, where I perceived a lady turned into a statue of stone. The crown of gold on her head, and a necklace of pearls about her neck, each of them as large as a nut, proclaimed her to be the queen. I quitted the chamber where the petrified queen was, and passed through several other apartments richly furnished, and at last came into a large room where there was a throne of massy gold, raised several steps above the floor, and enriched with large enchased emeralds, and upon the throne there was a bed of rich stuff embroidered with pearls. What surprised me most was a sparkling light which came from above the bed. Being curious to know whence it proceeded, I ascended the steps, and, lifting up my head, saw a diamond as large as the egg of an ostrich, lying upon a low stool; it was so pure that I could not find the least blemish in it, and it sparkled with so much brilliancy that when I saw it by daylight I could not endure its luster.

At the head of the bed there stood on each side a lighted flambeau, but for what use I could not comprehend; however, it made me imagine

*I took courage and went nearer, when I found they were all
turned into stone.*

that there must be some one living in the place; for I could not believe that the torches continued thus burning of themselves.

The doors being all open, I surveyed some other apartments, that were as beautiful as those I had already seen. In short, the wonders that everywhere appeared so wholly engrossed my attention that I forgot my ship and my sisters, and thought of nothing but gratifying my curiosity. In the meantime night came on, and I tried to return by the way I had entered, but I could not find it; I lost myself among the apartments; and perceiving I was come back again to the large room, where the throne, the couch, the large diamond, and the torches stood, I resolved to take my night's lodging there, and to depart the next morning early, to get aboard my ship. I laid myself down upon a costly couch, not without some dread to be alone in a desolate place; and this fear hindered my sleep.

About midnight I heard a man reading the Koran, in the same tone as it is read in our mosques. I immediately arose, and taking a torch in my hand passed from one chamber to another, on that side from whence the voice proceeded, until looking through a window I found it to be an oratory. It had, as we have in our mosques, a niche, to direct us whither we are to turn to say our prayers; there were also lamps hung up, and two candlesticks with large tapers of white wax burning.

I saw a little carpet laid down like those we have to kneel upon when we say our prayers, and a comely young man sat on this carpet, with great devotion reading the Koran, which lay before him on a desk. At this sight I was transported with admiration. I wondered how it came to pass that he should be the only living creature in a town where all the people were turned into stone, and I do not doubt but there was something in the circumstance very extraordinary.

The door being only half shut I opened it, went in, and standing upright before the niche, I exclaimed, "Bismillah! Praise be to God." The young man turned toward me, and, having saluted me, inquired what had brought me to this desolate city. I told him in a few words my history, and I prayed him to tell me why he alone was left alive in the midst of such terrible desolation. At these words he shut the Koran, put it into a rich case, and laid it in the niche. Then he thus addressed me:

"Know that this city was the metropolis of a mighty kingdom, over which the sultan, who was my father, reigned. That prince, his whole court, the inhabitants of the city, and all his other subjects, were magi, worshipers of fire instead of God.

"But though I was born of an idolatrous father and mother I had the good fortune in my youth to have a nurse who was a good Mussulman, believing in God and in His prophet. 'Dear Prince,' would she oftentimes say, 'there is but one true God; take heed that you do not acknowledge and adore any other.' She taught me to read Arabic, and the book she gave me to study was the Koran. As soon as I was capable of understanding it, she explained to me all the passages of this excellent book, unknown to my father or any other person. She died, but not before she had perfectly instructed me in the Mussulman religion. After her death, I persisted in worshiping according to its directions; and I abhor the adoration of fire.

"About three years and some months ago, a thundering voice was suddenly sounded so distinctly through the whole city that nobody could miss hearing it. The words were these: 'Inhabitants, abandon the worship of fire, and worship the only God who shows mercy.' This voice was heard three years successively, but no one was converted. On the last day of that year, at the break of day, all the inhabitants were changed in an instant into stone, each one in the condition and posture in which he happened to be. The sultan, my father, and the queen, my mother, shared the same fate.

"I am the only person who did not suffer under that heavy judgment, and ever since I have continued to serve God with more fervency than before. I am persuaded, dear lady, that He has sent you hither for my comfort, for which I render Him infinite thanks, for I must own that I have become weary of this solitary life."

On hearing these words, I said, "Prince, who can doubt that Providence has brought me into your port, to afford you an opportunity of withdrawing from this dismal place? I am a lady at Bagdad, where I have considerable property; and I dare engage to promise you sanctuary there, until the mighty Commander of the Faithful, caliph of our prophet, whom you acknowledge, shows you the honor that is due to your merit. This renowned prince lives at Bagdad, and as soon as he is informed of your arrival in his capital you will find it not in vain to implore his assistance. Stay no longer in a city where you can only renew your grief; my vessel is at your service, which you may absolutely command as you shall think fit."

He accepted the offer, and as soon as it was day we left the palace, and went aboard my ship, where we found my sisters, the captain, and the slaves, all much troubled at my absence. After I had presented my sisters to the prince, I told them what had hindered my return the day before, how I had met with the young prince, his story, and the cause of the desolation of so fine a city.

The seamen were taken up several days in unloading the merchandise I brought with me, and embarking in its stead many of the precious things in the palace, especially jewels, gold, and money. We left the furniture and goods, which consisted of an infinite quantity of silver vessels, because our vessel could not carry it, for it would have required several vessels more to convey to Bagdad all the riches that we might have taken with us.

After we had laden the vessel with what we thought most desirable, we took such provisions and water aboard as were necessary for our voyage. At last we set sail with a favorable wind.

The young prince, my sisters, and myself passed our time very agreeably. But, alas! this good understanding did not last long, for my sisters grew jealous of the friendship between the prince and myself, and maliciously asked me, one day, what we should do with him when we came to Bagdad. Resolving to put this question off with a joke, I answered, "I will take him for my husband." Upon that, turning myself to the prince, I said, "Sir, I humbly beg of you to give your consent, for as soon as we come to Bagdad I design to offer you my person to be your slave, to do you all the service that is in my power, and to resign myself wholly to your commands."

The prince replied, "I know not, madam, whether you be in jest or no; but for my part, I seriously declare before these ladies, your sisters, that from this moment I heartily accept your offer, not with any intention to have you as a slave, but as my lady and wife." At these words my sisters changed color, and I could perceive afterward that they did not love me as before.

We entered the Persian Gulf, and had come within a short distance of Bussorah (where I hoped, considering the fair wind, we might have arrived the day following), when, in the night, while I was asleep, my sisters watched their opportunity and threw me overboard. They did the same to the prince, who was drowned.

I floated some minutes on the water, and by good fortune, or rather miracle, I felt ground. I went toward a dark spot, that, by what I could discern, seemed to be land, and which, when day appeared, I found to be a desert island, lying about twenty miles from Bussorah. I soon dried my clothes in the sun, and as I walked along I found several kinds of fruit, and likewise fresh water, which gave me some hopes of preserving my life.

I had just laid myself down to rest in a shade, when I perceived a very large winged serpent coming toward me, with an irregular waving movement, and hanging out its tongue, which induced me to conclude it had received some injury. I instantly arose, and perceived that it was pursued by a larger serpent which had hold of its tail, and was endeavoring to devour it.

This perilous situation of the first serpent excited my pity; and instead of retreating, I took up a stone that lay near me, and threw it with all my strength at its pursuer, whom I hit upon the head and killed. The other, finding itself at liberty, took wing and flew away. I looked after it for some time till it disappeared. I then sought another shady spot for repose, and fell asleep.

Judge what was my surprise, when I awoke, to see standing by me a black woman of lively and agreeable features, who held in her hand two dogs of the same color, fastened together. I sat up, and asked her who she was.

"I am," said she, "the serpent whom you lately delivered from my mortal enemy, and I wish to requite the important services you have rendered me. These two black dogs are your sisters, whom I have transformed into this shape. But this punishment will not suffice; and my will is that you treat them hereafter in the way I shall direct."

As soon as she had thus spoken the fairy took me under one of her arms, and the two black dogs under the other, and conveyed us to my house in Bagdad, where I found in my storehouses all the riches with which my vessel had been laden. Before she left me, she delivered to me the two dogs, and said, "If you would not be changed into a similar form, I command you to give each of your sisters every night one hundred lashes with a rod, as the punishment of the crime they have committed against yourself and the young prince, whom they have drowned." I was forced to promise obedience. Since that time I have whipped them every night, though with regret, whereof your majesty has been a witness. My tears testify with how much sorrow and reluctance I perform this painful duty. If there be anything else relating to myself that you desire to know, my sister Amina will give you full information in the relation of her story.

After the caliph had heard Zobeide with much astonishment, he desired his grand vizier to request Amina to acquaint him wherefore her breast was disfigured with so many scars.

THE HISTORY OF AMINA

Commander of the Faithful, that I may not repeat those things which your majesty has already been informed of by my sister, I will only mention that my mother, having taken a house to pass her widowhood in private, first bestowed me in marriage on the heir of one of the richest men in this city.

I had not been married quite a year before my husband died. I thus became a widow, and was in possession of all his property, which amounted to above ninety thousand sequins. When the first six months of my mourning was over, I caused to be made for me ten different dresses, of such magnificence that each came to a thousand sequins; and at the end of the year I began to wear them.

One day, while I was alone, a lady desired to speak to me. I gave orders that she should be admitted. She was a very old woman. She saluted me by kissing the ground, and said to me, kneeling, "Dear lady, the confidence I have in your charity makes me thus bold. I have an orphan daughter, whose wedding is on this night. She and I are both strangers, and have no acquaintance in this town, which much perplexes me. Therefore, most beautiful lady, if you would vouchsafe to honor the wedding with your presence, we shall be infinitely obliged, because the family with whom we shall be allied will then know that we are not regarded here as unworthy and despised persons. But, alas, madam, if you refuse this request, how great will be our mortification! We know not where else to apply."

This poor woman's address, which she spoke with tears, moved my compassion.

"Good woman," said I, "do not afflict yourself; I will grant you the favor you desire. Tell me whither I must go, and I will meet you as soon as I am dressed." The old woman was so transported with joy at my answer that she kissed my feet before I had time to prevent her.

"Compassionate lady," said she, rising, "God will reward the kindness you have shown to your servants, and make your heart as joyful as you have made theirs. You need not at present trouble yourself; I will call for you in the evening."

As soon as she was gone I took the suit I liked best, with a necklace of large pearls, bracelets, pendants for my ears, and rings set with the finest and most sparkling diamonds, and prepared to attend the ceremony.

When the night closed in, the old woman called upon me, with a countenance full of joy, and said, "Dear lady, the relations of my son-in-law, who are the principal ladies of the city, are now met together. You may come when you please; I am ready to conduct you."

We immediately set out; she walked before me, and I was followed by a number of my women and slaves, richly robed for the occasion. We stopped in a wide street, newly swept and watered, at a spacious gate with a lamp, by the light of which I read this inscription, in golden letters, over the entrance: "This is the continual abode of pleasure and joy."

The old woman knocked, and the gate was opened immediately.

I was conducted toward the lower end of the court, into a large hall, where I was received by a young lady of exceeding beauty. She drew near, and after having embraced me, made me sit down by her upon a sofa, on which was raised a throne of precious wood set with diamonds.

"Madam," said she, "you are brought hither to assist at a wedding;

but I hope it will be a different wedding from what you expected. I have a brother, one of the handsomest men in the world. His fate depends wholly upon you, and he will be the unhappiest of men if you do not take pity on him. If my prayers, madam, can prevail, I shall join them with his, and humbly beg you will not refuse the proposal of being his wife."

After the death of my husband I had not thought of marrying again; but I had no power to refuse the solicitation of so charming a lady. As soon as I had given consent by my silence, accompanied with a blush, the young lady clapped her hands, and immediately a curtain was withdrawn, from behind which came a young man of so majestic an air, and so graceful a countenance, that I thought myself happy to have made such a choice. He sat down by me, and I found from his conversation that his merits far exceeded the account of him given by his sister.

When she perceived that we were satisfied with one another, she clapped her hands a second time, and a cadi with four witnesses, entered, who wrote and signed our contract of marriage.

There was only one condition that my new husband imposed upon me, that I should not be seen by nor speak to any other man but himself; and he vowed to me that, if I complied in this respect, I should have no reason to complain of him. Our marriage was concluded and finished after this manner; so I became the principal actress in a wedding to which I had only been invited as a guest.

About a month after our marriage, having occasion for some stuffs, I asked my husband's permission to go out to buy them, which he granted; and I took with me the old woman of whom I spoke before, she being one of the family, and two of my own female slaves.

When we came to the street where the merchants reside, the old woman said, "Dear mistress, since you want silk stuffs, I must take you to a young merchant of my acquaintance, who has a great variety; and that you may not fatigue yourself by running from shop to shop, I can assure you that you will find in his what no other can furnish." I was easily persuaded, and we entered a shop belonging to a young merchant. I sat down, and bade the old woman desire him to show me the finest silk stuffs he had. The woman desired me to speak myself; but I told her it was one of the articles of my marriage contract not to speak to any man but my husband, which I ought to keep.

The merchant showed me several stuffs, of which one pleased me better than the rest; and I bade her ask the price. He answered the old woman: "I will not sell it for gold or money; but I will make her a present of it, if she will give me leave to kiss her cheek."

I ordered the old woman to tell him that he was very rude to propose such a freedom. But instead of obeying me, she said, "What the merchant desires of you is no such great matter; you need not speak, but only present him your cheek."

The stuff pleased me so much that I was foolish enough to take her advice. The old woman and my slaves stood up, that nobody might see, and I put up my veil; but instead of kissing me, the merchant bit me so violently as to draw blood.

The pain and my surprise were so great that I fell down in a swoon, and continued insensible so long that the merchant had time to escape. When I came to myself I found my cheek covered with blood. The old woman and my slaves took care to cover it with my veil, and the people who came about us could not perceive it, but supposed I had only had a fainting fit.

The old woman who accompanied me being extremely troubled at this accident, endeavored to comfort me.

"My dear mistress," said she, "I beg your pardon, for I am the cause of this misfortune, having brought you to this merchant, because he is my countryman; but I never thought he would be guilty of such a villainous action. But do not grieve. Let us hasten home, and I will apply a remedy that shall in three days so perfectly cure you that not the least mark shall be visible."

The pain had made me so weak that I was scarcely able to walk. But at last I got home, where I again fainted, as I went into my chamber. Meanwhile, the old woman applied her remedy. I came to myself, and went to bed.

My husband came to me at night, and seeing my head bound up, asked me the reason. I told him I had the headache, which I hoped would have satisfied him; but he took a candle, and saw my cheek was hurt.

"How comes this wound?" he said.

Though I did not consider myself as guilty of any great offense, yet I could not think of owning the truth. Besides, to make such an avowal to a husband, I considered as somewhat indecorous.

I therefore said, "That as I was going, under his permission, to purchase a silk stuff, a camel, carrying a load of wood, came so near to me in a narrow street, that one of the sticks grazed my cheek, but had not done me much hurt."

"If that is the case," said my husband, "to-morrow morning, before sunrise, the grand vizier Giafar shall be informed of this insolence, and cause all the camel drivers to be put to death."

"Pray, sir," said I, "let me beg of you to pardon them, for they are not guilty."

"How, madam," he demanded, "what, then, am I to believe? Speak; for I am resolved to know the truth from your own mouth."

"Sir," I replied, "I was taken with a giddiness, and fell down, and that is the whole matter."

At these words my husband lost all patience.

"I have," said he, "too long listened to your tales."

As he spoke, he clapped his hands, and in came three slaves. "Strike," said he; "cut her in two, and then throw her into the Tigris. This is the punishment I inflict on those to whom I have given my heart, when they falsify their promise."

I had recourse to entreaties and prayers; but I supplicated in vain, when the old woman, who had been his nurse, coming in just at that moment, fell down upon her knees and endeavored to appease his wrath.

"My son," said she, "since I have been your nurse, and brought you up, let me beg you to consider, 'he who kills shall be killed,' and that you will stain your reputation and forfeit the esteem of mankind."

She spoke these words in such an affecting manner, accompanied with tears, that she prevailed upon him at last to abandon his purpose.

"Well, then," said he to his nurse, "for your sake I will spare her life; but she shall bear about her person some marks to make her remember her offense."

When he had thus spoken, one of the slaves, by his order, gave me upon my sides and breast so many blows with a little cane, that he tore away both skin and flesh, which threw me into a swoon. In this state he caused the same slaves, the executioners of his will, to carry me into the house, where the old woman took care of me. I kept my bed for four months. At last I recovered. The scars which, contrary to my wish, you saw yesterday, have remained ever since.

As soon as I was able to walk and go abroad, I resolved to retire to the house which was left me by my first husband, but I could not find the site whereon it stood, as my second husband had caused it to be leveled with the ground.

Being thus left destitute and helpless, I had recourse to my dear sister Zobeide. She received me with her accustomed goodness, and advised me to bear with patience my affliction, from which, she said, none are free. In confirmation of her remark, she gave me an account of the loss of the young prince her husband, occasioned by the jealousy of her two sisters. She told me also by what accident they were transformed into dogs; and in the last place, after a thousand testimonials of her love toward me, she introduced me to my youngest sister, who had likewise taken sanctuary with her after the death of her mother; and we have continued to live together in the house in which we received the guests whom your highness found assembled on your visit last night.

The caliph publicly expressed his admiration of what he had heard, and inquired of Zobeide, "Madam, did not this fairy whom you delivered, and who imposed such a rigorous command upon you, tell you where her place of abode was, or that she would restore your sisters to their natural shape?"

"Commander of the Faithful," answered Zobeide, "the fairy did leave with me a bundle of hair, saying that her presence would one day be of use to me; and then, if I only burned two tufts of this hair, she would be with me in a moment."

"Madam," demanded the caliph, "where is the bundle of hair?"

She answered, "Ever since that time I have been so careful of it that I always carry it about me."

Upon which she pulled it out of the case which contained it, and showed it to him.

"Well, then," said the caliph, "let us bring the fairy hither; you could not call her in a better time, for I long to see her."

Zobeide having consented, fire was brought in, and she threw the whole bundle of hair into it. The palace at that instant began to shake, and the fairy appeared before the caliph in the form of a lady very richly dressed.

"Commander of the Faithful," said she to the prince, "you see I am ready to receive your commands. At your wish I will not only restore these two sisters to their former shape, but I will also cure this lady of her scars, and tell you who it was that abused her."

The caliph sent for the two dogs from Zobeide's house, and when they came a glass of water was brought to the fairy by her desire. She pronounced over it some words, which nobody understood; then, throwing some part of it upon Amina and the rest upon the dogs, the latter became two ladies of surprising beauty, and the scars that were upon Amina disappeared.

After this the fairy said to the caliph, "Commander of the Faithful, I must now discover to you the unknown husband you inquire after. He is Prince Amin, your eldest son, who by stratagem brought this lady to his house, where he married her. As to the blows he caused to be given her, he is in some measure excusable; for this lady, his spouse, by the excuses she made, led him to believe she was more in fault than she really was."

At these words she saluted the caliph, and vanished.

The caliph, much satisfied with the changes that had happened through his means, acted in such a manner as will perpetuate his memory to all ages. First, he sent for his son Amin, and told him that he was informed of his secret marriage and how he had ill-treated Amina upon a very slight cause. Upon this, the prince, upon his father's commands, received her again immediately.

After which Haroun al Raschid declared that he would give his own heart and hand to Zobeide, and offered the other three sisters to the calenders, sons of sultans, who accepted them for their brides with much joy. The caliph assigned each of them a magnificent palace in the city of Bagdad, promoted them to the highest dignities of his empire, and admitted them to his councils.

The chief cadi of Bagdad being called, with witnesses, he wrote the contracts of marriage; and the caliph, in promoting by his patronage the happiness of many persons who had suffered such incredible calamities, drew a thousand blessings upon himself.

THE STORY OF THE THREE SISTERS

There was an emperor of Persia, named Khoonoo-shah. He often walked in disguise through the city, attended by a trusty minister, when he met with many adventures. On one of these occasions, as he was passing through a street in that part of the town inhabited only by the meaner sort, he heard some people talking very loud; and going close to the house whence the noise proceeded, he perceived a light, and three sisters sitting on a sofa, conversing together after supper. By what the eldest said, he presently understood the subject of their conversation was wishes:

"For," said she, "since we have got upon wishes, mine shall be to have the sultan's baker for my husband, for then I shall eat my fill of that bread which by way of excellence is called the sultan's. Let us see if your tastes are as good as mine."

"For my part," replied the second sister, "I wish I was wife to the sultan's chief cook, for then I should eat of the most excellent dishes; and, as I believe the sultan's bread is common in the palace, I should not want any of that. Therefore, you see," addressing herself to her eldest sister, "that I have better taste than you."

The youngest sister, who was very beautiful, and had more charms and wit than the two elder, spoke in her turn: "For my part, sisters," said she, "I shall not limit my desires to such trifles, but take a higher flight; and since we are upon wishing, I wish to be the emperor's queen consort. I would make him father of a prince whose hair should be gold on one side of his head, and silver on the other; when he cried, the tears from his eyes should be pearl; and when he smiled, his vermilion lips should look like a rose-bud fresh blown."

The three sisters' wishes, particularly that of the youngest, seemed so singular to the sultan that he resolved to gratify them in their desires; but without communicating his design to his grand vizier he charged him only to take notice of the house, and bring the three sisters before him the following day.

The grand vizier, in executing the emperor's orders, would give the sisters but just time to dress themselves to appear before him, without telling them the reason. He brought them to the palace and presented them to the emperor, who said to them, "Do you remember the wishes you expressed last night, when you were all in so pleasant a mood? Speak the truth; I must know what they were."

At these unexpected words of the emperor the three sisters were much confounded. They cast down their eyes and blushed. Modesty, and fear lest they might have offended the emperor by their conversation, kept them silent.

The emperor, perceiving their confusion, said, to encourage them, "Fear nothing; I did not send for you to distress you; and since I see that, without my intending it, is the effect of the question I asked, as I know the wish of each I will relieve you from your fears. You," added he, "who wished to be my wife shall have your desire this day; and you," continued he, addressing himself to the two elder sisters, "shall also be married, to my chief baker and cook."

The nuptials were all celebrated that day, as the emperor had resolved, but in a different manner. The youngest sister's were solemnized with all the rejoicings usual at the marriages of the emperors of Persia; and those of the other two sisters according to the quality and distinction of their husbands; the one as the sultan's chief baker, and the other as head cook.

The two elder sisters felt strongly the disproportion of their marriages to that of their younger sister. This consideration made them far from being content, though they were arrived at the utmost height of their late wishes, and much beyond their hopes. They gave themselves up to an excess of jealousy, and frequently met together to consult how they might revenge themselves on the queen. They proposed a great many ways, which they could not accomplish, but dissimulated all the time to flatter the queen with every demonstration of affection and respect.

Some months after her marriage, the queen gave birth to a young prince, as bright as the day; but her sisters, to whom the child was given at his birth, wrapped him up in a basket and floated it away on a canal that ran near the palace, and declared that the queen had given birth to a little dog. This made the emperor very angry.

In the meantime, the basket in which the little prince was exposed was carried by the stream toward the garden of the palace. By chance the intendant of the emperor's gardens, one of the principal and most considerable officers of the kingdom, was walking by the side of this canal, and perceiving a basket floating called to a gardener, who was not far off, to bring it to shore that he might see what it contained. The gardener, with a rake which he had in his hand, drew the basket to the side of the canal, took it up, and gave it to him.

The intendant of the gardens was extremely surprised to see in the basket a child, which, though he knew it could be but just born, had very fine features. This officer had been married several years, but though he had always been desirous of having children, Heaven had never blessed him with any. He made the gardener follow him with the child; and when he came to his own house, which was situated at the entrance into the gardens of the palace, went into his wife's apartment. "Wife," said he, "as we have no children of our own, God hath sent us one. I recommend him to you; provide him a nurse, and take as much care of him as if he were our own son; for, from this moment, I acknowledge him as such." The intendant's wife received the child with great joy.

The following year the queen consort gave birth to another prince, on whom the unnatural sisters had no more compassion than on his brother; but exposed him likewise in a basket, and set him adrift in the

*The gardener, with a rake which he had in his hand,
drew the basket to the side of the canal . . .*

canal, pretending this time that the sultaness was delivered of a cat. It was happy also for this child that the intendant of the gardens was walking by the canal side. He carried this child to his wife, and charged her to take as much care of it as of the former, which was as agreeable to her inclination as it was to that of the intendant.

This time the Emperor of Persia was more enraged against the queen than before, and she had felt the effects of his anger, as the grand vizier's remonstrances had not prevailed.

The next year the queen gave birth to a princess, which innocent babe underwent the same fate as the princes her brothers; for the two sisters, being determined not to desist from their detestable schemes till they had seen the queen their younger sister at least cast off, turned out, and humbled, exposed this infant also on the canal. But the princess, as had been the two princes her brothers, was preserved from death by the compassion and charity of the intendant of the gardens.

To this inhumanity the two sisters added a lie and deceit, as before. They procured a piece of wood, of which they said the queen had been delivered.

Khoonoo-shah could no longer contain himself at this third disappointment. He ordered a small shed to be built near the chief mosque, and the queen to be confined in it, so that she might be subjected to the scorn of those who passed by; which usage, as she did not deserve it, she bore with a patient resignation that excited the admiration as well as compassion of those who judged of things better than the vulgar.

The two princes and the princess were in the meantime nursed and brought up by the intendant of the gardens and his wife with all the tenderness of a father and mother; and as they advanced in age, they all showed marks of superior dignity, by a certain air which could only belong to exalted birth. All this increased the affection of the intendant and his wife, who called the eldest prince Bahman, and the second Perviz, both of them names of the most ancient emperors of Persia, and the princess Periezadeh, which name also had been borne by several queens and princesses of the kingdom.

As soon as the two princes were old enough, the intendant provided proper masters to teach them to read and write; and the princess, their sister, who was often with them—showing a great desire to learn—the intendant, pleased with her quickness, employed the same master to teach her also. Her emulation, vivacity, and wit made her in a little time as proficient as her brothers. At the hours of recreation, the princess learned to sing and to play upon all sorts of instruments; and when the princes were learning to ride, she would not permit them to have that advantage over her, but went through all the exercises with them, learning to ride also, to bend the bow, and dart the reed or javelin, and oftentimes outdid them in the race and other contests of agility.

The intendant of the gardens was so overjoyed to find his adopted children so well requited the expense he had been at in their education, that he resolved to be at a still greater; for as he had till then been content only with his lodge at the entrance to the garden, and kept no country house, he purchased a country seat at a short distance from the city, surrounded by a large tract of arable land, meadows, and woods, and furnished it in the richest manner, and added gardens, according to a plan drawn by himself, and a large park, stocked with fallow deer, that the princes and princess might divert themselves with hunting when they chose.

When this country seat was finished, the intendant of the gardens went and cast himself at the emperor's feet, and after representing his long service and the infirmities of age, which he found growing upon him, begged permission to resign his charge and retire. The emperor gave him leave, and asked what he should do to recompense him. "Sire," replied the intendant of the gardens, "I have received so many obligations from your majesty and the late emperor your father, of happy memory, that I desire no more than the honor of being assured of your continued favor."

He took his leave of the emperor, and retired with the two princes and the princess to the country retreat he had built. His wife had been dead some years, and he himself had not lived in his new abode above six months when he was surprised by so sudden a death that he had not time to give them the least account of the manner in which he had saved them from destruction.

The Princes Bahman and Perviz, and the Princess Periezadeh, who knew no other father than the intendant of the emperor's gardens, regretted and bewailed him as such, and paid all the honors in his funeral obsequies which love and filial gratitude required of them. Satisfied with the plentiful fortune he had left them, they lived together in perfect union, free from the ambition of distinguishing themselves at court, or aspiring to places of honor and dignity, which they might easily have obtained.

One day when the two princes were hunting, and the princess had remained at home, an old woman, a devotee, came to the gate, and desired leave to go in to say her prayers, it being then the hour. The servants asked the princess's permission, who ordered them to show her into the oratory, which the intendant of the emperor's gardens had taken care to fit up in his house, for want of a mosque in the neighborhood. After the good woman had finished her prayers, she was brought before the princess in the great hall, which in beauty and richness exceeded all the other apartments.

As soon as the princess saw the devout woman, she asked her many questions upon the exercise of devotion which she practiced, and how she lived; all which were answered with great modesty. Talking of several things, at last she asked the woman what she thought of the house, and how she liked it.

"Madam," answered the devout woman, "if you will give me leave to speak my mind freely, I will take the liberty to tell you that this house would be incomparable if it had three things which are wanting to complete it. The first of these three things is the speaking-bird, so singular a creature that it draws around it all the singing-birds in the neighborhood, which come to accompany his song. The second is the singing-tree, the leaves of which are so many mouths, which form an harmonious concert of different voices, and never cease. The third is the yellow-water of a gold color, a single drop of which being poured into a vessel properly prepared, it increases so as to fill it immediately, and rises up in the middle like a fountain, which continually plays, and yet the basin never overflows."

"Ah! my good mother," cried the princess, "how much am I obliged to you for the knowledge of these curiosities! They are surprising, and I never before heard there were such wonderful rarities in the world; but as I am persuaded that you know, I expect that you will do me the favor to inform me where they are to be found."

"Madam," replied the good woman, "I am glad to tell you that these curiosities are all to be met with in the same spot on the confines of this kingdom, toward India. The road lies before your house, and whoever you send needs but follow it for twenty days, and on the twentieth let him only ask the first person he meets where the speaking-bird, singing-tree, and yellow-water are, and he will be informed."

After saying this she rose from her seat, took her leave, and went her way.

The Princess Periezadeh's thoughts were so absorbed in her desire to obtain possession of these three wonders, that her brothers, on their return from hunting, instead of finding her lively and gay, as she used to be, were amazed to see her pensive and melancholy, and weighed down by some trouble.

"Sister," said Prince Bahman, "what has become of all your mirth and gayety? Are you not well? Or has some misfortune befallen you? Tell us that we may give you some relief."

The princess at first returned no answer to these inquiries; but on being pressed by her brothers, thus replied: "I always believed that this house which our father built us was so complete that nothing was wanting. But this day I have learned that it wants three rarities, the speaking-bird, the singing-tree, and the yellow-water. If it had these, no country seat in the world could be compared with it." Then she informed them wherein consisted the excellency of these rarities, and requested her brothers to send some trustworthy person in search of these three curiosities.

"Sister," replied Prince Bahman, "it is enough that you have an earnest desire for the things you mention to oblige us to try to obtain them. I will take that charge upon myself; only tell me the place, and the way to it, and I will set out to-morrow. You, brother, shall stay at home with our sister, and I commend her to your care."

Prince Bahman spent the remainder of the day in making preparations for his journey, and informing himself from the princess of the directions which the devout woman had left her. The next morning he mounted his horse, and Perviz and the princess embraced him and wished him a good journey. But in the midst of their adieus, the princess recollected what she had not thought of before.

"Brother," said she, "I had quite forgotten the perils to which you may be exposed. Who knows whether I shall ever see you again! Alight, I beseech you, and give up this journey. I would rather be deprived of the sight and possession of the speaking-bird, singing-tree, and yellow-water, than run the risk of never seeing you more."

"Sister," replied Bahman, smiling at the sudden fears of the princess, "my resolution is fixed, and you must allow me to execute it. However, as events are uncertain, and I may fail in this undertaking, all I can do is to leave you this knife. It has a peculiar property. If when you pull it out of the sheath it is clean as it is now, it will be a sign that I am alive; but if you find it stained with blood, then you may believe me to be dead."

The princess could prevail nothing more with Bahman. He bade adieu to her and Prince Perviz for the last time, and rode away. When he got into the road, he never turned to the right hand nor to the left, but went directly forward toward India. The twentieth day he perceived on the roadside a very singular old man, who sat under a tree some small distance from a thatched house, which was his retreat from the weather.

His eyebrows were as white as snow, as was also his beard, which was so long as to cover his mouth, while it reached down to his feet. The nails of his hands and feet were grown to an immense length; a flat broad umbrella covered his head. He wore no clothes, but only a mat thrown round his body.

This old man was a dervish, for many years retired from the world, and devoted to contemplation, so that at last he became what we have described.

Prince Bahman, who had been all that morning expecting to meet some one who could give him information of the place he was in search of, stopped when he came near the dervish, alighted, in conformity to the directions which the devout woman had given the Princess Periezadeh, and, leading his horse by the bridle, advanced toward him, and saluting him, said, "God prolong your days, good father, and grant you the accomplishment of your desires."

The dervish returned the prince's salutation, but spoke so unintelligibly that he could not understand one word he said. Prince Bahman perceiving that this difficulty proceeded from the dervish's hair hanging over his mouth, and unwilling to go any farther without the instructions he wanted, pulled out a pair of scissors he had about him, and having tied his horse to a branch of the tree, said, "Good dervish, I want to have some talk with you, but your hair prevents my understanding what you say, and if you will consent, I will cut off some part of it and of your eyebrows, which disfigure you so much that you look more like a bear than a man."

The dervish did not oppose the offer; and when the prince had cut off as much hair as he thought fit, he perceived that the dervish had a good complexion, and that he did not seem so very old.

"Good dervish," said he, "if I had a glass I would show you how young you look: you are now a man, but before nobody could tell what you were."

The kind behavior of Prince Bahman made the dervish smile, and return his compliment.

"Sir," said he, "whoever you are, I am obliged by the good office you have performed, and am ready to show my gratitude by doing anything in my power for you. Tell me wherein I may serve you."

"Good dervish," replied Prince Bahman, "I am in search of the speaking-bird, the singing-tree, and the yellow-water. I know these three rarities are not far from here, but cannot tell exactly the place where they are to be found; if you know, I conjure you to show me the way, that I may not lose my labor after so long a journey."

The prince, while he spoke, observed that the dervish changed countenance, held down his eyes, looked very serious, and instead of making any reply, remained silent: which obliged him to say to him again, "Good father, tell me whether you know what I ask you, that I may not lose my time, but inform myself somewhere else."

At last the dervish broke silence. "Sir," said he to Prince Bahman, "I know the way you ask of me; but the danger you are going to expose yourself to is greater than you may suppose. A number of gentlemen of as much bravery and courage as yourself have passed this way, and asked me the same question. I can assure you they have all perished, for I have not seen one come back. Therefore, if you have any regard for your life, take my advice, go no farther, but return home."

"Nothing," replied Prince Bahman to the dervish, "shall make me change my intention. Whoever attacks me, I am brave and well armed."

"But they who will attack you are not to be seen," said the dervish. "How will you defend yourself against invisible persons?"

"It is no matter," answered the prince; "all you can say shall not persuade me to forego my purpose. Since you know the way, I once more conjure you to inform me."

When the dervish found he could not prevail upon Prince Bahman to relinquish his journey, he put his hand into a bag that lay by him and pulled out a bowl, which he presented to him. "Since you will not be led by my advice," said he, "take this bowl: when you have mounted your horse, throw it before you, and follow it to the foot of a mountain.

There, as soon as the bowl stops, alight, leave your horse with the bridle over his neck, and he will stand in the same place till you return. As you ascend you will see on your right and left a great number of large black stones, and will hear on all sides a confusion of voices, which will utter a thousand injurious threats to discourage you, and prevent your reaching the summit of the mountain. Be not afraid; but above all things, do not turn your head to look behind you; for in an instant you will be changed into such a black stone as those you see, which are all youths who have failed in this enterprise. If you escape the danger, of which I give you but a faint idea, and get to the top of the mountain, you will see a cage, and in that cage is the bird you seek; ask him which are the singing-tree and the yellow-water, and he will tell you. I have nothing more to say, except to beg you again not to expose your life, for the difficulty is almost insuperable."

After these words, the prince mounted his horse, took his leave of the dervish with a respectful salute, and threw the bowl before him.

The bowl rolled away unceasingly, with as much swiftness as when Prince Bahman first hurled it from his hand, which obliged him to put his horse to the gallop to avoid losing sight of it, and when it had reached the foot of the mountain it stopped. The prince alighted from his horse, laid the bridle on his neck, and, having first surveyed the mountain and seen the black stones, began to ascend. He had not gone four steps before he heard the voices mentioned by the dervish, though he could see nobody. Some one said, "Where is he going?" "What would he have?" "Do not let him pass"; others, "Stop him," "Catch him," "Kill him"; and others, with a voice like thunder, "Thief!" "Assassin!" "Murderer!" while some, in a gibing tone, cried, "No, no, do not hurt him; let the pretty fellow pass. The cage and bird are kept for him."

Notwithstanding all these troublesome voices, Prince Bahman ascended with courage and resolution for some time, but the voices redoubled with so loud a din near him, both behind, before, and on all sides, that at last he was seized with dread, his legs trembled under him, he staggered, and finding that his strength failed him, he forgot the dervish's advice, turned about to run down the hill, and was that instant changed into a black stone. His horse likewise, at the same moment, underwent the same change.

From the time of Prince Bahman's departure, the Princess Periezadeh always wore the knife and sheath in her girdle, and pulled it out several times a day, to know whether her brother was yet alive. She had the consolation to find he was in perfect health, and to talk of him frequently with Prince Perviz.

On the fatal day that Prince Bahman was transformed into a stone, as Prince Perviz and the princess were talking together in the evening, as usual, the prince desired his sister to pull out the knife to know how their brother did. The princess readily complied, and seeing the blood run down the point, was seized with so much horror that she threw it down.

"Ah! my dear brother," cried she, "woe's me! I have been the cause of your death, and shall never see you more! Why did I tell you of the speaking-bird, the singing-tree, and yellow-water! Why did I allow my peace to be disturbed by the idle tales of a silly old woman!"

Prince Perviz was as much afflicted at the death of Prince Bahman as the princess; but as he knew that she still passionately desired possession of the speaking-bird, the singing-tree, and the golden-water, he interrupted her, saying, "Sister, our regret for our brother is vain and useless; our grief and lamentations cannot restore him to life. It is the will of God. We must submit to it, and adore the decrees of the Almighty without searching into them. Why should you now doubt of the truth of what the holy woman told you? Our brother's death is probably owing to some error on his part. I am determined to know the truth, and am resolved myself to undertake this search. To-morrow I shall set out."

The princess did all she could to dissuade Prince Perviz, conjuring him not to expose her to the danger of losing two brothers; but all the remonstrances she could urge had no effect upon him. Before he went, that she might know what success he had, he left her a string of a hundred pearls, telling her, that if they would not run when she should count them upon the string, but remain fixed, that would be a certain sign he had undergone the same fate as his brother; but at the same time told her he hoped it would never happen, but that he should have the happiness to see her again to their mutual satisfaction.

Prince Perviz, on the twentieth day after his departure, met the same dervish in the same place as had his brother Bahman before him, and asked of him the same question. The dervish urged the same difficulties and remonstrances as he had done to Prince Bahman, telling him that a young gentleman, who very much resembled him, was with him a short time before, and had not yet returned.

"Good dervish," answered Prince Perviz, "I know whom you speak of; he was my elder brother, and I am informed of the certainty of his death, but know not the cause."

"I can tell you," replied the dervish. "He was changed into a black stone, as all I speak of have been; and you must expect the same fate unless you observe more exactly than he has done the advice I gave him; but I once more entreat you to renounce your resolution."

"Dervish," said Prince Perviz, "I cannot sufficiently express how much I am obliged to you for your kind caution; but I cannot now relinquish this enterprise; therefore I beg of you to do me the same favor you have done my brother."

On this the dervish gave the prince a bowl with the same instructions he had delivered to his brother, and so let him depart.

Prince Perviz thanked the dervish, and when he had remounted, and taken leave, threw the bowl before his horse, and spurring him at the same time, followed it. When the bowl came to the bottom of the hill it stopped, the prince alighted, and stood some time to recollect the dervish's directions. He encouraged himself, and then began to walk up with a determination to reach the summit; but before he had gone above six steps, he heard a voice, which seemed to be near, as of a man behind him, say in an insulting tone, "Stay, rash youth, that I may punish you for your presumption."

Upon this affront, the prince, forgetting the dervish's advice, clapped his hand upon his sword, drew it, and turned about to avenge himself; but had scarcely time to see that nobody followed him before he and his horse were changed into black stones.

In the meantime, the Princess Periezadeh, several times a day after her brother's departure, counted her chaplet. She did not omit it at night, but when she went to bed put it about her neck; and in the morning when she awoke counted over the pearls again to see if they would slide.

The day that Prince Perviz was transformed into a stone she was counting over the pearls as she used to do, when all at once they became immovably fixed, a certain token that the prince, her brother, was dead. As she had determined what to do in case it should so happen, she lost no time in outward demonstrations of grief, but proceeded at once to put her plan into execution. She disguised herself in her brother's robes, and having procured arms and equipment she mounted her horse the next morning. Telling her servants she should return in two or three days, she took the same road as her brothers.

On the twentieth day she also met the dervish as her brothers had done, and asked him the same question and received from him the same answer, with a caution against the folly of sacrificing her life in such a search.

When the dervish had done, the princess replied, "By what I comprehend from your discourse, the difficulties of succeeding in this affair are, first, the getting up to the cage without being frightened at the terrible din of voices I shall hear; and, secondly, not to look behind me. For this last direction, I hope I shall be mistress enough of myself to observe it. As to the first, I desire to know of you if I may use a stratagem against those voices which you describe, and which are so well calculated to excite terror."

"And what stratagem is it you would employ?" said the dervish.

"To stop my ears with cotton," answered the princess, "that the voices, however loud and terrible, may make the less impression upon my imagination, and my mind remain free from that disturbance which might cause me to lose the use of my reason."

"Princess," replied the dervish, "if you persist in your design, you may make the experiment. You will be fortunate if it succeeds; but I would advise you not to expose yourself to the danger."

After the princess had thanked the dervish, and taken her leave of him, she mounted her horse, threw down the bowl which he had given her, and followed it till it stopped at the foot of the mountain.

The princess alighted, stopped her ears with cotton, and after she had well examined the path leading to the summit, began with a moderate pace, and walked up with intrepidity. She heard the voices, and perceived the great service the cotton was to her. The higher she went, the louder and more numerous the voices seemed; but they were not capable of making any impression upon her. She heard a great many affronting speeches and insultingaccusations,

whichsheonlylaughedat.Atlastshesawthecageandthebird,whileatthesame moment the clamor and thunders of the invisible voices greatly increased.

The princess, encouraged by the sight of the object of which she was in search, redoubled her speed, and soon gained the summit of the mountain, where the ground was level; then running directly to the cage, and clapping her hand upon it, cried, "Bird, I have you, and you shall not escape me."

At the same moment the voices ceased.

While Periezadeh was pulling the cotton out of her ears the bird said to her, "Heroic princess, since I am destined to be a slave, I would rather be yours than any other person's, since you have obtained me so courageously. From this instant I pay an entire submission to all your commands. I know who you are, for you are not what you seem, and I will one day tell you more. In the meantime, say what you desire, and I am ready to obey you."

"Bird," said Periezadeh, "I have been told that there is not far off a golden-water, the property of which is very wonderful; before all things, I ask you to tell me where it is."

The bird showed her the place, which was just by, and she went and filled a little silver flagon which she had brought with her. She returned to the bird, and said, "Bird, this is not enough; I want also the singing-tree. Tell me where it is."

"Turn about," said the bird, "and you will see behind you a wood, where you will find this tree. Break off a branch, and carry it to plant in your garden; it will take root as soon as it is put into the earth, and in a little time will grow to a fine tree."

The princess went into the wood, and by the harmonious concert she heard, soon discovered the singing-tree.

When the princess had obtained possession of the branch of the singing-tree, she returned again to the bird, and said, "Bird, what you have yet done for me is not sufficient. My two brothers, in their search for thee, have been transformed into black stones on the side of the mountain. Tell me how I may obtain their disenchantment."

The bird seemed most reluctant to inform the princess on this point; but on her threatening to take his life, he bade her sprinkle every stone on her way down the mountain with a little of the water from the golden fountain. She did so, and every stone she thus touched resumed the shape of a man or of a horse ready caparisoned. Among these were her two brothers, Bahman and Perviz, who exchanged with her the most affectionate embraces.

Having explained to her brothers and the band of noble youths who had been enchanted in their search after these three wonders, the means of their recovery, Periezadeh placed herself at their head, and bade them follow her to the old dervish, to thank him for his reception and wholesome advice, which they had all found to be sincere. But he was dead, whether from old age or because he was no longer needed to show the way to the obtaining the three rarities which the Princess Periezadeh had secured, did not appear. The procession, headed by Periezadeh, pursued its route, but lessened in its numbers every day. The youths, who had come from different countries, took leave of the princess and her brothers one after another, as they approached the various roads by which they had come.

As soon as the princess reached home, she placed the cage in the garden; and the bird no sooner began to warble than he was surrounded by nightingales, chaffinches, larks, linnets, goldfinches, and every species of birds of the country. And the branch of the singing-tree was no sooner set in the midst of the parterre, a little distance from the house, than it took root, and in a short time became a large tree, the leaves of which gave as harmonious a concert as those of the tree from which it was gathered. A large basin of beautiful marble was placed in the garden; and when it was finished the princess poured into it all the yellow-water from the flagon, which instantly increased and swelled so much that it soon reached up to the edges of the basin, and afterward formed in the middle a fountain twenty feet high which fell again into the basin perpetually without running over.

The report of these wonders was presently spread abroad, and as the gates of the house and those of the gardens were shut to nobody, a great number of people came to admire them.

Some days after, when the Princes Bahman and Perviz had recovered from the fatigue of their journey, they resumed their former way of living; and as their usual diversion was hunting, they mounted their horses and went for the first time since their return, not to their own demesne, but two or three leagues from their house. As they pursued their sport, the Emperor of Persia came in pursuit of game upon the same ground. When they perceived by the number of horsemen in different places that he would soon be up, they resolved to discontinue their chase, and retire to avoid encountering him; but in the very road they took they chanced to meet him in so narrow a way that they could not retreat without being seen. In their surprise they had only time to alight, and prostrate themselves before the emperor. He stopped and commanded them to rise. The princes rose up, and stood before him with an easy and graceful air. The emperor, after he had admired their good air and mien, asked them who they were, and where they lived.

"Sire," said Prince Bahman, "we are the sons of the late intendant of your majesty's gardens, and live in a house which he built a little before he died, till it should please you to give us some employment."

"By what I perceive," replied the emperor, "you love hunting."

"Sire," replied Prince Bahman, "it is our common exercise, and what none of your majesty's subjects who intend to bear arms in your armies ought, according to the ancient custom of the kingdom, to neglect."

The emperor, charmed with so prudent an answer, said, "It is so, and I should be glad to see your expertness in the chase; choose your own game."

The princes mounted their horses again, and followed the emperor; but had not gone far before they saw many wild beasts together. Prince Bahman chose a lion, and Prince Perviz a bear; and pursued them with so much intrepidity, that the emperor was surprised. They came up with their game nearly at the same time, and darted their javelins with so much skill and address, that they pierced, the one the lion and the other the bear, so effectually that the emperor saw them fall one after the other. Immediately afterward Prince Bahman pursued another bear, and Prince Perviz another lion, and killed them in a short time, and would have beaten out for fresh game, but the emperor would not let them, and sent to them to come to him.

When they approached, he said, "If I would have given you leave, you would soon have destroyed all my game; but it is not that which I would preserve, but your persons; for I am so well assured your bravery may one time or other be serviceable to me, that from this moment your lives will be always dear to me."

The emperor, in short, conceived so great a fondness for the two princes that he invited them immediately to make him a visit; to which Prince Bahman replied, "Your majesty does us an honor we do not deserve; and we beg you will excuse us."

The emperor, who could not comprehend what reason the princes could have to refuse this token of his favor, pressed them to tell him why they excused themselves.

"Sire," said Prince Bahman, "we have a sister younger than ourselves, with whom we live in such perfect union that we undertake nothing before we consult her, nor she anything without asking our advice."

"I commend your brotherly affection," answered the emperor. "Consult your sister, then meet me here to-morrow, and give me an answer."

The princes went home, but neglected to speak of their adventure in meeting the emperor, and hunting with him, and also of the honor he had done them by asking them to go home with him; yet did not the next morning fail to meet him at the place appointed.

"Well," said the emperor, "have you spoken to your sister? And has she consented to the pleasure I expect of seeing you?"

The two princes looked at each other and blushed.

"Sire," said Prince Bahman, "we beg your majesty to excuse us; for both my brother and I forgot."

"Then remember to-day," replied the emperor, "and be sure to bring me an answer to-morrow."

The princes were guilty of the same fault a second time, and the emperor was so good-natured as to forgive their negligence; but to prevent their forgetfulness the third time, he pulled three little golden balls out of a purse, and put them into Prince Bahman's bosom.

"These balls," said he, smiling, "will prevent you forgetting a third time what I wish you to do, since the noise they will make by falling on the floor, when you undress, will remind you, if you do not recollect it before."

The event happened just as the emperor foresaw; and without these balls the princes had not thought of speaking to their sister of this affair. For as Prince Bahman unloosened his girdle to go to bed the balls dropped on the floor, upon which he ran into Prince Perviz's chamber, when both went into the Princess Periezadeh's apartment, and after they had asked her pardon for coming at so unseasonable a time, they told her all the circumstances of their meeting the emperor.

The princess was somewhat surprised at this intelligence. "It was on my account, I know," she said, "you refused the emperor, and I am infinitely obliged to you for doing so. For, my dear brothers, I know by this your affection for me is equal to my own. But you know monarchs will be obeyed in their desires, and it may be dangerous to oppose them; therefore, if to follow my inclination I should dissuade you from showing the complaisance the emperor expects from you, it may expose you to his resentment, and may render myself and you miserable. These are my sentiments; but before we conclude upon anything let us consult the speaking-bird, and hear what he says; he is wise, and has promised his assistance in all difficulties."

The princess sent for the cage, and after she had related the circumstances to the bird in the presence of her brothers, asked him what they should do in this perplexity.

The bird answered, "The princes, your brothers, must conform to the emperor's pleasure, and in their turn invite him to come and see your house."

Next morning the princes met the emperor again, who called and asked them, while they were yet afar off, if they had remembered to speak to their sister. Prince Bahman approached, and answered, "Sire, your majesty may dispose of us as you please. We are ready to obey you; for we have not only obtained our sister's consent with great ease, but she took it amiss that we should pay her that deference in a matter wherein our duty to your majesty was concerned. But if we have offended, we hope you will pardon us."

"Do not be uneasy on that account," replied the emperor. "So far from taking amiss what you have done, I highly approve of your conduct, and hope you will have the same deference and attachment to my person, if I have ever so little share in your friendship."

The princes, confounded at the emperor's goodness, returned no other answer but a low obeisance, to show the great respect with which they received it.

The emperor gave orders to return at once to his palace. He made the princes ride one on each side of him, an honor which grieved the grand vizier, who was much mortified to see them preferred before him.

When the emperor entered his capital, the eyes of the people, who stood in crowds in the streets, were fixed upon the two Princes Bahman and Perviz; and they were earnest to know who they might be, whether foreigners or natives, and many wished that the emperor had been blessed with two such handsome princes.

The first thing that the emperor did when he arrived at his palace was to conduct the princes into the principal apartments. With due discrimination, like persons conversant in such matters, they praised the beauty and symmetry of the rooms, and the richness of the furniture and ornaments. Afterward, a magnificent repast was served up, and the emperor made them sit with him, and was so much pleased with the wit, judgment, and discernment shown by the two princes that he said, "Were these my own children, and I had improved their talents by suitable education, they could not have been more accomplished or better informed."

When night approached, the two princes prostrated themselves at the emperor's feet; and having thanked him for the favors he had heaped upon them, asked his permission to retire, which was granted by the emperor.

Before they went out of the emperor's presence, Prince Bahman said, "Sire, may we presume to request that you will do us and our sister the honor to visit us the first time you take the diversion of hunting in that neighborhood? Our house is not worthy your presence; but monarchs sometimes have vouchsafed to take shelter in a cottage."

"My children," replied the emperor, "your house cannot be otherwise than beautiful, and worthy of its owners. I will call and see it with pleasure, which will be the greater for having for my hosts you and your sister, who is already dear to me from the accounts you give me of the rare qualities with which she is endowed; and this satisfaction I will defer no longer than to-morrow. Early in the morning I will be at the place where I shall never forget that I first saw you. Meet me, and you shall be my guides."

When the Princes Bahman and Perviz had returned home they gave the princess an account of the distinguished reception the emperor had accorded them, and told her that he would call at their house the next day.

"If it be so," replied the princess, "we must think of preparing a repast fit for his majesty; and for that purpose I think it would be proper we should consult the speaking-bird; he will tell us perhaps what meats the emperor likes best."

The princes approved of her plan, and after they had retired, she consulted the bird alone.

"Bird," said she, "the emperor will to-morrow come to see our house, and we are to entertain him. Tell us what we shall do to acquit ourselves to his satisfaction."

"Good mistress," replied the bird, "you have excellent cooks; let them do the best they can. But above all things, let them prepare a dish of cucumbers stuffed full of pearls, which must be set before the emperor in the first course, before all the other dishes."

"Cucumbers stuffed full of pearls!" cried Princess Periezadeh, with amazement. "Surely, bird, you do not know what you say. It is an unheard-of dish! Besides, all the pearls I possess are not enough for such a dish."

"Mistress," said the bird, "do what I say, and as for the pearls, go early to-morrow morning to the foot of the first tree on your right hand in the park, dig under it, and you will find more than you want."

The princess immediately ordered a gardener to be ready to attend her in the morning, and led him at daybreak to the tree which the bird had told her of, and bade him dig at its foot. When the gardener came to a certain depth, he found some resistance to the spade, and presently discovered a gold box, about a foot square, which he gave into the princess's hands. As it was fastened only with neat little hasps, she soon opened it, and found it full of pearls. Very well satisfied with having found this treasure, after she had shut the box again she put it under her arm, and went back to the house; while the gardener threw the earth into the hole at the foot of the tree as it had been before.

The princess, as she returned to the house, met her two brothers and gave them an account of her having consulted the bird, and the answer he had given her to prepare a dish of cucumbers stuffed full of pearls, and how he had told her where to find this box. The princes and princess, though they could not by any means guess at the reason of the bird ordering them to prepare such a dish, yet agreed to follow his advice exactly.

As soon as the princess entered the house she called for the head cook; and after she had given him directions about the entertainment for the emperor, said to him, "Besides all this, you must dress an extraordinary dish to set before the emperor himself. This dish must be of cucumbers stuffed with these pearls." And at the same time she opened the box and showed him the pearls.

The chief cook, who had never heard of such a dish, started back, and could make no reply, but took the box and retired. Afterward the princess gave directions to all the domestics to have everything in order, both in house and gardens, to receive the emperor.

Next day the two princes went to the place appointed; and as soon as the Emperor of Persia arrived the chase began, which lasted till the heat of the sun obliged him to leave off. While Prince Bahman stayed to conduct the emperor to their house, Prince Perviz rode before to show the way, and when he came in sight of the house, spurred his horse, to inform the Princess Periezadeh that the emperor was approaching; but she had been told by some attendants whom she had placed to give notice, and the prince found her waiting ready to receive him.

When the emperor had entered the courtyard, and alighted at the portico, the princess came and threw herself at his feet.

The emperor stooped to raise her, and after he had gazed some time on her beauty, said, "The brothers are worthy of the sister, and she is worthy of them. I am not amazed that the brothers would do nothing without their sister's consent; but," added he, "I hope to be better acquainted with you, my daughter, after I have seen the house."

The princess led the emperor through all the rooms except the hall; and after he had considered them very attentively and admired their variety, "My daughter," said he to the princess, "do you call this a country house? The finest and largest cities would soon be deserted if all country houses were like yours. I am no longer surprised that you take so much delight in it, and despise the town. Now let me see the garden, which I doubt not is answerable to the house."

The princess opened a door which led into the garden; and conducted him to the spot where the harmonious tree was planted, and there the emperor heard a concert, different from all he had ever heard before.

Stopping to see where the musicians were, he could discern nobody far or near, but still distinctly heard the music, which ravished his senses. "My daughter," said he to the princess, "where are the musicians whom I hear? Are they underground, or invisible in the air? Such excellent performers will lose nothing by being seen; on the contrary, they would please the more."

"Sire," answered the princess, smiling, "they are not musicians, but the leaves of the tree your majesty sees before you, which form this concert; and if you will give yourself the trouble to go a little nearer, you will be convinced, for the voices will be the more distinct."

The emperor went nearer, and was so charmed with the sweet harmony that he could never have been tired with hearing it.

"Daughter," said he, "tell me, I pray you, whether this wonderful tree was found in your garden by chance, or was a present made to you, or have you procured it from some foreign country? It must certainly have come from a great distance, otherwise, curious as I am after natural rarities, I should have heard of it. What name do you call it by?"

"Sire," replied the princess, "this tree has no other name than that of the singing-tree, and is not a native of this country. Its history is connected with the yellow-water and the speaking-bird, which came to me at the same time, and which your majesty may see after you have rested yourself. And if it please you, I will relate to you the history of these rarities."

"My daughter," replied the emperor, "my fatigue is so well recompensed by the wonderful things you have shown me, that I do not feel it the least. I am impatient to see the yellow-water and to admire the speaking-bird."

When the emperor came to the yellow-water his eyes were fixed so steadfastly upon the fountain that he could not take them off. At last, addressing himself to the princess, he said, "Whence is this wonderful water? Where its source? By what art is it made to play so high that nothing in the world can be compared to it? I conclude that it is foreign, as well as the singing-tree."

"Sire," replied the princess, "it is as your majesty conjectures; and to let you know that this water has no communication with any spring, I must inform you that the basin is one entire stone, so that the water cannot come in at the sides or underneath. But what your majesty will think most wonderful is, that all this water proceeded but from one small flagon, emptied into this basin, which increased to the quantity you see, by a property peculiar to itself, and formed this fountain."

"Well," said the emperor, going from the fountain, "this is enough for one time. I promise myself the pleasure to come and visit it often. Now let us go and see the speaking-bird."

As he went toward the hall, the emperor perceived a prodigious number of singing-birds in the trees around, filling the air with their songs and warblings, and asked why there were so many there, and none on the other trees in the garden.

"The reason, sire," answered the princess, "is, because they come from all parts to accompany the song of the speaking-bird, which your majesty may see in a cage in one of the windows of the hall we are approaching; and if you attend, you will perceive that his notes are sweeter than those of any of the other birds, even the nightingale's."

The emperor went into the hall; and as the bird continued singing, the princess raised her voice, and said, "My slave, here is the emperor. Pay your compliments to him."

The bird left off singing that instant, all the other birds ceasing also, and it said, "God save the emperor. May he long live!"

As the entertainment was served at the sofa near the window where the bird was placed, the sultan replied, as he was taking his seat, "Bird, I thank you, and am overjoyed to find in you the sultan and king of birds."

As soon as the emperor saw the dish of cucumbers set before him, thinking it was stuffed in the best manner, he reached out his hand and took one; but when he cut it, was in extreme surprise to find it stuffed with pearls.

"What novelty is this?" said he. "And with what design were these cucumbers stuffed thus with pearls, since pearls are not to be eaten!"

He looked at the two princes and the princess to ask them the meaning; when the bird, interrupting him, said, "Can your majesty be in such great astonishment at cucumbers stuffed with pearls, which you see with your own eyes, and yet so easily believe that the queen your wife was the mother of a dog, a cat, and of a piece of wood?"

"I believed those things," replied the emperor, "because the nurses assured me of the facts."

"Those nurses, sire," replied the bird, "were the queen's two sisters, who, envious of her happiness in being preferred by your majesty before them, to satisfy their envy and revenge have abused your majesty's credulity. If you interrogate them, they will confess their crime. The two brothers and the sister whom you see before you are your own children, whom they exposed, and who were saved by the intendant of your gardens, who adopted and brought them up as his own children."

"Bird," cried the emperor, "I believe the truth which you discover to me. The inclination which drew me to them told me plainly they must be my own kin. Come then, my sons, come, my daughter, let me embrace you, and give you the first marks of a father's love and tenderness."

The emperor then rose, and after having embraced the two princes and the princess, and mingled his tears with theirs, said, "It is not enough, my children. You must embrace each other, not as the children of the intendant of my gardens, to whom I have been so much obliged for preserving your lives, but as my own children, of the royal blood of the monarchs of Persia, whose glory, I am persuaded, you will maintain."

After the two princes and the princess had embraced mutually with new satisfaction, the emperor sat down again with them, and finished his meal in haste; and when he had done, said, "My children, you see in me your father; to-morrow I will bring the queen your mother. Therefore prepare to receive her."

The emperor afterward mounted his horse, and returned with expedition to his capital. The first thing he did, as soon as he had alighted and entered his palace, was to command the grand vizier to seize the queen's two sisters. They were taken from their houses separately, convicted and condemned, and the fatal sentence was put in execution within an hour.

In the meantime the Emperor Khoonoo-shah, followed by all the lords of his court who were then present, went on foot to the door of the great mosque; and after he had taken the queen out of the strict confinement she had languished under for so many years, embracing her in the miserable condition to which she was then reduced, he said to her, with tears in his eyes:

"I come to entreat your pardon for the injustice I have done you, and to make you the reparation I ought. I have punished your cruel sisters who put the abominable cheat upon me; and I hope soon to present to you two accomplished princes and a lovely princess, our children. Come and resume your former rank, with all the honors which are your due."

All this was done and said before great crowds of people, who flocked from all parts at the first news of what was passing, and immediately spread the joyful intelligence through the city.

Next morning early the emperor and queen, whose mournful humiliating dress was changed for magnificent robes, went with all their court to the house built by the intendant of the gardens, where the emperor presented the Princes Bahman and Perviz and the Princess Periezadeh to their enraptured mother.

"These, much injured wife," said he, "are the two princes your sons, and this the princess your daughter; embrace them with the same tenderness I have done, since they are worthy both of me and you."

The tears flowed plentifully down the cheeks of all, but especially of the queen, from her exceeding joy at having two such princes for her sons, and such a princess for her daughter, on whose account she had so long endured the severest afflictions.

The two princes and the princess had prepared a magnificent repast for the emperor and queen and their court. As soon as that was over, the emperor led the queen into the garden, and showed her the harmonious-tree and the beautiful yellow-fountain. She had already seen and heard the speaking-bird in his cage, and the emperor had spared no panegyric in his praise during the repast.

When there was nothing to detain the emperor any longer, he took horse, and with the Princes Bahman and Perviz on his right hand, and the queen and the princess at his left, preceded and followed by all the officers of his court according to their rank, returned to his capital. Crowds of people came out to meet them, and with acclamations of joy ushered them into the city, where all eyes were fixed not only upon the queen, the two princes, and the princess, but also upon the bird which the princess carried before her in his cage, admiring his sweet notes which had drawn all the other birds about him, which followed him, flying from tree to tree in the country, and from one housetop to another in the city.

The Princes Bahman and Perviz and the Princess Periezadeh were at length brought to the palace with this pomp, and nothing was to be seen or heard all that night but illuminations and rejoicings both in the palace and in the utmost parts of the city, which lasted for many days, and extended throughout the empire of Persia.

Crowds of people came out to meet them, and with acclamations
of joy ushered them into the city.

THE STORY OF ALADDIN; OR, THE WONDERFUL LAMP

In one of the large and rich cities of China there once lived a tailor named Mustapha. He was very poor. He could hardly, by his daily labor, maintain himself and his family, which consisted only of his wife and a son.

His son, who was called Aladdin, was a very careless and idle fellow. He was disobedient to his father and mother, and would go out early in the morning and stay out all day, playing in the streets and public places with idle children of his own age. When he was old enough to learn a trade his father took him into his own shop, and taught him how to use his needle; but all his father's endeavors to keep him to his work were vain, for no sooner was his back turned than the boy was gone for that day. Mustapha chastised him, but Aladdin was incorrigible, and his father, to his great grief, was forced to abandon him to his idleness. He was so much troubled about him, that he fell sick and died in a few months.

Aladdin, who was now no longer restrained by the fear of a father, gave himself over entirely to his idle habits, and was never out of the streets from his companions. This course he followed till he was fifteen years old, without giving his mind to any useful pursuit, or the least reflection on what would become of him. As he was one day playing in the street with his evil associates, according to custom, a stranger passing by stood to observe him.

This stranger was a sorcerer, known as the African magician, as he had been but two days arrived from Africa, his native country.

The African magician, observing in Aladdin's countenance something which assured him that he was a fit boy for his purpose, inquired his name and history of his companions. When he had learned all he desired to know, he went up to him, and taking him aside from his comrades, said, "Child, was not your father called Mustapha the tailor?"

"Yes, sir," answered the boy, "but he has been dead a long time."

At these words the African magician threw his arms about Aladdin's neck, and kissed him several times, with tears in his eyes, saying, "I am your uncle. Your worthy father was my own brother. I knew you at first sight, you are so like him."

Then he gave Aladdin a handful of small money, saying, "Go, my son, to your mother. Give my love to her, and tell her that I will visit her to-morrow, that I may see where my good brother lived so long, and ended his days."

Aladdin ran to his mother, overjoyed at the money his uncle had given him.

"Mother," said he, "have I an uncle?"

"No, child," replied his mother, "you have no uncle by your father's side or mine."

"I am just now come," said Aladdin, "from a man who says he is my uncle, and my father's brother. He cried, and kissed me, when I told him my father was dead, and gave me money, sending his love to you, and promising to come and pay you a visit, that he may see the house my father lived and died in."

"Indeed, child," replied the mother, "your father had no brother, nor have you an uncle."

The next day the magician found Aladdin playing in another part of the town, and embracing him as before, put two pieces of gold into his hand, and said to him, "Carry this, child, to your mother. Tell her that I will come and see her to-night, and bid her get us something for supper. But first show me the house where you live."

Aladdin showed the African magician the house, and carried the two pieces of gold to his mother, who went out and bought provisions; and considering she wanted various utensils, borrowed them of her neighbors. She spent the whole day in preparing the supper; and at night, when it was ready, said to her son, "Perhaps the stranger knows not how to find our house; go and bring him, if you meet with him."

Aladdin was just ready to go, when the magician knocked at the door, and came in loaded with wine and all sorts of fruits, which he brought for a dessert. After he had given what he brought into Aladdin's hands, he saluted his mother, and desired her to show him the place where his brother Mustapha used to sit on the sofa; and when she had so done, he fell down, and kissed it several times, crying out, with tears in his eyes, "My poor brother! How unhappy am I, not to have come soon enough to give you one last embrace!"

Aladdin's mother desired him to sit down in the same place, but he declined.

"No," said he, "I shall not do that; but give me leave to sit opposite to it, that although I see not the master of a family so dear to me, I may at least behold the place where he used to sit."

When the magician had made choice of a place, and sat down, he began to enter into discourse with Aladdin's mother.

"My good sister," said he, "do not be surprised at your never having seen me all the time you have been married to my brother Mustapha of happy memory. I have been forty years absent from this country, which is my native place as well as my late brother's. During that time I have traveled into the Indies, Persia, Arabia, and Syria, and afterward crossed over into Africa, where I took up my abode in Egypt. At last, as it is natural for a man, I was desirous to see my native country again, and to embrace my dear brother; and finding I had strength enough to undertake so long a journey, I made the necessary preparations, and set out. Nothing ever afflicted me so much as hearing of my brother's death. But God be praised for all things! It is a comfort for me to find, as it were, my brother in a son, who has his most remarkable features."

The African magician, perceiving that the widow wept at the remembrance of her husband, changed the conversation, and turning toward her son, asked him, "What business do you follow? Are you of any trade?"

At this question the youth hung down his head, and was not a little abashed when his mother answered, "Aladdin is an idle fellow. His father, when alive, strove all he could to teach him his trade, but could not succeed; and since his death, notwithstanding all I can say to him, he does nothing but idle away his time in the streets, as you saw him, without considering he is no longer a child; and if you do not make him ashamed of it, I despair of his ever coming to any good. For my part, I am resolved, one of these days, to turn him out of doors, and let him provide for himself."

After these words, Aladdin's mother burst into tears; and the magician said, "This is not well, nephew; you must think of helping yourself, and getting your livelihood. There are many sorts of trades; perhaps you do not like your father's, and would prefer another; I will endeavor to help you. If you have no mind to learn any handicraft, I will take a shop for you, furnish it with all sorts of fine stuffs and linens; and then with the money you make of them you can lay in fresh goods, and live in an honorable way. Tell me freely what you think of my proposal; you shall always find me ready to keep my word."

This plan just suited Aladdin, who hated work. He told the magician he had a greater inclination to that business than to any other, and that he should be much obliged to him for his kindness. "Well, then," said the African magician, "I will carry you with me to-morrow, clothe you as handsomely as the best merchants in the city, and afterward we will open a shop as I mentioned."

The widow, after his promise of kindness to her son, no longer doubted that the magician was her husband's brother. She thanked him for his good intentions; and after having exhorted Aladdin to render himself worthy of his uncle's favor, she served up supper, at which they talked of several indifferent matters; and then the magician took his leave and retired.

He came again the next day, as he had promised, and took Aladdin with him to a merchant, who sold all sorts of clothes for different ages and ranks, ready made, and a variety of fine stuffs, and bade Aladdin choose those he preferred, which he paid for.

When Aladdin found himself so handsomely equipped, he returned his uncle thanks, who thus addressed him: "As you are soon to be a merchant, it is proper you should frequent these shops, and become acquainted with them."

He then showed him the largest and finest mosques, carried him to the khans or inns where the merchants and travelers lodged, and afterward to the sultan's palace, where he had free access; and at last brought him to his own khan, where, meeting with some merchants he had become acquainted with since his arrival, he gave them a treat, to bring them and his pretended nephew acquainted.

This entertainment lasted till night, when Aladdin would have taken leave of his uncle to go home. The magician would not let him go by himself, but conducted him to his mother, who, as soon as she saw him so well dressed, was transported with joy, and bestowed a thousand blessings upon the magician.

Early the next morning the magician called again for Aladdin, and said he would take him to spend that day in the country, and on the next he would purchase the shop. He then led him out at one of the gates of the city, to some magnificent palaces, to each of which belonged beautiful gardens, into which anybody might enter. At every building he came to he asked Aladdin if he did not think it fine; and the youth was ready to answer, when any one presented itself, crying out, "Here is a finer house, uncle, than any we have yet seen."

By this artifice the cunning magician led Aladdin some way into the country; and as he meant to carry him farther, to execute his design, pretending to be tired, he took an opportunity to sit down in one of the gardens, on the brink of a fountain of clear water which discharged itself by a lion's mouth of bronze into a basin.

"Come, nephew," said he, "you must be weary as well as I. Let us rest ourselves, and we shall be better able to pursue our walk."

The magician next pulled from his girdle a handkerchief with cakes and fruit, and during this short repast he exhorted his nephew to leave off bad company, and to seek that of wise and prudent men, to improve by their conversation. "For," said he, "you will soon be at man's estate, and you cannot too early begin to imitate their example."

When they had eaten as much as they liked, they got up, and pursued their walk through gardens separated from one another only by small ditches, which marked out the limits without interrupting the communication; so great was the confidence the inhabitants reposed in each other.

By this means the African magician drew Aladdin insensibly beyond the gardens, and crossed the country, till they nearly reached the mountains.

At last they arrived between two mountains of moderate height and equal size, divided by a narrow valley, where the magician intended to execute the design that had brought him from Africa to China.

"We will go no farther now," said he to Aladdin. "I will show you here some extraordinary things, which, when you have seen, you will thank me for; but while I strike a light, gather up all the loose dry sticks you can see, to kindle a fire with."

Aladdin found so many dried sticks that he soon collected a great heap. The magician presently set them on fire; and when they were in a blaze he threw in some incense, pronouncing several magical words, which Aladdin did not understand.

He had scarcely done so when the earth opened just before the magician, and disclosed a stone with a brass ring fixed in it. Aladdin was so frightened that he would have run away, but the magician caught hold of him, and gave him such a box on the ear that he knocked him down. Aladdin got up trembling, and, with tears in his eyes, said to the magician, "What have I done, uncle, to be treated in this severe manner?"

"I am your uncle," answered the magician; "I supply the place of your father, and you ought to make no reply. But, child," added he, softening, "do not be afraid; for I shall not ask anything of you, but that, if you obey me punctually, you will reap the advantages which I intend you. Know, then, that under this stone there is hidden a treasure, destined to be yours, and which will make you richer than the greatest monarch in the world. No person but yourself is permitted to lift this stone, or enter the cave; so you must punctually execute what I may command, for it is a matter of great consequence both to you and to me."

Aladdin, amazed at all he saw and heard, forgot what was past, and rising said, "Well, uncle, what is to be done? Command me. I am ready to obey."

"I am overjoyed, child," said the African magician, embracing him. "Take hold of the ring, and lift up that stone."

"Indeed, uncle," replied Aladdin, "I am not strong enough; you must help me."

"You have no occasion for my assistance," answered the magician; "if I help you, we shall be able to do nothing. Take hold of the ring, and lift it up; you will find it will come easily." Aladdin did as the magician bade him, raised the stone with ease, and laid it on one side.

When the stone was pulled up there appeared a staircase about three or four feet deep, leading to a door.

"Descend those steps, my son," said the African magician, "and open that door. It will lead you into a palace, divided into three great halls. In each of these you will see four large brass cisterns placed on each side, full of gold and silver; but take care you do not meddle with them. Before you enter the first hall, be sure to tuck up your robe, wrap it about you, and then pass through the second into the third without stopping. Above all things, have a care that you do not touch the walls so much as with your clothes; for if you do, you will die instantly. At the end of the third hall you will find a door which opens into a garden planted with fine trees loaded with fruit. Walk directly across the garden to a terrace, where you will see a niche before you, and in that niche a lighted lamp. Take the lamp down and put it out. When you have thrown away the wick and poured out the liquor, put it in your waistband and bring it to me. Do not be afraid that the liquor will spoil your clothes, for it is not oil, and the lamp will be dry as soon as it is thrown out."

After these words the magician drew a ring off his finger, and put it on one of Aladdin's, saying, "It is a talisman against all evil, so long as you obey me. Go, therefore, boldly, and we shall both be rich all our lives."

Aladdin descended the steps, and, opening the door, found the three halls just as the African magician had described. He went through them with all the precaution the fear of death could inspire, crossed the garden without stopping, took down the lamp from the niche, threw out the wick and the liquor, and, as the magician had desired, put it in his waistband. But as he came down from the terrace, seeing it was perfectly dry, he stopped in the garden to observe the trees, which were loaded with extraordinary fruit of different colors on each tree. Some bore fruit entirely white, and some clear and transparent as crystal; some pale red, and others deeper; some green, blue, and purple, and others yellow; in short, there was fruit of all colors. The white were pearls; the clear and transparent, diamonds; the deep red, rubies; the paler, ballas rubies; the green, emeralds; the blue, turquoises; the purple, amethysts; and the yellow, sapphires. Aladdin, ignorant of their value, would have preferred figs, or grapes, or pomegranates; but as he had  his uncle's permission, he resolved to gather some of every sort. Having filled the two new purses his uncle had bought for him with his clothes, he wrapped some up in the skirts of his vest, and crammed his bosom as full as it could hold.

Aladdin, having thus loaded himself with riches of which he knew not the value, returned through the three halls with the utmost precaution, and soon arrived at the mouth of the cave, where the African magician awaited him with the utmost impatience.

As soon as Aladdin saw him, he cried out, "Pray, uncle, lend me your hand, to help me out."

"Give me the lamp first," replied the magician; "it will be troublesome to you."

"Indeed, uncle," answered Aladdin, "I cannot now; but I will as soon as I am up."

The African magician was determined that he would have the lamp before he would help him up; and Aladdin, who had encumbered himself so much with his fruit that he could not well get at it, refused to give it to him till he was out of the cave. The African magician, provoked at this obstinate refusal, flew into a passion, threw a little of his incense into the fire, and pronounced two magical words, when the stone which had closed the mouth of the staircase moved into its place, with the earth over it in the same manner as it lay at the arrival of the magician and Aladdin.

This action of the magician plainly revealed to Aladdin that he was no uncle of his, but one who designed him evil. The truth was that he had learned from his magic books the secret and the value of this wonderful lamp, the owner of which would be made richer than any earthly ruler, and hence his journey to China. His art had also told him that he was not permitted to take it himself, but must receive it as a voluntary gift from the hands of another person. Hence he employed young Aladdin, and hoped by a mixture of kindness and authority to make him obedient to his word and will. When he found that his attempt had failed, he set out to return to Africa, but avoided the town, lest any person who had seen him leave in company with Aladdin should make inquiries after the youth.

Aladdin, being suddenly enveloped in darkness, cried, and called out to his uncle to tell him he was ready to give him the lamp. But in vain, since his cries could not be heard.

He descended to the bottom of the steps, with a design to get into the palace, but the door, which was opened before by enchantment, was now shut by the same means. He then redoubled his cries and tears, sat down on the steps without any hopes of ever seeing light again, and in an expectation of passing from the present darkness to a speedy death.

In this great emergency he said, "There is no strength or power but in the great and high God"; and in joining his hands to pray he rubbed the ring which the magician had put on his finger. Immediately a genie of frightful aspect appeared, and said, "What wouldst thou have? I am ready to obey thee. I serve him who possesses the ring on thy finger; I, and the other slaves of that ring."

At another time Aladdin would have been frightened at the sight of so extraordinary a figure, but the danger he was in made him answer without hesitation, "Whoever thou art, deliver me from this place." He had no sooner spoken these words than he found himself on the very spot where the magician had last left him, and no sign of cave or opening, nor disturbance of the earth. Returning thanks to God for being once more in the world, he made the best of his way home. When he got within his mother's door, joy at seeing her and weakness for want of sustenance made him so faint that he remained for a long time as dead. As soon as he recovered, he related to his mother all that had happened to him, and they were both very vehement in their complaints of the cruel magician.

Aladdin slept very soundly till late the next morning, when the first thing he said to his mother was, that he wanted something to eat, and wished she would give him his breakfast.

"Alas! child," said she, "I have not a bit of bread to give you; you ate up all the provisions I had in the house yesterday; but I have a little cotton which I have spun; I will go and sell it, and buy bread and something for our dinner."

"Mother," replied Aladdin, "keep your cotton for another time, and give me the lamp I brought home with me yesterday. I will go and sell it, and the money I shall get for it will serve both for breakfast and dinner, and perhaps supper too."

Aladdin's mother took the lamp and said to her son, "Here it is, but it is very dirty. If it were a little cleaner I believe it would bring something more."

She took some fine sand and water to clean it. But she had no sooner

Immediately a genie of frightful aspect appeared, and said,
"What wouldst thou have?"

begun to rub it, than in an instant a hideous genie of gigantic size appeared before her, and said to her in a voice of thunder, "What wouldst thou have? I am ready to obey thee as thy slave, and the slave of all those who have that lamp in their hands; I, and the other slaves of the lamp."

Aladdin's mother, terrified at the sight of the genie, fainted; when Aladdin, who had seen such a phantom in the cavern, snatched the lamp out of his mother's hand, and said to the genie boldly, "I am hungry. Bring me something to eat."

The genie disappeared immediately, and in an instant returned with a large silver tray, holding twelve covered dishes of the same metal, which contained the most delicious viands; six large white bread cakes on two plates, two flagons of wine, and two silver cups. All these he placed upon a carpet and disappeared; this was done before Aladdin's mother recovered from her swoon.

Aladdin had fetched some water, and sprinkled it in her face to recover her. Whether that or the smell of the meat effected her cure, it was not long before she came to herself.

"Mother," said Aladdin, "be not afraid. Get up and eat. Here is what will put you in heart, and at the same time satisfy my extreme hunger."

His mother was much surprised to see the great tray, twelve dishes, six loaves, the two flagons and cups, and to smell the savory odor which exhaled from the dishes.

"Child," said she, "to whom are we obliged for this great plenty and liberality? Has the sultan been made acquainted with our poverty, and had compassion on us?"

"It is no matter, mother," said Aladdin. "Let us sit down and eat; for you have almost as much need of a good breakfast as I myself. When we have done, I will tell you."

Accordingly, both mother and son sat down and ate with the better relish as the table was so well furnished. But all the time Aladdin's mother could not forbear looking at and admiring the tray and dishes, though she could not judge whether they were silver or any other metal, and the novelty more than the value attracted her attention.

The mother and son sat at breakfast till it was dinner time, and then they thought it would be best to put the two meals together. Yet, after this they found they should have enough left for supper, and two meals for the next day.

When Aladdin's mother had taken away and set by what was left, she went and sat down by her son on the sofa, saying, "I expect now that you will satisfy my impatience, and tell me exactly what passed between the genie and you while I was in a swoon."

He readily complied with her request.

She was in as great amazement at what her son told her as at the appearance of the genie, and said to him, "But, son, what have we to do with genies? I never heard that any of my acquaintance had ever seen one. How came that vile genie to address himself to me, and not to you, to whom he had appeared before in the cave?"

"Mother," answered Aladdin, "the genie you saw is not the one who appeared to me. If you remember, he that I first saw called himself the slave of the ring on my finger; and this you saw, called himself the slave of the lamp you had in your hand; but I believe you did not hear him, for I think you fainted as soon as he began to speak."

"What!" cried the mother, "was your lamp then the occasion of that cursed genie's addressing himself to me rather than to you? Ah! my son, take it out of my sight, and put it where you please. I had rather you would sell it than run the hazard of being frightened to death again by touching it; and if you would take my advice, you would part also with the ring, and not have anything to do with genies, who, as our prophet has told us, are only devils."

"With your leave, mother," replied Aladdin, "I shall now take care how I sell a lamp which may be so serviceable both to you and me. That false and wicked magician would not have undertaken so long a journey to secure this wonderful lamp if he had not known its value to exceed that of gold and silver. And since we have honestly come by it, let us make a profitable use of it, without making any great show and exciting the envy and jealousy of our neighbors. However, since the genies frighten you so much, I will take it out of your sight, and put it where I may find it when I want it. The ring I cannot resolve to part with; for without that you had never seen me again; and though I am alive now, perhaps, if it were gone, I might not be so some moments hence. Therefore I hope you will give me leave to keep it, and to wear it always on my finger."

Aladdin's mother replied that he might do what he pleased; for her part, she would have nothing to do with genies, and never say anything more about them.

By the next night they had eaten all the provisions the genie had brought; and the next day Aladdin, who could not bear the thought of hunger, putting one of the silver dishes under his vest, went out early to sell it. Addressing himself to a Jew whom he met in the streets, he took him aside, and pulling out the plate, asked him if he would buy it.

The cunning Jew took the

dish, examined it, and as soon as he found that it was good silver, asked Aladdin at how much he valued it.

Aladdin, who had never been used to such traffic, told him he would trust to his judgment and honor. The Jew was somewhat confounded at this plain dealing; and doubting whether Aladdin understood the material or the full value of what he offered to sell, took a piece of gold out of his purse and gave it him, though it was but the sixtieth part of the worth of the plate. Aladdin, taking the money very eagerly, retired with so much haste that the Jew, not content with the exorbitancy of his profit, was vexed he had not penetrated into his ignorance, and was going to run after him, to endeavor to get some change out of the piece of gold. But the boy ran so fast, and had got so far, that it would have been impossible to overtake him.

Before Aladdin went home he called at a baker's, bought some cakes of bread, changed his money, and on his return gave the rest to his mother, who went and purchased provisions enough to last them some time. After this manner they lived, until Aladdin had sold the twelve dishes singly, as necessity pressed, to the Jew, for the same money; who, after the first time, durst not offer him less, for fear of losing so good a bargain. When he had sold the last dish, he had recourse to the tray, which weighed ten times as much as the dishes, and would have carried it to his old purchaser, but that it was too large and cumbersome; therefore he was obliged to bring him home with him to his mother's, where, after the Jew had examined the weight of the tray, he laid down ten pieces of gold, with which Aladdin was very well satisfied.

When all the money was spent, Aladdin had recourse again to the lamp. He took it in his hands, looked for the part where his mother had rubbed it with the sand, and rubbed it also. The genie immediately appeared, and said, "What wouldst thou have? I am ready to obey thee as thy slave, and the slave of all those who have that lamp in their hands; I, and the other slaves of the lamp."

"I am hungry," said Aladdin. "Bring me something to eat."

The genie disappeared, and presently returned with a tray holding the same number of covered dishes as before, set it down, and vanished.

As soon as Aladdin found that their provisions were again expended, he took one of the dishes, and went to look for his Jew chapman. But as he was passing by a goldsmith's shop, the goldsmith perceiving him, called to him, and said, "My lad, I imagine that you have something to sell to the Jew, whom I often see you visit. Perhaps you do not know that he is the greatest rogue even among the Jews. I will give you the full worth of what you have to sell, or I will direct you to other merchants who will not cheat you."

This offer induced Aladdin to pull his plate from under his vest and show it to the goldsmith. At first sight he perceived that it was made of the finest silver, and asked if he had sold such as that to the Jew. When Aladdin told him he had sold him twelve such, for a piece of gold each, "What a villain!" cried the goldsmith. "But," added he, "my son, what is past cannot be recalled. By showing you the value of this plate, which is of the finest silver we use in our shops, I will let you see how much the Jew has cheated you."

The goldsmith took a pair of scales, weighed the dish, and assured him that his plate would fetch by weight sixty pieces of gold, which he offered to pay down immediately.

Aladdin thanked him for his fair dealing, and never after went to any other person.

Though Aladdin and his mother had an inexhaustible treasure in their lamp, and might have had whatever they wished for, yet they lived with the same frugality as before, and it may easily be supposed that the money for which Aladdin had sold the dishes and tray was sufficient to maintain them some time.

During this interval, Aladdin frequented the shops of the principal merchants, where they sold cloth of gold and silver, linens, silk stuffs, and jewelry, and, oftentimes joining in their conversation, acquired a knowledge of the world, and a desire to improve himself. By his acquaintance among the jewelers, he came to know that the fruits which he had gathered when he took the lamp were, instead of colored glass, stones of inestimable value; but he had the prudence not to mention this to any one, not even to his mother.

One day as Aladdin was walking about the town he heard an order proclaimed, commanding the people to shut up their shops and houses, and keep within doors while the Princess Buddir al Buddoor, the sultan's daughter, went to the bath and returned.

This proclamation inspired Aladdin with eager desire to see the princess's face, which he determined to gratify by placing himself behind the door of the bath, so that he could not fail to see her face.

Aladdin had not long concealed himself before the princess came. She was attended by a great crowd of ladies, slaves, and mutes, who walked on each side and behind her. When she came within three or four paces of the door of the bath, she took off her veil, and gave Aladdin an opportunity of a full view of her face.

The princess was a noted beauty; her eyes were large, lively, and sparkling; her smile bewitching; her nose faultless; her mouth small; her lips vermilion. It is not therefore surprising that Aladdin, who had never before seen such a blaze of charms, was dazzled and enchanted.

After the princess had passed by, and entered the bath, Aladdin quitted his hiding place, and went home. His mother perceived him to be more thoughtful and melancholy than usual, and asked what had happened to make him so, or if he were ill. He then told his mother all his adventure, and concluded by declaring,

"I love the princess more than I can express, and am resolved that I will ask her in marriage of the sultan."

Aladdin's mother listened with surprise to what her son told her. When he talked of asking the princess in marriage, she laughed aloud.

"Alas! child," said she, "what are you thinking of? You must be mad to talk thus."

"I assure you, mother," replied Aladdin, "that I am not mad, but in my right senses. I foresaw that you would reproach me with folly and extravagance; but I must tell you once more that I am resolved to demand the princess of the sultan in marriage; nor do I despair of success. I have the slaves of the lamp and of the ring to help me, and you know how powerful their aid is. And I have another secret to tell you; those pieces of glass, which I got from the trees in the garden of the subterranean palace, are jewels of inestimable value, and fit for the greatest monarchs. All the precious stones the jewelers have in Bagdad are not to be compared to mine for size or beauty; and I am sure that the offer of them will secure the favor of the sultan. You have a large porcelain dish fit to hold them; fetch it, and let us see how they will look, when we have arranged them according to their different colors."

Aladdin's mother brought the china dish. Then he took the jewels out of the two purses in which he had kept them, and placed them in order, according to his fancy. But the brightness and luster they emitted in the daytime, and the variety of the colors, so dazzled the eyes both of mother and son that they were astonished beyond measure. Aladdin's mother, emboldened by the sight of these rich jewels, and fearful lest her son should be guilty of greater extravagance, complied with his request, and promised to go early the next morning to the palace of the sultan. Aladdin rose before daybreak, awakened his mother, pressing her to go to the sultan's palace and to get admittance, if possible, before the grand vizier, the other viziers, and the great officers of state went in to take their seats in the divan, where the sultan always attended in person.

Aladdin's mother took the china dish, in which they had put the jewels the day before, wrapped it in two fine napkins, and set forward for the sultan's palace. When she came to the gates the grand vizier, the other viziers, and most distinguished lords of the court were just gone in; but notwithstanding the crowd of people was great, she got into the divan, a spacious hall, the entrance into which was very magnificent. She placed herself just before the sultan, and the grand vizier and the great lords, who sat in council on his right and left hand. Several causes were called, according to their order, pleaded and adjudged, until the time the divan generally broke up, when the sultan, rising, returned to his apartment, attended by the grand vizier; the other viziers and ministers of state then retired, as also did all those whose business had called them thither.

Aladdin's mother, seeing the sultan retire, and all the people depart, judged rightly that he would not sit again that day, and resolved to go home. On her arrival she said, with much simplicity, "Son, I have seen the sultan, and am very well persuaded he has seen me, too, for I placed myself just before him; but he was so much taken up with those who attended on all sides of him that I pitied him, and wondered at his patience. At last I believe he was heartily tired, for he rose up suddenly, and would not hear a great many who were ready prepared to speak to him, but went away, at which I was well pleased, for indeed I began to lose all patience, and was extremely fatigued with staying so long. But there is no harm done; I will go again to-morrow. Perhaps the sultan may not be so busy."

The next morning she repaired to the sultan's palace with the present as early as the day before; but when she came there, she found the gates of the divan shut.

She went six times afterward on the days appointed, placed herself always directly before the sultan, but with as little success as the first morning.

On the sixth day, however, after the divan was broken up, when the sultan returned to his own apartment he said to his grand vizier: "I have for some time observed a certain woman, who attends constantly every day that I give audience, with something wrapped up in a napkin; she always stands up from the beginning to the breaking up of the audience, and effects to place herself just before me. If this woman comes to our next audience, do not fail to call her, that I may hear what she has to say."

The grand vizier made answer by lowering his hand, and then lifting it up above his head, signifying his willingness to lose it if he failed.

On the next audience day, when Aladdin's mother went to the divan, and placed herself in front of the sultan as usual, the grand vizier immediately called the chief of the mace-bearers, and pointing to her bade him bring her before the sultan. The old woman at once followed the mace-bearer, and when she reached the sultan, bowed her head down to the carpet which covered the platform of the throne, and remained in that posture until he bade her rise.

She had no sooner done so, than he said to her, "Good woman, I have observed you to stand many days from the beginning to the rising of the divan. What business brings you here?"

At these words, Aladdin's mother prostrated herself a second time, and when she arose, said, "Monarch of monarchs, I beg of you to pardon the boldness of my petition, and to assure me of your pardon and forgiveness."

"Well," replied the sultan, "I will forgive you, be it what it may, and no hurt shall come to you. Speak boldly."

When Aladdin's mother had taken all these precautions, for fear of the sultan's anger, she told him faithfully the errand on which her son had sent her, and the event which led to his making so bold a request in spite of all her remonstrances.

The sultan hearkened to this discourse without showing the least anger. But before he gave her any answer, he asked her what she had brought tied up in the napkin. She took the china dish which she had set down at the foot of the throne, untied it, and presented it to the sultan.

The sultan's amazement and surprise were inexpressible, when he saw so many large, beautiful, and valuable jewels collected in the dish. He remained for some time lost in admiration. At last, when he had recovered himself, he received the present from Aladdin's mother's hand, saying, "How rich, how beautiful!"

After he had admired and handled all the jewels one after another, he turned to his grand vizier, and showing him the dish, said, "Behold, admire, wonder! And confess that your eyes never beheld jewels so rich and beautiful before."

The vizier was charmed.

"Well," continued the sultan, "what sayest thou to such a present? Is it not worthy of the princess my daughter? And ought I not to bestow her on one who values her at so great a price?"

"I cannot but own," replied the grand vizier, "that the present is worthy of the princess; but I beg of your majesty to grant me three months before you come to a final resolution. I hope, before that time, my son, whom you have regarded with your favor, will be able to make a nobler present than this Aladdin, who is an entire stranger to your majesty."

The sultan granted his request, and he said to the old woman, "Good woman, go home, and tell your son that I agree to the proposal you have made me; but I cannot marry the princess my daughter for three months. At the expiration of that time, come again."

Aladdin's mother returned home much more gratified than she had expected, and told her son with much joy the condescending answer she had received from the sultan's own mouth; and that she was to come to the divan again that day three months.

At hearing this news, Aladdin thought himself the most happy of all men, and thanked his mother for the pains she had taken in the affair, the good success of which was of so great importance to his peace that he counted every day, week, and even hour as it passed. When two of the three months were passed, his mother one evening, having no oil in the house, went out to buy some, and found a general rejoicing—the houses dressed with foliage, silks, and carpeting, and every one striving to show his joy according to his ability. The streets were crowded with officers in habits of ceremony, mounted on horses richly caparisoned, each attended by a great many footmen. Aladdin's mother asked the oil merchant what was the meaning of all this preparation of public festivity.

"Whence came you, good woman," said he, "that you don't know that the grand vizier's son is to marry the Princess Buddir al Buddoor, the sultan's daughter, to-night? She will presently return from the bath; and these officers whom you see are to assist at the cavalcade to the palace, where the ceremony is to be solemnized."

Aladdin's mother, on hearing this news, ran home very quickly.

"Child," cried she, "you are undone! The sultan's fine promises will come to naught. This night the grand vizier's son is to marry the Princess Buddir al Buddoor."

At this account Aladdin was thunderstruck. He bethought himself of the lamp, and of the genie who had promised to obey him; and without indulging in idle words against the sultan, the vizier, or his son, he determined, if possible, to prevent the marriage.

When Aladdin had got into his chamber he took the lamp, and rubbing it in the same place as before, immediately the genie appeared, and said to him, "What wouldst thou have? I am ready to obey thee as thy slave; I, and the other slaves of the lamp."

"Hear me," said Aladdin. "Thou hast hitherto obeyed me, but now I am about to impose on thee a harder task. The sultan's daughter, who was promised me as my bride, is this night married to the son of the grand vizier. Bring them both hither to me immediately they retire to their bedchamber."

"Master," replied the genie, "I obey you."

Aladdin supped with his mother as was their wont, and then went to his own apartment, and sat up to await the return of the genie, according to his commands.

In the meantime the festivities in honor of the princess's marriage were conducted in the sultan's palace with great magnificence. The ceremonies were at last brought to a conclusion, and the princess and the son of the vizier retired to the bedchamber prepared for them. No sooner had they entered it, and dismissed their attendants, than the genie, the faithful slave of the lamp, to the great amazement and alarm of the bride and bridegroom took up the bed, and by an agency invisible to them, transported it in an instant into Aladdin's chamber, where he set it down.

"Remove the bridegroom," said Aladdin to the genie, "and keep him a prisoner till to-morrow dawn, and then return with him here." On Aladdin being left alone with the princess, he endeavored to assuage her fears, and explained to her the treachery practiced upon him by the sultan her father. He then laid himself down beside her, putting a drawn scimitar between them, to show that he was determined to secure her safety, and to treat her with the utmost possible respect. At break of day, the genie appeared at the appointed hour, bringing back the bridegroom, whom by breathing upon he had left motionless and entranced at the door of Aladdin's chamber during the night, and at Aladdin's command transported the couch, with the bride and bridegroom on it, by the same invisible agency, into the palace of the sultan.

At the instant that the genie had set down the couch with the bride and bridegroom in their own chamber, the sultan came to the door to offer his good wishes to his daughter. The grand vizier's son, who was almost perished with cold, by standing in his thin under-garment all night, no sooner heard the knocking at the door than he got out of bed, and ran into the robing-chamber, where he had undressed himself the night before.

The sultan, having opened the door, went to the bed-side, and kissed the princess on the forehead, but was extremely surprised to see her look so melancholy. She only cast at him a sorrowful look, expressive of great affliction. He suspected there was something extraordinary in this silence, and thereupon went immediately to the sultaness's apartment, told her in what a state he found the princess, and how she had received him.

"Sire," said the sultaness, "I will go and see her. She will not receive me in the same manner."

The princess received her mother with sighs and tears, and signs of deep dejection. At last, upon her pressing on her the duty of telling her all her thoughts, she gave to the sultaness a precise description of all that happened to her during the night; on which the sultaness enjoined on her the necessity of silence and discretion, as no one would give credence to so strange a tale. The grand vizier's son, elated with the honor of being the sultan's son-in-law, kept silence on his part, and the events of the night were not allowed to cast the least gloom on the festivities on the following day, in continued celebration of the royal marriage.

When night came, the bride and bridegroom were again attended to their chamber with the same ceremonies as on the preceding evening. Aladdin, knowing that this would be so, had already given his commands to the genie of the lamp; and no sooner were they alone than their bed was removed in the same mysterious manner as on the preceding evening; and having passed the night in the same unpleasant way, they were in the morning conveyed to the palace of the sultan. Scarcely had they been replaced in their apartment, when the sultan came to make his compliments to his daughter. The princess could no longer conceal from him the unhappy treatment she had been subjected to, and told him all that had happened, as she had already related it to her mother.

The sultan, on hearing these strange tidings, consulted with the grand vizier; and finding from him that his son had been subjected by an invisible agency to even worse treatment, he determined to declare the marriage canceled, and all the festivities, which were yet to last for several days, countermanded and terminated.

This sudden change in the mind of the sultan gave rise to various speculations and reports. Nobody but Aladdin knew the secret, and he kept it with the most scrupulous silence. Neither the sultan nor the grand vizier, who had forgotten Aladdin and his request, had the least thought that he had any hand in the strange adventures that befell the bride and bridegroom.

On the very day that the three months contained in the sultan's promise expired, the mother of Aladdin again went to the palace, and stood in the same place in the divan. The sultan knew her again, and directed his vizier to have her brought before him.

After having prostrated herself, she made answer, in reply to the sultan: "Sire, I come at the end of three months to ask of you the fulfillment of the promise you made to my son."

The sultan little thought the request of Aladdin's mother was made to him in earnest, or that he would hear any more of the matter. He therefore took counsel with his vizier, who suggested that the sultan should attach such conditions to the marriage that no one of the humble condition of Aladdin could possibly fulfill. In accordance with this suggestion of the vizier, the sultan replied to the mother of Aladdin: "Good woman, it is true sultans ought to abide by their word, and I am ready to keep mine, by making your son happy in marriage with the princess my daughter. But as I cannot marry her without some further proof of your son being able to support her in royal state, you may tell him I will fulfill my promise as soon as he shall send me forty trays of massy gold, full of the same sort of jewels you have already made me a present of, and carried by the like number of black slaves, who shall be led by as many young and handsome white slaves, all dressed magnificently. On these conditions I am ready to bestow the princess my daughter upon him; therefore, good woman, go and tell him so, and I will wait till you bring me his answer."

Aladdin's mother prostrated herself a second time before the sultan's throne, and retired. On her way home, she laughed within herself at her son's foolish imagination. "Where," said she, "can he get so many large gold trays, and such precious stones to fill them? It is altogether out of his power, and I believe he will not be much pleased with my embassy this time."

When she came home, full of these thoughts, she told Aladdin all the circumstances of her interview with the sultan, and the conditions on which he consented to the marriage. "The sultan expects your answer immediately," said she; and then added, laughing, "I believe he may wait long enough!"

"Not so long, mother, as you imagine," replied Aladdin. "This demand is a mere trifle, and will prove no bar to my marriage with the princess. I will prepare at once to satisfy his request."

Aladdin retired to his own apartment and summoned the genie of the lamp, and required him to immediately prepare and present the gift, before the sultan closed his morning audience, according to the terms in which it had been prescribed. The genie professed his obedience to the owner of the lamp, and disappeared. Within a very short time, a train of forty black slaves, led by the same number of white slaves, appeared opposite the house in which Aladdin lived. Each black slave carried on his head a basin of massy gold, full of pearls, diamonds, rubies, and emeralds.

Aladdin then addressed his mother: "Madam, pray lose no time; before the sultan and the divan rise, I would have you return to the palace with this present as the dowry demanded for the princess, that he may judge by my diligence and exactness of the ardent and sincere desire I have to procure myself the honor of this alliance."

As soon as this magnificent procession, with Aladdin's mother at its head, had begun to march from Aladdin's house, the whole city was filled with the crowds of people desirous to see so grand a sight. The graceful bearing, elegant form, and wonderful likeness of each slave; their grave walk at an equal distance from each other, the luster of their jeweled girdles, and the brilliancy of the aigrettes of precious stones in their turbans, excited the greatest admiration in the spectators. As they had to pass through several streets to the palace, the whole length of the way was lined with files of spectators. Nothing, indeed, was ever seen so beautiful and brilliant in the sultan's palace, and the richest robes of the emirs of his court were not to be compared to the costly dresses of these slaves, whom they supposed to be kings.

As the sultan, who had been informed of their approach, had given orders for them to be admitted, they met with no obstacle, but went into the divan in regular order, one part turning to the right and the other to the left. After they were all entered, and had formed a semi-circle before the sultan's throne, the black slaves laid the golden trays on the carpet, prostrated themselves, touching the carpet with their foreheads, and at the same time the white slaves did the same. When they rose, the black slaves uncovered the trays, and then all stood with their arms crossed over their breasts.

In the meantime, Aladdin's mother advanced to the foot of the throne, and having prostrated herself, said to the sultan, "Sire, my son knows this present is much below the notice of Princess Buddir al Buddoor; but hopes, nevertheless, that your majesty will accept of it, and make it agreeable to the princess, and with the greater confidence since he has endeavored to conform to the conditions you were pleased to impose."

The sultan, overpowered by the sight of such more than royal magnificence, replied without hesitation to the words of Aladdin's mother: "Go and tell your son that I wait with open arms to embrace him; and the more haste he makes to come and receive the princess my daughter from my hands, the greater pleasure he will do me."

As soon as Aladdin's mother had retired, the sultan put an end to the audience. Rising from his throne, he ordered that the princess's attendants should come and carry the trays into their mistress's apartment, whither he went himself to examine them with her at his leisure. The fourscore slaves were conducted into the palace; and the sultan, telling the princess of their magnificent apparel, ordered them to be brought before her apartment, that she might see through the lattices he had not exaggerated in his account of them.

In the meantime Aladdin's mother reached home, and showed in her air and countenance the good news she brought to her son. "My son," said she, "you may rejoice you are arrived at the height of your desires. The sultan has declared that you shall marry the Princess Buddir al Buddoor. He waits for you with impatience."

Aladdin, enraptured with this news, made his mother very little reply, but retired to his chamber. There he rubbed his lamp, and the obedient genie appeared.

"Genie," said Aladdin, "convey me at once to a bath, and supply me with the richest and most magnificent robe ever worn by a monarch."

No sooner were the words out of his mouth than the genie rendered him, as well as himself, invisible, and transported him into a hummum of the finest marble of all sorts of colors; where he was undressed, without seeing by whom, in a magnificent and spacious hall. He was then well rubbed and washed with various scented waters. After he had passed through several degrees of heat, he came out quite a different man from what he was before. His skin was clear as that of a child, his body lightsome and free; and when he returned into the hall, he found, instead of his own poor raiment, a robe, the magnificence of which astonished him. The genie helped him to dress, and when he had done, transported him back to his own chamber, where he asked him if he had any other commands.

"Yes," answered Aladdin, "bring me a charger that surpasses in beauty and goodness the best in the sultan's stables; with a saddle, bridle, and other caparisons to correspond with his value. Furnish also twenty slaves, as richly clothed as those who carried the present to the sultan, to walk by my side and follow me, and twenty more to go before me in two ranks. Besides these, bring my mother six women slaves to attend her, as richly dressed at least as any of the Princess Buddir al Buddoor's, each carrying a complete dress fit for any sultaness. I want also ten thousand pieces of gold in ten purses; go, and make haste."

As soon as Aladdin had given these orders, the genie disappeared, but presently returned with the horse, the forty slaves, ten of whom carried each a purse containing ten thousand pieces of gold, and six women slaves, each carrying on her head a different dress for Aladdin's mother, wrapped up in a piece of silver tissue, and presented them all to Aladdin.

He presented the six women slaves to his mother, telling her they were her slaves, and that the dresses they had brought were for her use. Of the ten purses Aladdin took four, which he gave to his mother, telling her those were to supply her with necessaries; the other six he left in the hands of the slaves who brought them, with an order to throw them by handfuls among the people as they went to the sultan's palace. The six slaves who carried the purses he ordered likewise to march before him, three on the right hand and three on the left.

When Aladdin had thus prepared himself for his first interview with the sultan, he dismissed the genie, and immediately mounting his charger, began his march, and though he never was on horseback before, appeared with a grace the most experienced horseman might envy. The innumerable concourse of people through whom he passed made the air echo with their acclamations, especially every time the six slaves who carried the purses threw handfuls of gold among the populace.

On Aladdin's arrival at the palace, the sultan was surprised to find him more richly and magnificently robed than he had ever been himself, and was impressed with his good looks and dignity of manner, which were so different from what he expected in the son of one so humble as Aladdin's mother. He embraced him with all the demonstrations of joy, and when he would have fallen at his feet, held him by the hand, and made him sit near his throne. He shortly after led him, amidst the sounds of trumpets, hautboys, and all kinds of music, to a magnificent entertainment, at which the sultan and Aladdin ate by themselves, and the great lords of the court, according to their rank and dignity, sat at different tables.

After the feast, the sultan sent for the chief cadi, and commanded him to draw up a contract of marriage between the Princess Buddir al Buddoor and Aladdin. When the contract had been drawn, the sultan asked Aladdin if he would stay in the palace and complete the ceremonies of the marriage that day.

*The innumerable concourse of people through whom he passed
made the air echo with their acclamations.*

"Sire," said Aladdin, "though great is my impatience to enter on the honor granted me by your majesty, yet I beg you to permit me first to build a palace worthy to receive the princess your daughter. I pray you to grant me sufficient ground near your palace, and I will have it completed with the utmost expedition."

The sultan granted Aladdin his request, and again embraced him. After which he took his leave with as much politeness as if he had been bred up and had always lived at court.

Aladdin returned home in the order he had come, amidst the acclamations of the people, who wished him all happiness and prosperity. As soon as he dismounted, he retired to his own chamber, took the lamp, and summoned the genie as usual, who professed his allegiance.

"Genie," said Aladdin, "build me a palace fit to receive the Princess Buddir al Buddoor. Let its materials be made of nothing less than porphyry, jasper, agate, lapis lazuli, and the finest marble. Let its walls be massive gold and silver bricks and laid alternately. Let each front contain six windows, and let the lattices of these (except one, which must be left unfinished) be enriched with diamonds, rubies, and emeralds, so that they shall exceed everything of the kind ever seen in the world. Let there be an inner and outer court in front of the palace, and a spacious garden; but above all things, provide a safe treasure house, and fill it with gold and silver. Let there be also kitchens and storehouses, stables full of the finest horses, with their equerries and grooms, and hunting equipage, officers, attendants, and slaves, both men and women, to form a retinue for the princess and myself. Go and execute my wishes."

When Aladdin gave these commands to the genie, the sun was set. The next morning at daybreak the genie presented himself, and, having obtained Aladdin's consent, transported him in a moment to the palace he had made. The genie led him through all the apartments, where he found officers and slaves, habited according to their rank and the services to which they were appointed. The genie then showed him the treasury, which was opened by a treasurer, where Aladdin saw large vases of different sizes, piled up to the top with money, ranged all around the chamber. The genie thence led him to the stables, where were some of the finest horses in the world, and the grooms busy in dressing them; from thence they went to the storehouses, which were filled with all things necessary, both for food and ornament.

When Aladdin had examined every portion of the palace, and particularly the hall with the four-and-twenty windows, and found it far to exceed his fondest expectations, he said, "Genie, there is one thing wanting, a fine carpet for the princess to walk upon from the sultan's palace to mine. Lay one down immediately." The genie disappeared, and Aladdin saw what he desired executed in an instant. The genie then returned, and carried him to his own home.

When the sultan's porters came to open the gates, they were amazed to find what had been an unoccupied garden filled up with a magnificent palace, and a splendid carpet extending to it all the way from the sultan's palace. They told the strange tidings to the grand vizier, who informed the sultan.

"It must be Aladdin's palace," the sultan exclaimed, "which I gave him leave to build for my daughter. He has wished to surprise us, and let us see what wonders can be done in only one night."

Aladdin, on his being conveyed by the genie to his own home, requested his mother to go to the Princess Buddir al Buddoor, and tell her that the palace would be ready for her reception in the evening. She went, attended by her women slaves, in the same order as on the preceding day. Shortly after her arrival at the princess's apartment the sultan himself came in, and was surprised to find her, whom he knew only as his suppliant at his divan in humble guise, more richly and sumptuously attired than his own daughter. This gave him a higher opinion of Aladdin, who took such care of his mother, and made her share his wealth and honors.

Shortly after her departure, Aladdin, mounting his horse and attended by his retinue of magnificent attendants, left his paternal home forever, and went to the palace in the same pomp as on the day before. Nor did he forget to take with him the wonderful lamp, to which he owed all his good fortune, nor to wear the ring which was given him as a talisman.

The sultan entertained Aladdin with the utmost magnificence, and at night, on the conclusion of the marriage ceremonies, the princess took leave of the sultan her father. Bands of music led the procession, followed by a hundred state ushers, and the like number of black mutes, in two files, with their officers at their head. Four hundred of the sultan's young pages carried flambeaux on each side, which, together with the illuminations of the sultan's and Aladdin's palaces, made it as light as day. In this order the princess, conveyed in her litter, and accompanied also by Aladdin's mother, carried in a superb litter and attended by her women slaves, proceeded on the carpet which was spread from the sultan's palace to that of Aladdin.

On her arrival Aladdin was ready to receive her at the entrance, and led her into a large hall, illuminated with an infinite number of wax candles, where a noble feast was served up. The dishes were of massy gold, and contained the most delicate viands. The vases, basins, and goblets were gold also, and of exquisite workmanship, and all the other ornaments and embellishments of the hall were answerable to this display. The princess, dazzled to see so much riches collected in one place, said to Aladdin, "I thought, prince, that nothing in the world was so beautiful as the sultan my father's palace, but the sight of this hall alone is sufficient to show I was mistaken."

When the supper was ended, there entered a company of female dancers, who performed, according to the custom of the country, singing at the same time verses in praise of the bride and bridegroom. About midnight Aladdin's mother conducted the bride to the nuptial apartment, and he soon after retired.

The next morning the attendants of Aladdin presented themselves to dress him, and brought him another habit, as rich and magnificent as that worn the day before. He then ordered one of the horses to be got ready, mounted him, and went in the midst of a large troop of slaves to the sultan's palace to entreat him to take a repast in the princess's palace, attended by his grand vizier and all the lords of his court. The sultan consented with pleasure, rose up immediately, and, preceded by the principal officers of his palace, and followed by all the great lords of his court, accompanied Aladdin.

The nearer the sultan approached Aladdin's palace, the more he was struck with its beauty; but when he entered it, when he came into the hall and saw the windows, enriched with diamonds, rubies, emeralds, all large perfect stones, he was completely surprised, and said to his son-in-law, "This palace is one of the wonders of the world; for where in all the world besides shall we find walls built of massy gold and silver, and diamonds, rubies, and emeralds composing the windows? But what most surprises me is that a hall of this magnificence should be left with one of its windows incomplete and unfinished."

"Sire," answered Aladdin, "the omission was by design, since I wished that you should have the glory of finishing this hall."

"I take your intention kindly," said the sultan, "and will give orders about it immediately."

After the sultan had finished this magnificent entertainment, provided for him and for his court by Aladdin, he was informed that the jewelers and goldsmiths attended; upon which he returned to the hall, and showed them the window which was unfinished.

"I sent for you," said he, "to fit up this window in as great perfection as the rest. Examine them well, and make all the dispatch you can."

The jewelers and goldsmiths examined the three-and-twenty windows with great attention, and after they had consulted together, to know what each could furnish, they returned, and presented themselves before the sultan, whose principal jeweler, undertaking to speak for the rest, said, "Sire, we are all willing to exert our utmost care and industry to obey you; but among us all we cannot furnish jewels enough for so great a work."

"I have more than are necessary," said the sultan. "Come to my palace, and you shall choose what may answer your purpose."

When the sultan returned to his palace he ordered his jewels to be brought out, and the jewelers took a great quantity, particularly those Aladdin had made him a present of, which they soon used, without making any great advance in their work. They came again several times for more, and in a month's time had not finished half their work. In short, they used all the jewels the sultan had, and borrowed of the vizier, but yet the work was not half done.

Aladdin, who knew that all the sultan's endeavors to make this window like the rest were in vain, sent for the jewelers and goldsmiths, and not only commanded them to desist from their work, but ordered them to undo what they had begun, and to carry all their jewels back to the sultan and to the vizier. They undid in a few hours what they had been six weeks about, and retired, leaving Aladdin alone in the hall. He took the lamp, which he carried about him, rubbed it, and presently the genie appeared.

"Genie," said Aladdin, "I ordered thee to leave one of the four-and-twenty windows of this hall imperfect, and thou hast executed my commands exactly; now I would have thee make it like the rest."

The genie immediately disappeared. Aladdin went out of the hall, and returning soon after, found the window, as he wished it to be, like the others.

In the meantime the jewelers and goldsmiths repaired to the palace, and were introduced into the sultan's presence, where the chief jeweler presented the precious stones which he had brought back. The sultan asked them if Aladdin had given them any reason for so doing, and they answering that he had given them none, he ordered a horse to be brought, which he mounted, and rode to his son-in-law's palace, with some few attendants on foot, to inquire why he had ordered the completion of the window to be stopped.

Aladdin met him at the gate, and without giving any reply to his inquiries conducted him to the grand saloon, where the sultan, to his great surprise, found that the window, which was left imperfect, corresponded exactly with the others. He fancied at first that he was mistaken, and examined the two windows on each side, and afterward all the four-and-twenty; but when he was convinced that the window which several workmen had been so long about was finished in so short a time, he embraced Aladdin and kissed him between his eyes.

"My son," said he, "what a man you are to do such surprising things always in the twinkling of an eye! There is not your fellow in the world; the more I know, the more I admire you."

The sultan returned to the palace, and after this went frequently to the window to contemplate and admire the wonderful palace of his son-in-law.

Aladdin did not confine himself in his palace, but went with much state, sometimes to one mosque, and sometimes to another, to prayers, or to visit the grand vizier or the principal lords of the court. Every time he went out he caused two slaves, who walked by the side of his horse, to throw handfuls of money among the people as he passed through the streets and squares. This generosity gained him the love and blessings of the people, and it was common for them to swear by his head.

Thus Aladdin, while he paid all respect to the sultan, won by his affable behavior and liberality the affection of the people.

Aladdin had conducted himself in this manner several years, when the African magician, who had for some years dismissed him from his recollection, determined to inform himself with certainty whether he perished, as he supposed, in the subterranean cave or not. After he had resorted to a long course of magic ceremonies, and had formed a horoscope by which to ascertain Aladdin's fate, what was his surprise to find the appearances to declare that Aladdin, instead of dying in the cave, had made his escape, and was living in royal splendor by the aid of the genie of the wonderful lamp!

On the very next day the magician set out, and traveled with the utmost haste to the capital of China, where, on his arrival, he took up his lodgings in a khan.

He then quickly learned about the wealth, charities, happiness, and splendid palace of Prince Aladdin. Directly he saw the wonderful fabric, he knew that none but the genies, the slaves of the lamp, could have performed such wonders, and, piqued to the quick at Aladdin's high estate, he returned to the khan.

On his return he had recourse to an operation of geomancy to find out where the lamp was—whether Aladdin carried it about with him, or where he left it. The result of his consultation informed him, to his great joy, that the lamp was in the palace.

"Well," said he, rubbing his hands in glee, "I shall have the lamp, and I shall make Aladdin return to his original mean condition."

The next day the magician learned from the chief superintendent of the khan where he lodged that Aladdin had gone on a hunting expedition which was to last for eight days, of which only three had expired. The magician wanted to know no more. He resolved at once on his plans. He went to a coppersmith, and asked for a dozen copper lamps; the master of the shop told him he had not so many by him, but if he would have patience till the next day he would have them ready. The magician appointed his time, and desired him to take care that they should be handsome and well polished.

The next day the magician called for the twelve lamps, paid the man his full price, put them into a basket hanging on his arm, and went directly to Aladdin's palace. As he approached, he began crying, "Who will exchange old lamps for new?" And as he went along, a crowd of children collected, who hooted, and thought him, as did all who chanced to be passing by, a madman or a fool to offer to exchange new lamps for old.

The African magician regarded not their scoffs, hootings, or all they could say to him, but still continued crying, "Who will exchange old lamps for new?" He repeated this so often, walking backward and forward in front of the palace, that the princess, who was then in the hall of the four-and-twenty windows, hearing a man cry something, and seeing a great mob crowding about him, sent one of her women slaves to know what he cried.

The slave returned, laughing so heartily that the princess rebuked her. "Madam," answered the slave, laughing still, "who can forbear laughing, to see an old man with a basket on his arm, full of fine new lamps, asking to exchange them for old ones? The children and mob, crowding about him so that he can hardly stir, make all the noise they can in derision of him."

Another female slave, hearing this, said, "Now you speak of lamps, I know not whether the princess may have observed it, but there is an old one upon a shelf of the Prince Aladdin's robing room, and whoever owns it will not be sorry to find a new one in its stead. If the princess chooses, she may have the pleasure of trying if this old man is so silly as to give a new lamp for an old one, without taking anything for the exchange."

The princess, who knew not the value of the lamp and the interest that Aladdin had to keep it safe, entered into the pleasantry and commanded a slave to take it and make the exchange. The slave obeyed, went out of the hall, and no sooner got to the palace gates than he saw the African magician, called to him, and showing him the old lamp, said, "Give me a new lamp for this."

The magician never doubted but this was the lamp he wanted. There could be no other such in this palace, where every utensil was gold or silver. He snatched it eagerly out of the slave's hand, and thrusting it as far as he could into his breast, offered him his basket, and bade him choose which he liked best. The slave picked out one and carried it to the princess; but the change was no sooner made than the place rang with the shouts of the children, deriding the magician's folly.

The African magician stayed no longer near the palace, nor cried any more, "New lamps for old," but made the best of his way to his khan. His end was answered, and by his silence he got rid of the children and the mob.

As soon as he was out of sight of the two palaces he hastened down the least-frequented streets. Having no more occasion for his lamps or basket, he set all down in a spot where nobody saw him; then going down another street or two, he walked till he came to one of the city gates, and pursuing his way through the suburbs, which were very extensive, at length he reached a lonely spot, where he stopped till the darkness of the night, as the most suitable time for the design he had in contemplation.

When it became quite dark, he pulled the lamp out of his breast and rubbed it. At that summons the genie appeared, and said, "What wouldst thou have? I am ready to obey thee as thy slave, and the slave of all those who have that lamp in their hands; both I and the other slaves of the lamp."

"I command thee," replied the magician, "to transport me immediately, and the palace which thou and the other slaves of the lamp have built in this city, with all the people in it, to Africa."

The genie made no reply, but with the assistance of the other genies, the slaves of the lamp, immediately transported him and the palace, entire, to the spot whither he had been desired to convey it.

Early the next morning when the sultan, according to custom, went to contemplate and admire Aladdin's palace, his amazement was unbounded to find that it could nowhere be seen. He could not comprehend how so large a palace, which he had seen plainly every day for some years, should vanish so soon and not leave the least remains behind. In his perplexity he ordered the grand vizier to be sent for with expedition.

The grand vizier, who, in secret, bore no good will to Aladdin, intimated his suspicion that the palace was built by magic, and that Aladdin had made his hunting excursion an excuse for the removal of his palace with the same suddenness with which it had been erected. He induced the sultan to send a detachment of his guard, and to have Aladdin seized as a prisoner of state.

On his son-in-law being brought before him, the sultan would not hear a word from him, but ordered him to be put to death. But the decree caused so much discontent among the people, whose affection Aladdin had secured by his largesses and charities, that the sultan, fearful of an insurrection, was obliged to grant him his life.

When Aladdin found himself at liberty, he again addressed the sultan: "Sire, I pray you to let me know the crime by which I have thus lost the favor of thy countenance."

"Your crime!" answered the sultan. "Wretched man, do you not know it? Follow me, and I will show you."

The sultan then took Aladdin into the apartment from whence he was wont to look at and admire his palace, and said, "You ought to know where your palace stood; look, mind, and tell me what has become of it."

Aladdin did so, and being utterly amazed at the loss of his palace, was speechless. At last recovering himself, he said, "It is true, I do not see the palace. It is vanished; but I had no concern in its removal. I beg you to give me forty days, and if in that time I cannot restore it, I will offer my head to be disposed of at your pleasure."

"I give you the time you ask, but at the end of the forty days forget not to present yourself before me."

Aladdin went out of the sultan's palace in a condition of exceeding humiliation. The lords who had courted him in the days of his splendor now declined to have any communication with him. For three days he wandered about the city, exciting the wonder and compassion of the multitude by asking everybody he met if they had seen his palace, or could tell him anything of it. On the third day he wandered into the country, and as he was approaching a river he fell down the bank with so much violence that he rubbed the ring which the magician had given him so hard, by holding on to the rock to save himself, that immediately the same genie appeared whom he had seen in the cave where the magician had left him.

"What wouldst thou have?" said the genie. "I am ready to obey thee as thy slave, and the slave of all those that have that ring on their finger; both I and the other slaves of the ring."

Aladdin, agreeably surprised at an offer of help so little expected, replied, "Genie, show me where the palace I caused to be built now stands, or transport it back where it first stood."

"Your command," answered the genie, "is not wholly in my power; I am only the slave of the ring, and not of the lamp."

"I command thee, then," replied Aladdin, "by the power of the ring, to transport me to the spot where my palace stands, in what part of the world soever it may be."

These words were no sooner out of his mouth than the genie transported him into Africa, to the midst of a large plain, where his palace stood at no great distance from a city, and, placing him exactly under the window of the princess's apartment, left him.

Now it so happened that shortly after Aladdin had been transported by the slave of the ring to the neighborhood of his palace, that one of the attendants of the Princess Buddir al Buddoor, looking through the window, perceived him and instantly told her mistress. The princess, who could not believe the joyful tidings, hastened herself to the window, and seeing Aladdin, immediately opened it. The noise of opening the window made Aladdin turn his head that way, and perceiving the princess, he saluted her with an air that expressed his joy.

"To lose no time," said she to him, "I have sent to have the private door opened for you; enter, and come up."

The private door, which was just under the princess's apartment, was soon opened, and Aladdin was conducted up into the chamber. It is impossible to express the joy of both at seeing each other, after so cruel a separation. After embracing and shedding tears of joy, they sat down, and Aladdin said, "I beg of you, princess, to tell me what is become of an old lamp which stood upon a shelf in my robing chamber."

"Alas!" answered the princess, "I was afraid our misfortune might be owing to that lamp; and what grieves me most is that I have been the cause of it. I was foolish enough to exchange the old lamp for a new one, and the next morning I found myself in this unknown country, which I am told is Africa."

"Princess," said Aladdin, interrupting her, "you have explained all by telling me we are in Africa. I desire you only to tell me if you know where the old lamp now is."

"The African magician carries it carefully wrapped up in his bosom," said the princess; "and this I can assure you, because he pulled it out before me, and showed it to me in triumph."

"Princess," said Aladdin, "I think I have found the means to deliver you and to regain possession of the lamp, on which all my prosperity depends. To execute this design, it is necessary for me to go to the town. I shall return by noon, and will then tell you what must be done by you to insure success. In the meantime, I shall disguise myself, and I beg that the private door may be opened at the first knock."

When Aladdin was out of the palace, he looked round him on all sides, and perceiving a peasant going into the country, hastened after him. When he had overtaken him, he made a proposal to him to change clothes, which the man agreed to. When they had made the exchange, the countryman went about his business, and Aladdin entered the neighboring city. After traversing several streets, he came to that part of the town where the merchants and artisans had their particular streets according to their trades. He went into that of the druggists; and entering one of the largest and best furnished shops, asked the druggist if he had a certain powder, which he named.

The druggist, judging Aladdin by his habit to be very poor, told him he had it, but that it was very dear; upon which Aladdin, penetrating his thoughts, pulled out his purse, and showing him some gold, asked for half a dram of the powder, which the druggist weighed and gave him, telling him the price was a piece of gold. Aladdin put the money into his hand, and hastened to the palace, which he entered at once by the private door.

When he came into the princess's apartment he said to her, "Princess, you must take your part in the scheme which I propose for our deliverance. You must overcome your aversion for the magician, and assume a most friendly manner toward him, and ask him to oblige you by partaking of an entertainment in your apartments. Before he leaves, ask him to exchange cups with you, which he, gratified at the honor you do him, will gladly do, when you must give him the cup containing this powder. On drinking it he will instantly fall asleep, and we will obtain the lamp, whose slaves will do all our bidding, and restore us and the palace to the capital of China."

The princess obeyed to the utmost her husband's instructions. She assumed a look of pleasure on the next visit of the magician, and asked him to an entertainment, which he most willingly accepted. At the close of the evening, during which the princess had tried all

she could to please him, she asked him to exchange cups with her, and giving the signal, had the drugged cup brought to her, which she gave to the magician. Out of compliment to the princess he drank it to the very last drop, when he fell back lifeless on the sofa.

The princess, in anticipation of the success of her scheme, had so placed her women from the great hall to the foot of the staircase that the word was no sooner given that the African magician was fallen backward, than the door was opened, and Aladdin admitted to the hall. The princess rose from her seat, and ran, overjoyed, to embrace him; but he stopped her, and said, "Princess, retire to your apartment; and let me be left alone, while I endeavor to transport you back to China as speedily as you were brought from thence."

When the princess, her women, and slaves were gone out of the hall, Aladdin shut the door, and going directly to the dead body of the magician, opened his vest, took out the lamp, which was carefully wrapped up, and rubbing it, the genie immediately appeared.

"Genie," said Aladdin, "I command thee to transport this palace instantly to the place from whence it was brought hither."

The genie bowed his head in token of obedience, and disappeared. Immediately the palace was transported into China, and its removal was felt only by two little shocks, the one when it was lifted up, the other when it was set down, and both in a very short interval of time.

On the morning after the restoration of Aladdin's palace the sultan was looking out of his window, mourning over the fate of his daughter, when he thought that he saw the vacancy created by the disappearance of the palace to be again filled up.

On looking more attentively, he was convinced beyond the power of doubt that it was his son-in-law's palace. Joy and gladness succeeded to sorrow and grief. He at once ordered a horse to be saddled, which he mounted that instant, thinking he could not make haste enough to the place.

Aladdin rose that morning by daybreak, put on one of the most magnificent habits his wardrobe afforded, and went up into the hall of the twenty-four windows, from whence he perceived the sultan approaching, and received him at the foot of the great staircase, helping him to dismount.

He led the sultan into the princess's apartment. The happy father embraced her with tears of joy; and the princess, on her side, afforded similar testimonies of her extreme pleasure. After a short interval, devoted to mutual explanations of all that had happened, the sultan restored Aladdin to his favor, and expressed his regret for the apparent harshness with which he had treated him.

"My son," said he, "be not displeased at my proceedings against you; they arose from my paternal love, and therefore you ought to forgive the excesses to which it hurried me."

"Sire," replied Aladdin, "I have not the least reason to complain of your conduct, since you did nothing but what your duty required. This infamous magician, the basest of men, was the sole cause of my misfortune."

The African magician, who was thus twice foiled in his endeavor to ruin Aladdin, had a younger brother, who was as skillful a magician as himself and exceeded him in wickedness and hatred of mankind. By mutual agreement they communicated with each other once a year, however widely separate might be their place of residence from each other. The younger brother, not having received as usual his annual communication, prepared to take a horoscope and ascertain his brother's proceedings. He, as well as his brother, always carried a geomantic square instrument about him; he prepared the sand, cast the points, and drew the figures. On examining the planetary crystal, he found that his brother was no longer living, but had been poisoned; and by another observation, that he was in the capital of the kingdom of China; also, that the person who had poisoned him was of mean birth, though married to a princess, a sultan's daughter.

When the magician had informed himself of his brother's fate he resolved immediately to avenge his death, and at once departed for China; where, after crossing plains, rivers, mountains, deserts, and a long tract of country without delay, he arrived after incredible fatigues. When he came to the capital of China he took a lodging at a khan. His magic art soon revealed to him that Aladdin was the person who had been the cause of the death of his brother. He had heard, too, all the persons of repute in the city talking of a woman called Fatima, who was retired from the world, and of the miracles she wrought. As he fancied that this woman might be serviceable to him in the project he had conceived, he made more minute inquiries, and requested to be informed more particularly who that holy woman was, and what sort of miracles she performed.

"What!" said the person whom he addressed, "have you never seen or heard of her? She is the admiration of the whole town, for her fasting, her austerities, and her exemplary life. Except Mondays and Fridays, she never stirs out of her little cell; and on those days on which she comes into the town she does an infinite deal of good; for there is not a person who is diseased but she puts her hand on him and cures him."

Having ascertained the place where the hermitage of this holy woman was, the magician went at night, and plunged a poniard into her heart—killed this good woman. In the morning he dyed his face of the same hue as hers, and arraying himself in her garb, taking her veil, the large necklace she wore round her waist, and her stick, went straight to the palace of Aladdin.

As soon as the people saw the holy woman, as they imagined him to be, they presently gathered about him in a great crowd. Some begged his blessing, others kissed his hand, and others, more reserved, kissed only the hem of his garment; while others, suffering from disease, stooped for him to lay his hands upon them; which he did, muttering some words in form of prayer, and, in short, counterfeiting so well that everybody took him for the holy woman. He came at last to the square before Aladdin's palace. The crowd and the noise were so great that the princess, who was in the hall of the four-and-twenty windows, heard it, and asked what was the matter. One of her women told her it was a great crowd of people collected about the holy woman to be cured of diseases by the imposition of her hands.

The princess, who had long heard of this holy woman, but had never seen her, was very desirous to have some conversation with her. The chief officer perceiving this, told her it was an easy matter to bring the woman to her if she desired and commanded it; and the princess expressing her wishes, he immediately sent four slaves for the pretended holy woman.

As soon as the crowd saw the attendants from the palace, they made way; and the magician, perceiving also that they were coming for him, advanced to meet them, overjoyed to find his plot succeed so well.

"Holy woman," said one of the slaves, "the princess wishes to see you, and has sent us for you."

"The princess does me too great an honor," replied the false Fatima; "I am ready to obey her command." And at the same time he followed the slaves to the palace.

When the pretended Fatima had made his obeisance, the princess said, "My good mother, I have one thing to request, which you must not refuse me; it is, to stay with me, that you may edify me with your way of living, and that I may learn from your good example."

"Princess," said the counterfeit Fatima, "I beg of you not to ask what I cannot consent to without neglecting my prayers and devotion."

"That shall be no hindrance to you," answered the princess; "I have a great many apartments unoccupied; you shall choose which you like best, and have as much liberty to perform your devotions as if you were in your own cell."

The magician, who really desired nothing more than to introduce himself into the palace, where it would be a much easier matter for him to execute his designs, did not long excuse himself from accepting the obliging offer which the princess made him.

"Princess," said he, "whatever resolution a poor wretched woman as I am may have made to renounce the pomp and grandeur of this world, I dare not presume to oppose the will and commands of so pious and charitable a princess."

Upon this the princess, rising up, said, "Come with me. I will show you what vacant apartments I have, that you may make choice of that you like best."

The magician followed the princess, and of all the apartments she showed him, made choice of that which was the worst, saying that was too good for him, and that he only accepted it to please her.

Afterward the princess would have brought him back again into the great hall to make him dine with her; but he, considering that he should then be obliged to show his face, which he had always taken care to conceal with Fatima's veil, and fearing that the princess would find out that he was not Fatima, begged of her earnestly to excuse him, telling her that he never ate anything but bread and dried fruits, and desiring to eat that slight repast in his own apartment.

The princess granted his request, saying, "You may be as free here, good mother, as if you were in your own cell: I will order you a dinner, but remember, I expect you as soon as you have finished your repast."

After the princess had dined, and the false Fatima had been sent for by one of the attendants, he again waited upon her. "My good mother," said the princess, "I am overjoyed to see so holy a woman as yourself, who will confer a blessing upon this palace. But now I am speaking of the palace, pray how do you like it? And before I show it all to you, tell me first what you think of this hall."

Upon this question, the counterfeit Fatima surveyed the hall from one end to the other. When he had examined it well, he said to the princess, "As far as such a solitary being as I am, who am unacquainted with what the world calls beautiful, can judge, this hall is truly admirable; there wants but one thing."

"What is that, good mother?" demanded the princess; "tell me, I conjure you. For my part, I always believed, and have heard say, it wanted nothing; but if it does, it shall be supplied."

"Princess," said the false Fatima, with great dissimulation, "forgive me the liberty I have taken; but my opinion is, if it can be of any importance, that if a roc's egg were hung up in the middle of the dome, this hall would have no parallel in the four quarters of the world, and your palace would be the wonder of the universe."

"My good mother," said the princess, "what is a roc, and where may one get an egg?"

"Princess," replied the pretended Fatima, "it is a bird of prodigious size, which inhabits the summit of Mount Caucasus; the architect who built your palace can get you one."

After the princess had thanked the false Fatima for what she believed her good advice, she conversed with her upon other matters; but she could not forget the roc's egg, which she resolved to request of Aladdin when next he should visit his apartments. He did so in the course of that evening, and shortly after he entered, the princess thus addressed him: "I always believed that our palace was the most superb, magnificent, and complete in the world: but I will tell you now what it wants, and that is a roc's egg hung up in the midst of the dome."

"Princess," replied Aladdin, "it is enough that you think it wants such an ornament; you shall see by the diligence which I use in obtaining it, that there is nothing which I would not do for your sake."

Aladdin left the Princess Buddir al Buddoor that moment, and went up into the hall of four-and-twenty windows, where, pulling out of his bosom the lamp, which after the danger he had been exposed to he always carried about him, he rubbed it; upon which the genie immediately appeared.

"Genie," said Aladdin, "I command thee, in the name of this lamp, bring a roc's egg to be hung up in the middle of the dome of the hall of the palace."

Aladdin had no sooner pronounced these words than the hall shook as if ready to fall; and the genie said, in a loud and terrible voice, "Is it not enough that I and the other slaves of the lamp have done everything for you, but you, by an unheard-of ingratitude, must command me to bring my master, and hang him up in the midst of this dome? This attempt deserves that you, the princess, and the palace should be immediately reduced to ashes; but you are spared because this request does not come from yourself. Its true author is the brother of the African magician, your enemy whom you have destroyed. He is now in your palace, disguised in the habit of the holy woman Fatima, whom he has murdered; at his suggestion your wife makes this pernicious demand. His design is to kill you; therefore take care of yourself." After these words the genie disappeared.

Aladdin resolved at once what to do. He returned to the princess's apartment, and without mentioning a word of what had happened, sat down, and complained of a great pain which had suddenly seized his head. On hearing this, the princess told him how she had invited the holy Fatima to stay with her, and that she was now in the palace; and at the request of the prince, ordered her to be summoned to her at once.

When the pretended Fatima came, Aladdin said, "Come hither, good mother; I am glad to see you here at so fortunate a time. I am tormented with a violent pain in my head, and request your assistance, and hope you will not refuse me that cure which you impart to afflicted persons."

So saying, he arose, but held down his head. The counterfeit Fatima advanced toward him, with his hand all the time on a dagger concealed in his girdle under his gown. Observing this, Aladdin snatched the weapon from his hand, pierced him to the heart with his own dagger, and then pushed him down on the floor.

"My dear prince, what have you done?" cried the princess, in surprise. "You have killed the holy woman!"

"No, my princess," answered Aladdin, with emotion, "I have not killed Fatima, but a villain who would have assassinated me, if I had not prevented him. This wicked man," added he, uncovering his face, "is the

"His design is to kill you; therefore take care of yourself."

brother of the magician who attempted our ruin. He has strangled the true Fatima, and disguised himself in her clothes with intent to murder me."

Aladdin then informed her how the genie had told him these facts, and how narrowly she and the palace had escaped destruction though his treacherous suggestion which had led to her request.

Thus was Aladdin delivered from the persecution of the two brothers, who were magicians. Within a few years the sultan died in a good old age, and as he left no male children, the Princess Buddir al Buddoor succeeded him, and she and Aladdin reigned together many years, and left a numerous and illustrious posterity.

THE HISTORY OF ALI BABA, AND OF THE FORTY ROBBERS KILLED BY ONE SLAVE

There once lived in a town of Persia two brothers, one named Cassim and the other Ali Baba. Their father divided a small inheritance equally between them. Cassim married a very rich wife, and became a wealthy merchant. Ali Baba married a woman as poor as himself, and lived by cutting wood, and bringing it upon three asses into the town to sell.

One day, when Ali Baba was in the forest and had just cut wood enough to load his asses, he saw at a distance a great cloud of dust, which seemed to approach him. He observed it with attention, and distinguished soon after a body of horsemen, whom he suspected might be robbers. He determined to leave his asses to save himself. He climbed up a large tree, planted on a high rock, whose branches were thick enough to conceal him, and yet enabled him to see all that passed without being discovered.

The troop, who were to the number of forty, all well mounted and armed, came to the foot of the rock on which the tree stood, and there dismounted. Every man unbridled his horse, tied him to some shrub, and hung about his neck a bag of corn which they had brought behind them. Then each of them took off his saddle-bag, which seemed to Ali Baba from its weight to be full of gold and silver. One, whom he took to be their captain, came under the tree in which Ali Baba was concealed; and making his way through some shrubs, pronounced these words: "Open, Sesame!"

He climbed up a large tree, planted on a high rock, whose branches were thick enough to conceal him . . .

As soon as the captain of the robbers had thus spoken, a door opened in the rock; and after he had made all his troop enter before him, he followed them, when the door shut again of itself.

The robbers stayed some time within the rock, during which Ali Baba, fearful of being caught, remained in the tree.

At last the door opened again, and as the captain went in last, so he came out first, and stood to see them all pass by him; when Ali Baba heard him make the door close by pronouncing these words, "Shut, Sesame!" Every man at once went and bridled his horse, fastened his wallet, and mounted again. When the captain saw them all ready, he put himself at their head, and they returned the way they had come.

Ali Baba followed them with his eyes as far as he could see them; and afterward stayed a considerable time before he descended. Remembering the words the captain of the robbers used to cause the door to open and shut, he had the curiosity to try if his pronouncing them would have the same effect. Accordingly, he went among the shrubs, and perceiving the door concealed behind them, stood before it, and said, "Open, Sesame!" The door instantly flew wide open.

Ali Baba, who expected a dark, dismal cavern, was surprised to see a well-lighted and spacious chamber, which received the light from an opening at the top of the rock, and in which were all sorts of provisions, rich bales of silk, stuff, brocade, and valuable carpeting, piled upon one another, gold and silver ingots in great heaps, and money in bags. The sight of all these riches made him suppose that this cave must have been occupied for ages by robbers, who had succeeded one another.

Ali Baba went boldly into the cave, and collected as much of the gold coin, which was in bags, as he thought his three asses could carry. When he had loaded them with the bags, he laid wood over them in such a manner that they could not be seen. When he had passed in and out as often as he wished, he stood before the door, and pronouncing the words, "Shut, Sesame!" the door closed of itself. He then made the best of his way to town.

When Ali Baba got home he drove his asses into a little yard, shut the gates very carefully, threw off the wood that covered the panniers, carried the bags into his house, and ranged them in order before his wife. He then emptied the bags, which raised such a great heap of gold as dazzled his wife's eyes, and then he told her the whole adventure from beginning to end, and, above all, recommended her to keep it secret.

The wife rejoiced greatly at their good fortune, and would count all the gold piece by piece.

"Wife," replied Ali Baba, "you do not know what you undertake, when you pretend to count the money; you will never have done. I will dig a hole, and bury it. There is no time to be lost."

"You are in the right, husband," replied she, "but let us know, as nigh as possible, how much we have. I will borrow a small measure, and measure it, while you dig the hole."

Away the wife ran to her brother-in-law Cassim, who lived just by, and addressing herself to his wife, desired that she lend her a measure for a little while. Her sister-in-law asked her whether she would have a great or a small one. The other asked for a small one. She bade her stay a little, and she would readily fetch one.

The sister-in-law did so, but as she knew Ali Baba's poverty, she was curious to know what sort of grain his wife wanted to measure, and artfully putting some suet at the bottom of the measure, brought it to her, with an excuse that she was sorry that she had made her stay so long, but that she could not find it sooner.

Ali Baba's wife went home, set the measure upon the heap of gold, filled it, and emptied it often upon the sofa, till she had done, when she was very well satisfied to find the number of measures amounted to so many as they did, and went to tell her husband, who had almost finished digging the hole. When Ali Baba was burying the gold, his wife, to show her exactness and diligence to her sister-in-law, carried the measure back again, but without taking notice that a piece of gold had stuck to the bottom.

"Sister," said she, giving it to her again, "you see that I have not kept your measure long. I am obliged to you for it, and return it with thanks."

As soon as Ali Baba's wife was gone, Cassim's looked at the bottom of the measure, and was in inexpressible surprise to find a piece of gold sticking to it. Envy immediately possessed her breast.

"What!" said she, "has Ali Baba gold so plentiful as to measure it? Whence has he all this wealth?"

Cassim, her husband, was at his counting house. When he came home his wife said to him, "Cassim, I know you think yourself rich, but Ali Baba is infinitely richer than you. He does not count his money, but measures it."

Cassim desired her to explain the riddle, which she did, by telling him the stratagem she had used to make the discovery, and showed him the piece of money, which was so old that they could not tell in what prince's reign it was coined.

Cassim, after he had married the rich widow, had never treated Ali Baba as a brother, but neglected him; and now, instead of being pleased, he conceived a base envy at his brother's prosperity. He could not sleep all that night, and went to him in the morning before sunrise.

"Ali Baba," said he, "I am surprised at you. You pretend to be miserably poor, and yet you measure gold. My wife found this at the bottom of the measure you borrowed yesterday."

By this discourse, Ali Baba perceived that Cassim and his wife, through his own wife's folly, knew what they had so much reason to conceal; but what was done could not be undone. Therefore, without showing the least surprise or trouble, he confessed all, and offered his brother part of his treasure to keep the secret.

"I expect as much," replied Cassim haughtily; "but I must know exactly where this treasure is, and how I may visit it myself when I choose. Otherwise I will go and inform against you, and then you will not only get no more, but will lose all you have, and I shall have a share for my information."

Ali Baba told him all he desired, even to the very words he was to use to gain admission into the cave.

Cassim rose the next morning long before the sun, and set out for the forest with ten mules bearing great chests, which he designed to fill, and followed the road which Ali Baba had pointed out to him. He was not long before he reached the rock, and found out the place, by the tree and other marks which his brother had given him. When he reached the entrance of the cavern, he pronounced the words, "Open, Sesame!" The door immediately opened, and, when he was in, closed upon him. In examining the cave, he was in great admiration to find much more riches than he had expected from Ali Baba's relation. He quickly laid as many bags of gold as he could carry at the door of the cavern; but his thoughts were so full of the great riches he should possess that he could not think of the necessary word to make it open, but instead of "Sesame," said, "Open, Barley!" and was much amazed to find that the door remained fast shut. He named several sorts of grain, but still the door would not open.

Cassim had never expected such an incident, and was so alarmed at the danger he was in, that the more he endeavored to remember the

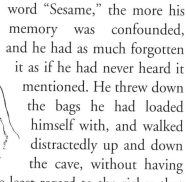

word "Sesame," the more his memory was confounded, and he had as much forgotten it as if he had never heard it mentioned. He threw down the bags he had loaded himself with, and walked distractedly up and down the cave, without having the least regard to the riches that were around him.

About noon the robbers visited their cave. At some distance they saw Cassim's mules straggling about the rock, with great chests on their backs. Alarmed at this, they galloped full speed to the cave. They drove away the mules, who strayed through the forest so far that they were soon out of sight, and went directly, with their naked sabers in their hands, to the door, which, on their captain pronouncing the proper words, immediately opened.

Cassim, who heard the noise of the horses' feet, at once guessed the arrival of the robbers, and resolved to make one effort for his life. He rushed to the door, and no sooner saw the door open, than he ran out and threw the leader down, but could not escape the other robbers, who with their scimitars soon deprived him of life.

The first care of the robbers after this was to examine the cave. They found all the bags which Cassim had brought to the door, to be ready to load his mules, and carried them again to their places, but they did not miss what Ali Baba had taken away before. Then holding a council, and deliberating upon this occurrence, they guessed that Cassim, when he was in, could not get out again, but could not imagine how he had learned the secret words by which alone he could enter. They could not deny the fact of his being there; and to terrify any person or accomplice who should attempt the same thing, they agreed to cut Cassim's body into four quarters—to hang two on one side, and two on the other, within the door of the cave. They had no sooner taken this resolution than they put it in execution; and when they had nothing more to detain them, left the place of their hoards well closed. They mounted their horses, went to beat the roads again, and to attack the caravans they might meet.

In the meantime, Cassim's wife was very uneasy when night came, and her husband was not returned. She ran to Ali Baba in great alarm, and said, "I believe, brother-in-law, that you know Cassim is gone to the forest, and upon what account. It is now night, and he has not returned. I am afraid some misfortune has happened to him."

Ali Baba told her that she need not frighten herself, for that certainly Cassim would not think it proper to come into the town till the night should be pretty far advanced.

Cassim's wife, considering how much it concerned her husband to keep the business secret, was the more easily persuaded to believe her brother-in-law. She went home again, and waited patiently till midnight. Then her fear redoubled, and her grief was the more sensible because she was forced to keep it to herself. She repented of her foolish curiosity, and cursed her desire of prying into the affairs of her brother and sister-in-law. She spent all the night in weeping; and as soon as it was day went to them, telling them, by her tears, the cause of her coming.

Ali Baba did not wait for his sister-in-law to desire him to go to see what was become of Cassim, but departed immediately with his three asses, begging of her first to moderate her grief. He went to the forest, and when he came near the rock, having seen neither his brother nor his mules on his way, was seriously alarmed at finding some blood spilt near the door, which he took for an ill omen; but when he had pronounced the word, and the door had opened, he was struck with horror at the dismal sight of his brother's body. He was not long in determining how he should pay the last dues to his brother; but without adverting to the little fraternal affection he had shown for him, went into the cave, to find something to enshroud his remains. Having loaded one of his asses with them, he covered them over with wood. The other two asses he loaded with bags of gold, covering them with wood also as before; and then, bidding the door shut, he came away; but was so cautious as to stop some time at the end of the forest, that he might not go into the town before night. When he came home he drove the two asses loaded with gold into his little yard, and left the care of unloading them to his wife, while he led the other to his sister-in-law's house.

Ali Baba knocked at the door, which was opened by Morgiana, a clever, intelligent slave, who was fruitful in inventions to meet the most difficult circumstances. When he came into the court he unloaded the ass, and taking Morgiana aside, said to her, "You must observe an inviolable secrecy. Your master's body is contained in these two panniers. We must bury him as if he had died a natural death. Go now and tell your mistress. I leave the matter to your wit and skillful devices."

Ali Baba helped to place the body in Cassim's house, again recommended to Morgiana to act her part well, and then returned with his ass.

Morgiana went out early the next morning to a druggist and asked for a sort of lozenge which was considered efficacious in the most dangerous disorders. The apothecary inquired who was ill. She replied, with a sigh, her good master Cassim himself; and that he could neither eat nor speak.

In the evening Morgiana went to the same druggist again, and with tears in her eyes, asked for an essence which they used to give to sick people only when in the last extremity.

"Alas!" said she, taking it from the apothecary, "I am afraid that this remedy will have no better effect than the lozenges; and that I shall lose my good master."

On the other hand, as Ali Baba and his wife were often seen to go between Cassim's and their own house all that day, and to seem melancholy, nobody was surprised in the evening to hear the lamentable shrieks and

cries of Cassim's wife and Morgiana, who gave out everywhere that her master was dead. The next morning at daybreak, Morgiana went to an old cobbler whom she knew to be always ready at his stall, and bidding him good morrow, put a piece of gold into his hand, saying, "Baba Mustapha, you must bring with you your sewing tackle, and come with me; but I must tell you, I shall blindfold you when you come to such a place."

Baba Mustapha seemed to hesitate a little at these words. "Oh! Oh!" replied he, "you would have me do something against my conscience, or against my honor?"

"God forbid," said Morgiana, putting another piece of gold into his hand, "that I should ask anything that is contrary to your honor! Only come along with me, and fear nothing."

Baba Mustapha went with Morgiana, who, after she had bound his eyes with a handkerchief at the place she had mentioned, conveyed him to her deceased master's house, and never unloosed his eyes till he had entered the room where she had put the corpse together. "Baba Mustapha," said she, "you must make haste and sew the parts of this body together; and when you have done, I will give you another piece of gold."

After Baba Mustapha had finished his task, she blindfolded him again, gave him the third piece of gold as she had promised, and recommending secrecy to him, carried him back to the place where she first bound his eyes, pulled off the bandage, and let him go home, but watched him

201

that he returned toward his stall, till he was quite out of sight, for fear he should have the curiosity to return and dodge her; she then went home.

Morgiana, on her return, warmed some water to wash the body, and at the same time Ali Baba perfumed it with incense, and wrapped it in the burying clothes with the accustomed ceremonies. Not long after the proper officer brought the bier, and when the attendants of the mosque, whose business it was to wash the dead, offered to perform their duty, she told them it was done already. Shortly after this the imaun and the other ministers of the mosque arrived. Four neighbors carried the corpse to the burying-ground, following the imaun, who recited some prayers. Ali Baba came after with some neighbors, who often relieved the others in carrying the bier to the burying-ground. Morgiana, a slave to the deceased, followed in the procession, weeping, beating her breast, and tearing her hair. Cassim's wife stayed at home mourning, uttering lamentable cries with the women of the neighborhood, who came, according to custom, during the funeral, and joining their lamentations with hers filled the quarter far and near with sounds of sorrow.

In this manner Cassim's melancholy death was concealed and hushed up between Ali Baba, his widow, and Morgiana his slave, with so much contrivance that nobody in the city had the least knowledge or suspicion of the cause of it. Three or four days after the funeral, Ali Baba removed his few goods openly to his sister's house, in which it was agreed that he should in future live; but the money he had taken from the robbers he conveyed thither by night. As for Cassim's warehouse, he intrusted it entirely to the management of his eldest son.

While these things were being done, the forty robbers again visited their retreat in the forest. Great, then, was their surprise to find Cassim's body taken away, with some of their bags of gold. "We are certainly discovered," said the captain. "The removal of the body and the loss of some of our money, plainly shows that the man whom we killed had an accomplice: and for our own lives' sake we must try to find him. What say you, my lads?"

All the robbers unanimously approved of the captain's proposal.

"Well," said the captain, "one of you, the boldest and most skillful among you, must go into the town, disguised as a traveler and a stranger, to try if he can hear any talk of the man whom we have killed, and endeavor to find out who he was, and where he lived. This is a matter of the first importance, and for fear of any treachery I propose that whoever undertakes this business without success, even though the failure arises only from an error of judgment, shall suffer death."

Without waiting for the sentiments of his companions, one of the robbers started up, and said, "I submit to this condition, and think it an honor to expose my life to serve the troop."

After this robber had received great commendations from the captain and his comrades, he disguised himself so that nobody would take him for what he was; and taking his leave of the troop that night, he went into the town just at daybreak. He walked up and down, till accidentally he came to Baba Mustapha's stall, which was always open before any of the shops.

Baba Mustapha was seated with an awl in his hand, just going to work. The robber saluted him, bidding him good morrow; and perceiving that he was old, said, "Honest man, you begin to work very early; is it possible that one of your age can see so well? I question, even if it were somewhat lighter, whether you could see to stitch."

"You do not know me," replied Baba Mustapha; "for old as I am, I have extraordinary good eyes; and you will not doubt it when I tell you that I sewed the body of a dead man together in a place where I had not so much light as I have now."

"A dead body!" exclaimed the robber, with affected amazement.

"Yes, yes," answered Baba Mustapha. "I see you want me to speak out, but you shall know no more."

The robber felt sure that he had discovered what he sought. He pulled out a piece of gold, and putting it into Baba Mustapha's hand, said to him, "I do not want to learn your secret, though I can assure you you might safely trust me with it. The only thing I desire of you is to show me the house where you stitched up the dead body."

"If I were disposed to do you that favor," replied Baba Mustapha, "I assure you I cannot. I was taken to a certain place, whence I was led blindfold to the house, and afterward brought back in the same manner. You see, therefore, the impossibility of my doing what you desire."

"Well," replied the robber, "you may, however, remember a little of the way that you were led blindfold. Come, let me blind your eyes at the same place. We will walk together; perhaps you may recognize some part, and as every one should be paid for his trouble here is another piece of gold for you; gratify me in what I ask you." So saying, he put another piece of gold into his hand.

The two pieces of gold were great temptations to Baba Mustapha. He looked at them a long time in his hand, without saying a word, but at last he pulled out his purse and put them in.

"I cannot promise," said he to the robber, "that I can remember the way exactly; but since you desire, I will try what I can do."

At these words Baba Mustapha rose up, to the great joy of the robber, and led him to the place where Morgiana had bound his eyes.

"It was here," said Baba Mustapha, "I was blindfolded; and I turned this way."

The robber tied his handkerchief over his eyes, and walked by him till he stopped directly at Cassim's house, where Ali Baba then lived.

The thief, before he pulled off the band, marked the door with a piece of chalk, which he had ready in his hand, and then asked him if he knew whose house that was; to which Baba Mustapha replied that as he did not live in that neighborhood, he could not tell.

The robber, finding that he could discover no more from Baba Mustapha, thanked him for the trouble he had taken, and left him to go back to his stall, while he returned to the forest, persuaded that he should be very well received.

A little after the robber and Baba Mustapha had parted, Morgiana went out of Ali Baba's house upon some errand, and upon her return, seeing the mark the robber had made, stopped to observe it.

"What can be the meaning of this mark?" said she to herself. "Somebody intends my master no good. However, with whatever intention it was done, it is advisable to guard against the worst."

Accordingly, she fetched a piece of chalk, and marked two or three doors on each side in the same manner, without saying a word to her master or mistress.

In the meantime, the robber rejoined his troop in the forest, and recounted to them his success, expatiating upon his good fortune in meeting so soon with the only person who could inform him of what he wanted to know. All the robbers listened to him with the utmost satisfaction. Then the captain, after commending his diligence, addressing himself to them all, said, "Comrades, we have no time to lose. Let us set off well armed, without its appearing who we are; but that we may not excite any suspicion, let only one or two go into the town together, and join at our rendezvous, which shall be the great square. In the meantime, our comrade who brought us the good news and I will go and find out the house, that we may consult what had best be done."

This speech and plan was approved of by all, and they were soon ready. They filed off in parties of two each, after some interval of time, and got into the town without being in the least suspected. The captain, and he who had visited the town in the morning as spy, came in the last. He led the captain into the street where he had marked Ali Baba's residence; and when they came to the first of the houses which Morgiana had marked, he pointed it out. But the captain observed that the next door was chalked in the same manner, and in the same place; and showing it to his guide, asked him which house it was, that, or the first. The guide was so confounded, that he knew not what answer to make; but he was still more puzzled when he and the captain saw five or six houses similarly marked. He assured the captain, with an oath, that he had marked but one, and could not tell who had chalked the rest, so that he could not distinguish the house which the cobbler had stopped at.

The captain, finding that their design had proved abortive, went directly to their place of rendezvous, and told his troop that they had lost their labor, and must return to their cave. He himself set them the example, and they all returned as they had come.

When the troop was all got together, the captain told them the reason of their returning; and presently the conductor was declared by all worthy of death. He condemned himself, acknowledging that he ought to have taken better precaution, and prepared to receive the stroke from him who was appointed to cut off his head.

But as the safety of the troop required the discovery of the second intruder into the cave, another of the gang, who promised himself that he should succeed better, presented himself, and his offer being accepted he went and corrupted Baba Mustapha as the other had done; and being shown the house, marked it in a place more remote from sight, with red chalk.

Not long after, Morgiana, whose eyes nothing could escape, went out, and seeing the red chalk, and arguing with herself as she had done before, marked the other neighbors' houses in the same place and manner.

The robber, on his return to his company, valued himself much on the precaution he had taken, which he looked upon as an infallible way of distinguishing Ali Baba's house from the others; and the captain and all of them thought it must succeed. They conveyed themselves into the town with the same precaution as before; but when the robber and his captain came to the street, they found the same difficulty; at which the captain was enraged, and the robber in as great confusion as his predecessor.

Thus the captain and his troop were forced to retire a second time, and much more dissatisfied; while the robber who had been the author of the mistake underwent the same punishment, which he willingly submitted to.

The captain, having lost two brave fellows of his troop, was afraid of diminishing it too much by pursuing this plan to get information of the residence of their plunderer. He found by their example that their heads were not so good as their hands on such occasions; and therefore resolved to take upon himself the important commission.

When the robber and his captain came to the street,
they found the same difficulty . . .

Accordingly, he went and addressed himself to Baba Mustapha, who did him the same service he had done to the other robbers. He did not set any particular mark on the house, but examined and observed it so carefully, by passing often by it, that it was impossible for him to mistake it.

The captain, well satisfied with his attempt, and informed of what he wanted to know, returned to the forest: and when he came into the cave, where the troop waited for him, said, "Now, comrades, nothing can prevent our full revenge, as I am certain of the house; and on my way hither I have thought how to put it into execution, but if any one can form a better expedient, let him communicate it."

He then told them his contrivance; and as they approved of it, ordered them to go into the villages about, and buy nineteen mules, with thirty-eight large leather jars, one full of oil, and the others empty.

In two or three days' time the robbers had purchased the mules and jars, and as the mouths of the jars were rather too narrow for his purpose, the captain caused them to be widened, and after having put one of his men into each, with the weapons which he thought fit, leaving open the seam which had been undone to leave them room to breathe, he rubbed the jars on the outside with oil from the full vessel.

Things being thus prepared, when the nineteen mules were loaded with thirty-seven robbers in jars, and the jar of oil, the captain, as their driver, set out with them, and reached the town by the dusk of the evening, as he had intended.

He led them through the streets, till he came to Ali Baba's, at whose door he designed to have knocked; but was prevented by his sitting there after supper to take a little fresh air. He stopped his mules, addressed himself to him, and said, "I have brought some oil a great way, to sell at tomorrow's market; and it is now so late that I do not know where to lodge. If I should not be troublesome to you, do me the favor to let me pass the night with you, and I shall be very much obliged by your hospitality."

Though Ali Baba had seen the captain of the robbers in the forest, and had heard him speak, it was impossible to know him in the disguise of an oil merchant. He told him he should be welcome, and immediately opened his gates for the mules to go into the yard. At the same time he called to a slave, and ordered him, when the mules were unloaded, to put them into the stable, and to feed them; and then went to Morgiana, to bid her get a good supper for his guest.

After they had finished supper, Ali Baba, charging Morgiana afresh to take care of his guest, said to her, "To-morrow morning I design to go to the bath before day; take care my bathing linen be ready, give them to Abdalla (which was the slave's name), and make me some good broth against I return." After this he went to bed.

In the meantime the captain of the robbers went into the yard, and took off the lid of each jar, and gave his people orders what to do. Beginning at the first jar, and so on to the last, he said to each man: "As soon as I throw some stones out of the chamber window where I lie, do not fail to come out, and I will immediately join you."

After this he returned into the house, when Morgiana, taking up a light, conducted him to his chamber, where she left him; and he, to avoid any suspicion, put the light out soon after, and laid himself down in his clothes, that he might be the more ready to rise.

Morgiana, remembering Ali Baba's orders, got his bathing linen ready, and ordered Abdalla to set on the pot for the broth; but while she was preparing it the lamp went out, and there was no more oil in the house, nor any candles. What to do she did not know, for the broth must be made. Abdalla, seeing her very uneasy, said, "do not fret and tease yourself, but go into the yard, and take some oil out of one of the jars."

Morgiana thanked Abdalla for his advice, took the oil pot, and went into the yard; when, as she came nigh the first jar, the robber within said softly, "Is it time?"

Though naturally much surprised at finding a man in the jar instead of the oil she wanted, she immediately felt the importance of keeping silence, as Ali Baba, his family, and herself were in great danger; and collecting herself, without showing the least emotion, she answered, "Not yet, but presently." She went quietly in this manner to all the jars, giving the same answer, till she came to the jar of oil.

By this means Morgiana found that her master Ali Baba had admitted thirty-eight robbers into his house, and that this pretended oil merchant was their captain. She made what haste she could to fill her oil pot, and returned into the kitchen, where, as soon as she had lighted her lamp, she took a great kettle, went again to the oil jar, filled the kettle, set it on a large wood fire, and as soon as it boiled, went and poured enough into every jar to stifle and destroy the robber within.

When this action, worthy of the courage of Morgiana, was executed without any noise, as she had projected, she returned into the kitchen with the empty kettle; and having put out the great fire she had made to boil the oil, and leaving just enough to make the broth, put out the lamp also, and remained silent, resolving not to go to rest till, through a window of the kitchen, which opened into the yard, she had seen what might follow.

She had not waited long before the captain of the robbers got up, opened the window, and, finding no light and hearing no noise or any one stirring in the house, gave the appointed signal, by throwing little stones, several of which hit the jars, as he doubted not by the sound they gave. He then listened, but not hearing or perceiving anything whereby he could judge that his companions stirred, he began to grow very uneasy, threw stones again a second and also a third time, and could not comprehend the reason that none of them should answer his signal. Much alarmed, he went softly down into the yard, and going to the first jar, while asking the robber, whom he thought alive, if he was in readiness, smelt the hot boiled oil, which sent forth a steam out of the jar. Hence he knew that his plot to murder Ali Baba and plunder his house was discovered. Examining all the jars, one after another, he found that all his gang were dead; and, enraged to despair at having failed in his design, he forced the lock of a door that led from the yard to the garden, and climbing over the walls made his escape.

When Morgiana saw him depart, she went to bed, satisfied and pleased to have succeeded so well in saving her master and family.

Ali Baba rose before day, and, followed by his slave, went to the baths, entirely ignorant of the important event which had happened at home.

When he returned from the baths he was very much surprised to see the oil jars, and to learn that the merchant was not gone with the mules. He asked Morgiana, who opened the door, the reason of it.

"My good master," answered she, "God preserve you and all your family. You will be better informed of what you wish to know when you have seen what I have to show you, if you will follow me."

As soon as Morgiana had shut the door, Ali Baba followed her, when she requested him to look into the first jar, and see if there was any oil. Ali Baba did so, and seeing a man, started back in alarm, and cried out.

"Do not be afraid," said Morgiana; "the man you see there can neither do you nor anybody else any harm. He is dead."

"Ah, Morgiana," said Ali Baba, "what is it you show me? Explain yourself."

"I will," replied Morgiana. "Moderate your astonishment,

212

and do not excite the curiosity of your neighbors; for it is of great importance to keep this affair secret. Look into all the other jars."

Ali Baba examined all the other jars, one after another; and when he came to that which had the oil in it, found it prodigiously sunk, and stood for some time motionless, sometimes looking at the jars and sometimes at Morgiana, without saying a word, so great was his surprise.

At last, when he had recovered himself, he said, "And what is become of the merchant?"

"Merchant!" answered she; "he is as much one as I am. I will tell you who he is, and what is become of him; but you had better hear the story in your own chamber; for it is time for your health that you had your broth after your bathing."

Morgiana then told him all she had done, from the first observing the mark upon the house, to the destruction of the robbers, and the flight of their captain.

On hearing of these brave deeds from the lips of Morgiana, Ali Baba said to her—"God, by your means, has delivered me from the snares of these robbers laid for my destruction. I owe, therefore, my life to you; and, for the first token of my acknowledgment, I give you your liberty from this moment, till I can complete your recompense as I intend."

Ali Baba's garden was very long, and shaded at the farther end by a great number of large trees. Near these he and the slave Abdalla dug a trench, long and wide enough to hold the bodies of the robbers; and as the earth was light, they were not long in doing it. When this was done, Ali Baba hid the jars and weapons; and as he had no occasion for the mules, he sent them at different times to be sold in the market by his slave.

While Ali Baba was taking these measures the captain of the forty robbers returned to the forest with inconceivable mortification. He did not stay long; the loneliness of the gloomy cavern became frightful to him. He determined, however, to avenge the death of his companions, and to accomplish the death of Ali Baba. For this purpose he returned to the town, and took a lodging in a khan, disguising himself as a merchant in silks. Under this assumed character he gradually conveyed a great many sorts of rich stuffs and fine linen to his lodging from the cavern, but with all the necessary precautions to conceal the place whence he brought them. In order to dispose of the merchandise, when he had thus amassed them together, he took a warehouse, which happened to be opposite to Cassim's, which Ali Baba's son had occupied since the death of his uncle.

He took the name of Cogia Houssain, and, as a newcomer, was, according to custom, extremely civil and complaisant to all the merchants his neighbors. Ali Baba's son was, from his vicinity, one of the first to converse with Cogia Houssain, who strove to cultivate his friendship more particularly. Two or three days after he was settled, Ali Baba came to see his son, and the captain of the robbers recognized him at once, and soon learned from his son who he was. After this he increased his assiduities, caressed him in the most engaging manner, made him some small presents, and often asked him to dine and sup with him, when he treated him very handsomely.

Ali Baba's son did not choose to lie under such obligation to Cogia Houssain; but was so much straitened for want of room in his house that he could not entertain him. He therefore acquainted his father, Ali Baba, with his wish to invite him in return.

Ali Baba with great pleasure took the treat upon himself. "Son," said he, "to-morrow being Friday, which is a day that the shops of such great merchants as Cogia Houssain and yourself are shut, get him to accompany you, and as you pass by my door, call in. I will go and order Morgiana to provide a supper."

The next day Ali Baba's son and Cogia Houssain met by appointment, took their walk, and as they returned, Ali Baba's son led Cogia Houssain through the street where his father lived, and when they came to the house, stopped and knocked at the door.

"This, sir," said he, "is my father's house, who, from the account I have given him of your friendship, charged me to procure him the honor of your acquaintance; and I desire you to add this pleasure to those for which I am already indebted to you."

Though it was the sole aim of Cogia Houssain to introduce himself into Ali Baba's house, that he might kill him without hazarding his own life or making any noise, yet he excused himself, and offered to take his leave; but a slave having opened the door, Ali Baba's son took him obligingly by the hand, and, in a manner, forced him in.

Ali Baba received Cogia Houssain with a smiling countenance, and in the most obliging manner he could wish. He thanked him for all the favors he had done his son; adding, withal, the obligation was the greater as he was a young man, not much acquainted with the world, and that he might contribute to his information.

Cogia Houssain returned the compliment by assuring Ali Baba that though his son might not have acquired the experience of older men, he had good sense equal to the experience of many others. After a little more conversation on different subjects, he offered again to take his leave, when Ali Baba, stopping him, said, "Where are you going, sir, in so much haste? I beg you will do me the honor to sup with me, though my entertainment may not be worthy your acceptance. Such as it is, I heartily offer it."

"Sir," replied Cogia Houssain, "I am thoroughly persuaded of your good will; but the truth is, I can eat no victuals that have any salt in them; therefore judge how I should feel at your table."

"If that is the only reason," said Ali Baba, "it ought not to deprive me of the honor of your company; for, in the first place, there is no salt ever put into my bread, and as to the meat we shall have to-night, I promise you there shall be none in that. Therefore you must do me the favor to stay. I will return immediately."

Ali Baba went into the kitchen, and ordered Morgiana to put no salt to the meat that was to be dressed that night; and to make quickly two or three ragouts besides what he had ordered, but be sure to put no salt in them.

Morgiana, who was always ready to obey her master, could not help being surprised at his strange order.

"Who is this strange man," said she, "who eats no salt with his meat? Your supper will be spoiled, if I keep it back so long."

"Do not be angry, Morgiana," replied Ali Baba. "He is an honest man, therefore do as I bid you."

Morgiana obeyed, though with no little reluctance, and had a curiosity to see this man who ate no salt. To this end, when she had finished what she had to do in the kitchen, she helped Abdalla to carry up the dishes; and looking at Cogia Houssain, she knew him at first sight, notwithstanding his disguise, to be the captain of the robbers, and examining him very carefully, perceived that he had a dagger under his garment.

"I am not in the least amazed," said she to herself, "that this wicked man, who is my master's greatest enemy, would eat no salt with him, since he intends to assassinate him; but I will prevent him."

Morgiana, while they were at supper, determined in her own mind to execute one of the boldest acts ever meditated. When Abdalla came for the dessert of fruit, and had put it with the wine and glasses before Ali Baba, Morgiana retired, dressed herself neatly with a suitable headdress like a dancer, girded her waist with a silver-gilt girdle, to which there hung a poniard with a hilt and guard of the same metal, and put a handsome mask on her face. When she had thus disguised herself, she said to Abdalla, "Take your tabor, and let us go and divert our master and his son's friend, as we do sometimes when he is alone."

Abdalla took his tabor, and played all the way into the hall before Morgiana, who, when she came to the door, made a low obeisance by way of asking leave to exhibit her skill, while Abdalla left off playing.

"Come in, Morgiana," said Ali Baba, "and let Cogia Houssain see what you can do, that he may tell us what he thinks of your performance."

Cogia Houssain, who did not expect this diversion after supper, began to fear he should not be able to take advantage of the opportunity he thought he had found; but hoped, if he now missed his aim, to secure it another time, by keeping up a friendly correspondence with the father and son; therefore, though he could have wished Ali Baba would have declined the dance, he pretended to be obliged to him for it, and had the complaisance to express his satisfaction at what he saw, which pleased his host.

As soon as Abdalla saw that Ali Baba and Cogia Houssain had done talking, he began to play on the tabor, and accompanied it with an air, to which Morgiana, who was an excellent performer, danced in such a manner as would have created admiration in any company.

After she had danced several dances with much grace, she drew the poniard, and holding it in her hand, began a dance in which she outdid herself by the many different figures, light movements, and the surprising leaps and wonderful exertions with which she accompanied it. Sometimes she presented the poniard to one breast, sometimes to another, and oftentimes seemed to strike her own. At last, she snatched the tabor from Abdalla with her left hand, and holding the dagger in her right presented the other side of the tabor, after the manner of those who get a livelihood by dancing, and solicit the liberality of the spectators.

Ali Baba put a piece of gold into the tabor, as did also his son; and Cogia Houssain, seeing that she was coming to him, had pulled his purse out of his bosom to make her a present; but while he was putting his hand into it, Morgiana, with a courage and resolution worthy of herself, plunged the poniard into his heart.

Ali Baba and his son, shocked at this action, cried out aloud.

"Unhappy woman!" exclaimed Ali Baba, "what have you done, to ruin me and my family?"

"It was to preserve, not to ruin you," answered Morgiana; "for see here," continued she, opening the pretended Cogia Houssain's garment, and showing the dagger, "what an enemy you had entertained! Look well at him, and you will find him to be both the fictitious oil merchant, and the captain of the gang of forty robbers. Remember, too, that he would eat no salt with you; and what would you have more to persuade you of his wicked design? Before I saw him, I suspected him as soon as you told me you had such a guest. I knew him, and you now find that my suspicion was not groundless."

Ali Baba, who immediately felt the new obligation he had to Morgiana for saving his life a second time, embraced her: "Morgiana," said he, "I gave you your liberty, and then promised you that my gratitude should not stop there, but that I would soon give you higher proofs of its sincerity, which I now do by making you my daughter-in-law."

Then addressing himself to his son, he said, "I believe you, son, to be so dutiful a child, that you will not refuse Morgiana for your wife. You see that Cogia Houssain sought your friendship with a treacherous design to take away my life; and if he had succeeded, there is no doubt but he would have sacrificed you also to his revenge. Consider, that by marrying Morgiana you marry the preserver of my family and your own."

The son, far from showing any dislike, readily consented to the marriage; not only because he would not disobey his father, but also because it was agreeable to his inclination. After this they thought of burying the captain of the robbers with his comrades, and did it so privately that nobody discovered their bones till many years after, when no one had any concern in the publication of this remarkable history. A few days afterward, Ali Baba celebrated the nuptials of his son and Morgiana with great solemnity, a sumptuous feast, and the usual dancing and spectacles; and had the satisfaction to see that his friends and neighbors, whom he invited, had no knowledge of the true motives of the marriage; but that those who were not unacquainted with Morgiana's good qualities commended his generosity and goodness of heart. Ali Baba did not visit the robber's cave for a whole year, as he supposed the other two, whom he could get no account of, might be alive.

At the year's end, when he found they had not made any attempt to disturb him, he had the curiosity to make another journey. He mounted his horse, and when he came to the cave he alighted, tied his horse to a tree, and approaching the entrance, pronounced the words, "Open, Sesame!" and the door opened. He entered the cavern, and by the condition he found things in, judged that nobody had been there since the captain had fetched the goods for his shop. From this time he believed he was the only person in the world who had the secret of opening the cave, and that all the treasure was at his sole disposal. He put as much gold into his saddle-bag as his horse would carry, and returned to town. Some years later he carried his son to the cave, and taught him the secret, which he handed down to his posterity, who, using their good fortune with moderation, lived in great honor and splendor.

THE STORY OF SINDBAD THE SAILOR

In the reign of the same caliph, Haroun al Raschid, of whom we have already heard, there lived at Bagdad a poor porter, called Hindbad. One day, when the weather was excessively hot, he was employed to carry a heavy burden from one end of the town to the other. Being much fatigued, he took off his load, and sat upon it, near a large mansion.

He was much pleased that he stopped at this place, for the agreeable smell of wood of aloes and of pastils, that came from the house, mixing with the scent of the rose water, completely perfumed and embalmed the air. Besides, he heard from within a concert of instrumental music, accompanied with the harmonious notes of nightingales and other birds. This charming melody, and the smell of several sorts of savory dishes, made the porter conclude there was a feast, with great rejoicings within. His business seldom leading him that way, he knew not to whom the mansion belonged; but he went to some of the servants, whom he saw standing at the gate in magnificent apparel, and asked the name of the proprietor.

"How," replied one of them, "do you live in Bagdad, and know not that this is the house of Sindbad the sailor, that famous voyager, who has sailed round the world?"

The porter lifted up his eyes to heaven, and said, loud enough to be heard, "Almighty Creator of all things, consider the difference between Sindbad and me! I am every day exposed to fatigues and calamities, and can scarcely get coarse barley bread for myself and my family, while happy Sindbad profusely expends immense riches, and leads a life of continual pleasure. What has he done to obtain from Thee a lot so agreeable? And what have I done to deserve one so wretched?"

While the porter was thus indulging his melancholy, a servant came out of the house, and taking him by the arm, bade him follow him, for Sindbad, his master, wanted to speak to him.

The servant brought him into a great hall, where a number of people sat round a table covered with all sorts of savory dishes. At the upper end sat a comely, venerable gentleman, with a long white beard, and behind him stood a number of officers and domestics, all ready to attend his pleasure. This person was Sindbad. Hindbad, whose fear was increased at the sight of so many people, and of a banquet so sumptuous, saluted the company, trembling. Sindbad bade him draw near, and seating him at his right hand, served him himself, and gave him excellent wine, of which there was abundance upon the sideboard.

Now Sindbad had himself heard the porter complain through the window, and this it was that induced him to have him brought in. When the repast was over, Sindbad addressed his conversation to Hindbad, and inquired his name and employment, and said, "I wish to hear from your own mouth what it was you lately said in the street."

At this request, Hindbad hung down his head in confusion, and replied, "My lord, I confess that my fatigue put me out of humor and occasioned me to utter some indiscreet words, which I beg you to pardon."

"Do not think I am so unjust," resumed Sindbad, "as to resent such a complaint. But I must rectify your error concerning myself. You think, no doubt, that I have acquired without labor and trouble the ease and indulgence which I now enjoy. But do not mistake; I did not attain to this happy condition without enduring for several years more trouble of body and mind than can well be imagined. Yes, gentlemen," he added, speaking to the whole company, "I assure you that my sufferings have been of a nature so extraordinary as would deprive the greatest miser of his love of riches; and as an opportunity now offers, I will, with your leave, relate the dangers I have encountered, which I think will not be uninteresting to you."

THE FIRST VOYAGE OF SINDBAD THE SAILOR

My father was a wealthy merchant of much repute. He bequeathed me a large estate, which I wasted in riotous living. I quickly perceived my error, and that I was misspending my time, which is of all things the most valuable. I remembered the saying of the great Solomon, which I had frequently heard from my father, "A good name is better than precious ointment," and again, "Wisdom is good with an inheritance." Struck with these reflections, I resolved to walk in my father's ways, and I entered into a contract with some merchants, and embarked with them on board a ship we had jointly fitted out.

We set sail, and steered our course toward the Indies, through the Persian Gulf, which is formed by the coasts of Arabia Felix on the right, and by those of Persia on the left. At first I was troubled with seasickness, but speedily recovered my health, and was not afterward subject to that complaint.

In our voyage we touched at several islands, where we sold or exchanged our goods. One day, while under sail, we were becalmed near a small island, but little elevated above the level of the water, and resembling a green meadow. The captain ordered his sails to be furled, and permitted such persons as were so inclined to land; of this number I was one.

But while we were enjoying ourselves in eating and drinking, and recovering ourselves from the fatigue of the sea, the island on a sudden trembled, and shook us terribly.

The trembling of the island was perceived on board the ship, and we were called upon to re-embark speedily, or we should all be lost; for what we took for an island proved to be the back of a sea monster. The nimblest got into the sloop, others betook themselves to swimming; but as for myself, I was still upon the island when it disappeared into the sea, and I had only time to catch hold of a piece of wood that we had brought out of the ship to make a fire. Meanwhile the captain, having received those on board who were in the sloop, and taken up some of those that swam, resolved to improve the favorable gale that had just risen, and hoisting his sails pursued his voyage, so that it was impossible for me to recover the ship.

Thus was I exposed to the mercy of the waves all the rest of the day and the following night. By this time I found my strength gone, and despaired of saving my life, when happily a wave threw me against an island. The bank was high and rugged, so that I could scarcely have got up had it not been for some roots of trees which I found within reach. When the sun arose, though I was very feeble, both from hard labor and want of food, I crept along to find some herbs fit to eat, and had the good luck not only to procure some, but likewise to discover a spring

Thus was I exposed to the mercy of the waves all the rest of the day and the following night.

of excellent water, which contributed much to recover me. After this I advanced farther into the island, and at last reached a fine plain, where I perceived some horses feeding. I went toward them, when I heard the voice of a man, who immediately appeared, and asked me who I was. I related to him my adventure, after which, taking me by the hand, he led me into a cave, where there were several other people, no less amazed to see me than I was to see them.

I partook of some provisions which they offered me. I then asked them what they did in such a desert place; to which they answered that they were grooms belonging to the maharaja, sovereign of the island, and that every year they brought thither the king's horses for pasturage. They added that they were to return home on the morrow, and had I been one day later I must have perished, because the inhabited part of the island was a great distance off, and it would have been impossible for me to have got thither without a guide.

Next morning they returned to the capital of the island, took me with them, and presented me to the maharaja. He asked me who I was, and by what adventure I had come into his dominions. After I had satisfied him, he told me he was much concerned for my misfortune, and at the same time ordered that I should want for nothing; which commands his officers were so generous and careful as to see exactly fulfilled.

Being a merchant, I frequented men of my own profession, and particularly inquired for those who were strangers, that perchance I might hear news from Bagdad, or find an opportunity to return. For the maharaja's capital is situated on the seacoast, and has a fine harbor, where ships arrive daily from the different quarters of the world. I frequented also the society of the learned Indians, and took delight to hear them converse; but withal, I took care to make my court regularly to the maharaja, and conversed with the governors and petty kings, his tributaries, that were about him. They put a thousand questions respecting my country; and I, being willing to inform myself as to their laws and customs, asked them concerning everything which I thought worth knowing.

There belongs to this king an island named Cassel. They assured me that every night a noise of drums was heard there, whence the mariners fancied that it was the residence of Gegial. I determined to visit this wonderful place, and in my way thither saw fishes of one hundred and two hundred cubits long, that occasion more fear than hurt; for they are so timorous that they will fly upon the rattling of two sticks or boards. I saw likewise other fish, about a cubit in length, that had heads like owls.

As I was one day at the port after my return, the ship arrived in which I had embarked at Bussorah. I at once knew the captain, and I went and asked him for my bales. "I am Sindbad," said I, "and those bales marked with his name are mine."

When the captain heard me speak thus, "Heavens!" he exclaimed, "whom can we trust in these times! I saw Sindbad perish with my own eyes, as did also the passengers on board, and yet you tell me you are that Sindbad. What impudence is this! And what a false tale to tell, in order to possess yourself of what does not belong to you!"

"Have patience," replied I. "Do me the favor to hear what I have to say."

The captain was at length persuaded that I was no cheat; for there came people from his ship who knew me, paid me great compliments, and expressed much joy at seeing me alive. At last he recollected me himself, and embracing me, "Heaven be praised," said he, "for your happy escape! I cannot express the joy it affords me. There are your goods; take and do with them as you please."

I took out what was most valuable in my bales, and presented them to the maharaja, who, knowing my misfortune, asked me how I came by such rarities. I acquainted him with the circumstance of their recovery. He was pleased at my good luck, accepted my present, and in return gave me one much more considerable. Upon this I took leave of him, and went aboard the same ship after I had exchanged my goods for the commodities of that country. I carried with me wood of aloes, sandals, camphor, nutmegs, cloves, pepper, and ginger.

We passed by several islands, and at last arrived at Bussorah, from whence I came to this city, with the value of one hundred thousand sequins.

Sindbad stopped here, and ordered the musicians to proceed with their concert, which the story had interrupted. When it was evening, Sindbad sent for a purse of one hundred sequins, and giving it to the porter, said, "Take this, Hindbad, return to your home, and come back to-morrow to hear more of my adventures." The porter went away, astonished at the honor done him, and the present made him. The account of this adventure proved very agreeable to his wife and children, who did not fail to return thanks for what Providence had sent them by the hand of Sindbad.

Sindbad put on his best robe next day, and returned to the bountiful traveler, who received him with a pleasant air, and welcomed him heartily. When all the guests had arrived, dinner was served, and continued a long time. When it was ended, Sindbad, addressing himself to the company, said, "Gentlemen, be pleased to listen to the adventures of my second voyage. They deserve your attention even more than those of the first."

Upon which every one held his peace, and Sindbad proceeded.

THE SECOND VOYAGE OF SINDBAD THE SAILOR

I designed, after my first voyage, to spend the rest of my days at Bagdad, but it was not long ere I grew weary of an indolent life, and I put to sea a second time, with merchants of known probity. We embarked on board a good ship, and, after recommending ourselves to God, set sail. We traded from island to island, and exchanged commodities with great profit. One day we landed on an island covered with several sorts of fruit trees, but we could see neither man nor animal. We walked in the meadows, along the streams that watered them. While some diverted themselves with gathering flowers, and others fruits, I took my wine and provisions, and sat down near a stream betwixt two high trees, which formed a thick shade. I made a good meal, and afterward fell sleep. I cannot tell how long I slept, but when I awoke the ship was gone.

In this sad condition I was ready to die with grief. I cried out in agony, beat my head and breast, and threw myself upon the ground, where I lay some time in despair. I upbraided myself a hundred times for not being content with the produce of my first voyage, that might have sufficed me all my life. But all this was in vain, and my repentance came too late. At last I resigned myself to the will of God. Not knowing what to do, I climbed to the top of a lofty tree, from whence I looked about on all sides, to see if I could discover anything that could give me hope. When I gazed toward the sea I could see nothing but sky and water; but looking over the land, I beheld something white; and coming down, I took what provision I had left and went toward it, the distance being so great that I could not distinguish what it was.

As I approached, I thought it to be a white dome, of a prodigious height and extent; and when I came up to it, I touched it, and found it to be very smooth. I went round to see if it was open on any side, but saw it was not, and that there was no climbing up to the top, as it was so smooth. It was at least fifty paces round.

By this time the sun was about to set, and all of a sudden the sky became as dark as if it had been covered with a thick cloud. I was much astonished at this sudden darkness, but much more when I found it was occasioned by a bird of a monstrous size, that came flying toward me. I remembered that I had often heard mariners speak of a miraculous bird called the roc, and conceived that the great dome which I so much admired must be its egg. In short, the bird alighted, and sat over the egg. As I perceived her coming, I crept close to the egg, so that I had before me one of the legs of the bird, which was as big as the trunk of a tree. I tied myself strongly to it with my turban, in hopes that the roc next morning would carry me with her out of this desert island. After having passed the night in this condition, the bird flew away as soon as it was daylight, and carried me so high that I could not discern the earth; she afterward descended with so much rapidity that I lost my senses. But when I found myself on the ground, I speedily untied the knot, and had scarcely done so, when the roc, having taken up a serpent of a monstrous length in her bill, flew away.

The spot where it left me was encompassed on all sides by mountains, that seemed to reach above the clouds, and so steep that there was no possibility of getting out of the valley. This was a new perplexity; so that when I compared this place with the desert island from which the roc had brought me, I found that I had gained nothing by the change.

As I walked through this valley, I perceived it was strewn with diamonds, some of which were of surprising bigness. I took pleasure in looking upon them; but shortly I saw at a distance such objects as greatly diminished my satisfaction, and which I could not view without terror, namely, a great number of serpents, so monstrous that the least of them was capable of swallowing an elephant. They retired in the daytime to their dens, where they hid themselves from the roc, their enemy, and came out only in the night.

I spent the day in walking about in the valley, resting myself at times in such places as I thought most convenient. When night came on I went into a cave, where I thought I might repose in safety. I secured the entrance, which was low and narrow, with a great stone, to preserve me from the serpents; but not so far as to exclude the light. I supped on part of my provisions, but the serpents, which began hissing round me, put me into such extreme fear that I did not sleep. When day appeared the serpents retired, and I came out of the cave, trembling. I can justly say that I walked upon diamonds without feeling any inclination to touch them. At last I sat down, and notwithstanding my apprehensions, not having closed my eyes during the night, fell asleep, after having eaten a little more of my provisions. But I had scarcely shut my eyes when something that fell by me with a great noise awakened me.

As I walked through this valley, I perceived it was strewn with diamonds, some of which were of surprising bigness.

This was a large piece of raw meat; and at the same time I saw several others fall down from the rocks in different places.

I had always regarded as fabulous what I had heard sailors and others relate of the valley of diamonds, and of the stratagems employed by merchants to obtain jewels from thence; but now I found that they had stated nothing but the truth. For the fact is, that the merchants come to the neighborhood of this valley, when the eagles have young ones, and throwing great joints of meat into the valley, the diamonds, upon whose points they fall, stick to them; the eagles, which are stronger in this country than anywhere else, pounce with great force upon those pieces of meat, and carry them to their nests on the precipices of the rocks to feed their young: the merchants at this time run to their nests, disturb and drive off the eagles by their shouts, and take away the diamonds that stick to the meat.

I perceived in this device the means of my deliverance.

Having collected together the largest diamonds I could find, and put them into the leather bag in which I used to carry my provisions, I took the largest of the pieces of meat, tied it close round me with the cloth of my turban, and then laid myself upon the ground, with my face downward, the bag of diamonds being made fast to my girdle.

I had scarcely placed myself in this posture when one of the eagles, having taken me up with the piece of meat to which I was fastened, carried me to his nest on the top of the mountain. The merchants immediately began their shouting to frighten the eagles; and when they had obliged them to quit their prey, one of them came to the nest where I was. He was much alarmed when he saw me; but recovering himself, instead of inquiring how I came thither, began to quarrel with me, and asked why I stole his goods.

"You will treat me," replied I, "with more civility when you know me better. Do not be uneasy; I have diamonds enough for you and myself, more than all the other merchants together. Whatever they have they owe to chance; but I selected for myself, in the bottom of the valley, those which you see in this bag."

I had scarcely done speaking, when the other merchants came crowding about us, much astonished to see me; but they were much more surprised when I told them my story.

They conducted me to their encampment; and there, having opened my bag, they were surprised at the largeness of my diamonds, and confessed that they had never seen any of such size and perfection. I prayed the merchant who owned the nest to which I had been carried (for every merchant had his own) to take as many for his share as he pleased. He contented himself with one, and that, too, the least of them; and when I pressed him to take more, without fear of doing me any injury, "No," said he, "I am very well satisfied with this, which is valuable enough to save me the trouble of making any more voyages, and will raise as great a fortune as I desire."

I spent the night with the merchants, to whom I related my story a second time, for the satisfaction of those who had not heard it. I could not moderate my joy when I found myself delivered from the danger I have mentioned. I thought myself in a dream, and could scarcely believe myself out of danger.

The merchants had thrown their pieces of meat into the valley for several days; and each of them being satisfied with the diamonds that had fallen to his lot, we left the place the next morning, and traveled near high mountains, where there were serpents of a prodigious length, which we had the good fortune to escape. We took shipping at the first port we reached, and touched at the isle of Roha, where the trees grow that yield camphor. This tree is so large, and its branches so thick, that one hundred men may easily sit under its shade. The juice, of which the camphor is made, exudes from a hole bored in the upper part of the tree, and is received in a vessel, where it thickens to a consistency, and becomes what we call camphor. After the juice is thus drawn out, the tree withers and dies.

In this island is also found the rhinoceros, an animal less than the elephant but larger than the buffalo. It has a horn upon its nose, about a cubit in length; this horn is solid, and cleft through the middle. The rhinoceros fights with the elephant, runs his horn into his belly, and carries him off upon his head; but the blood and the fat of the elephant running into his eyes and making him blind, he falls to the ground; and then, strange to relate, the roc comes and carries them both away in her claws, for food for her young ones.

I pass over many other things peculiar to this island, lest I should weary you. Here I exchanged some of my diamonds for merchandise. From hence we went to other islands, and at last, having touched at several trading towns of the continent, we landed at Bussorah, from whence I proceeded to Bagdad. There I immediately gave large presents to the poor, and lived honorably upon the vast riches I had brought, and gained with so much fatigue.

Thus Sindbad ended the relation of the second voyage, gave Hindbad another hundred sequins, and invited him to come the next day to hear the account of the third.

THE THIRD VOYAGE OF SINDBAD THE SAILOR

I soon again grew weary of living a life of idleness, and hardening myself against the thought of any danger, I embarked with some merchants on another long voyage. We touched at several ports, where we traded. One day we were overtaken by a dreadful tempest, which drove us from our course. The storm continued several days, and brought us before the port of an island, which the captain was very unwilling to enter; but we were obliged to cast anchor. When we had furled our sails the captain told us that this and some other neighboring islands were inhabited by hairy savages, who would speedily attack us; and though they were but dwarfs we must make no resistance, for they were more in number than the locusts; and if we happened to kill one, they would all fall upon us and destroy us.

We soon found that what the captain had told us was but too true. An innumerable multitude of frightful savages, about two feet high, covered all over with red hair, came swimming toward us, and encompassed our ship. They chattered as they came near, but we understood not their language. They climbed up the sides of the ship with such agility as surprised us. They took down our sails, cut the cable, and hauling to the shore, made us all get out, and afterward carried the ship into another island, from whence they had come.

As we advanced, we perceived at a distance a vast pile of building, and made toward it. We found it to be a palace, elegantly built, and very lofty, with a gate of ebony of two leaves, which we opened. We saw before us a large apartment, with a porch, having on one side a heap of human bones, and on the other a vast number of roasting spits. We trembled at this spectacle, and were seized with deadly apprehension, when suddenly the gate of the apartment opened with a loud crash, and there came out the horrible figure of a black man, as tall as a lofty palm tree. He had but one eye, and that in the middle of his forehead, where it blazed bright as a burning coal. His foreteeth were very long and sharp, and stood out of his mouth, which was as deep as that of a horse. His upper lip hung down upon his breast. His ears resembled those of an elephant, and covered his shoulders; and his nails were as long and crooked as the talons of the greatest birds. At the sight of so frightful a genie we became insensible, and lay like dead men.

At last we came to ourselves, and saw him sitting in the porch looking at us. When he had considered us well, he advanced toward us, and laying his hand upon me, took me up by the nape of my neck, and turned me around, as a butcher would do a sheep's head. After having examined me, and perceiving me to be so lean that I was nothing but skin and bone, he let me go. He took up all the rest one by one, and viewed them in the same manner. The captain being the fattest, he held him with one hand, as I would do a sparrow, and thrust a spit through him; he then kindled a great fire, roasted, and ate him in his apartment for his supper. Having finished his repast, he returned to his porch, where he lay and fell asleep, snoring louder than thunder.

He slept thus till morning. As for ourselves, it was not possible for us to enjoy any rest, so that we passed the night in the most painful apprehension that can be imagined. When day appeared the giant awoke, got up, went out, and left us in the palace.

The next night we determined to revenge ourselves on the brutish giant, and did so in the following manner. After he had again finished his inhuman supper on another of our seamen, he lay down on his back, and fell asleep. As soon as we heard him snore according to his custom, nine of the boldest among us, and myself, took each of us a spit, and putting the points of them into the fire till they were burning hot, we thrust them into his eye all at once, and blinded him. The pain made him break out into a frightful yell: he started up, and stretched out his hands in order to sacrifice some of us to his rage, but we ran to such places as he could not reach; and after having sought for us in vain, he groped for the gate, and went out, howling in agony.

We immediately left the palace, and came to the shore, where with some timber that lay about in great quantities, we made some rafts, each large enough to carry three men. We waited until day to get upon them, for we hoped if the giant did not appear by sunrise, and give over his howling, which we still heard, that he would prove to be dead; and if that happened to be the case, we resolved to stay on that island, and not to risk our lives upon the rafts. But day had scarcely appeared when we perceived our cruel enemy, with two others, almost of the same size, leading him; and a great number more coming before him at a quick pace.

We did not hesitate to take to our rafts, but put to sea with all the speed we could. The giants, who perceived this, took up great stones, and running to the shore they entered the water up to the middle, and threw so exactly that they sank all the rafts but that I was upon; and all my companions, except the two with me, were drowned. We rowed with all our might, and got out of the reach of the giants. But when we got out to sea we were exposed to the mercy of the waves and winds, and spent that day and the following night under the most painful uncertainty as to our fate; but next morning we had the good fortune to be thrown upon an island, where we landed with much joy. We found excellent fruit, which afforded us great relief, and recruited our strength.

At night we went to sleep on the seashore; but were awakened by the noise of a serpent of surprising length and thickness, whose scales made a rustling noise as he wound himself along. It swallowed up one of my comrades, notwithstanding his loud cries and the efforts he made to extricate himself from it. Dashing him several times against the ground, it crushed him, and we could hear it gnaw and tear the poor fellow's bones, though we had fled to a considerable distance. The following day, to our great terror, we saw the serpent again, when I exclaimed, "O Heaven, to what dangers are we exposed! We rejoiced yesterday at having escaped from the cruelty of a giant and the rage of the waves; now are we fallen into another danger equally dreadful."

As we walked about, we saw a large tall tree, upon which we designed to pass the following night for our security; and having satisfied our hunger with fruit, we mounted it accordingly. Shortly after, the serpent came hissing to the foot of the tree, raised itself up against the trunk of it, and meeting with my comrade, who sat lower than I, swallowed him at once, and went off.

I remained upon the tree till it was day, and then came down, more like a dead man than one alive, expecting the same fate as had befallen my two companions. This filled me with horror, and I advanced some steps to throw myself into the sea; but I withstood this dictate of despair, and submitted myself to the will of God, who disposes of our lives at His pleasure.

In the meantime I collected together a great quantity of small wood, brambles, and dry thorns, and making them up into fagots, made a wide circle with them round the tree, and also tied some of them to the branches over my head. Having done this, when the evening came I shut myself up within this circle, with the melancholy satisfaction that I had neglected nothing which could preserve me from the cruel destiny with which I was threatened. The serpent failed not to come at the usual hour, and went round the tree, seeking for an opportunity to devour me, but was prevented by the rampart I had made; so that he lay till day, like a cat watching in vain for a mouse that has fortunately reached a place of safety. When day appeared, he retired, but I dared not leave my fort until the sun arose.

God took compassion on my hopeless state; for just as I was going, in a fit of desperation, to throw myself into the sea, I perceived a ship in the distance. I called as loud as I could, and unfolding the linen of my turban, displayed it, that they might observe me. This had the desired effect. The crew perceived me, and the captain sent his boat for me. As soon as I came on board, the merchants and seamen flocked about me, to know how I came into that desert island; and after I had related to them all that had befallen me, the oldest among them said they had several times heard of the giants that dwelt on that island, and that they were cannibals; and as to the serpents, they added that there were abundant in the island; that they hid themselves by day, and came abroad by night. After having testified their joy at my escaping so many dangers, they brought me the best of their provisions; and took me before the captain, who, seeing that I was in rags, gave me one of his own suits. Looking steadfastly upon him, I knew him to be the person who, on my second voyage, had left me in the island where I fell asleep, and had sailed without me, or without sending to seek for me.

I was not surprised that he, believing me to be dead, did not recognize me.

"Captain," said I, "look at me, and you may know that I am Sindbad, whom you left in that desert island."

The captain, having considered me attentively, recognized me.

"God be praised!" said he, embracing me; "I rejoice that fortune has rectified my fault. There are your goods, which I always took care to preserve."

I took them from him, and made him my acknowledgments for his care of them.

We continued at sea for some time, touched at several islands, and at last landed at that of Salabat, where sandalwood is obtained, which is much used in medicine.

From the isle of Salabat we went to another, where I furnished myself with cloves, cinnamon, and other spices. As we sailed from this island we saw a tortoise twenty cubits in length and breadth. We observed also an amphibious animal like a cow, which gave milk; its skin is so hard, that they usually make bucklers of it. I saw another, which had the shape and color of a camel.

In short, after a long voyage I arrived at Bussorah, and from thence returned to Bagdad with so much wealth that I knew not its extent. I gave a great deal to the poor, and bought another considerable estate.

Thus Sindbad finished the history of his third voyage. He gave another hundred sequins to Hindbad, and invited him to dinner again the next day, to hear:

THE FOURTH VOYAGE OF SINDBAD THE SAILOR

After I had rested from the dangers of my third voyage, my passion for trade and my love of novelty soon again prevailed. I therefore settled my affairs, and provided a stock of goods fit for the traffic I designed to engage in. I took the route to Persia, traveled over several provinces, and then arrived at a port, where I embarked. On putting out to sea, we were overtaken by such a sudden gust of wind as obliged the captain to lower his yards, and take all other necessary precautions to prevent the danger that threatened us. But all was in vain; our endeavors had no effect. The sails were split in a thousand pieces, and the ship was stranded, several of the merchants and seamen were drowned, and the cargo was lost.

I had the good fortune, with several of the merchants and mariners, to get upon some planks, and we were carried by the current to an island which lay before us. There we found fruit and spring water, which preserved our lives. We stayed all night near the place where we had been cast ashore.

Next morning, as soon as the sun was up, we explored the island, and saw some houses, which we approached. As soon as we drew near we were encompassed by a great number of negroes, who seized us, shared us among them, and carried us to their respective habitations.

I and five of my comrades were carried to one place; here they made us sit down, and gave us a certain herb, which they made signs to us to eat.

My comrades, not taking notice that the blacks ate none of it themselves, thought only of satisfying their hunger, and ate with greediness. But I, suspecting some trick, would not so much as taste it, which happened well for me; for in a little time after I perceived my companions had lost their senses, and that when they spoke to me they knew not what they said.

The negroes fed us afterward with rice, prepared with oil of coconuts; and my comrades, who had lost their reason, ate of it greedily. I also partook of it, but very sparingly. They gave us that herb at first on purpose to deprive us of our senses, that we might not be aware of the sad destiny prepared for us; and they supplied us with rice to fatten us; for, being cannibals, their design was to eat us as soon as we grew fat. This accordingly happened, for they devoured my comrades, who were not sensible of their condition; but my senses being entire, you may easily guess that instead of growing fat, as the rest did, I grew leaner every day. The fear of death turned all my food into poison. I fell into a languishing distemper, which proved my safety; for the negroes, having killed and eaten my companions, seeing me to be withered, lean, and sick, deferred my death.

Meanwhile I had much liberty, so that scarcely any notice was taken of what I did, and this gave me an opportunity one day to get at a distance from the houses, and to make my escape. An old man who saw me, and suspected my design, called to me as loud as he could to return; but instead of obeying him, I redoubled my speed, and quickly got out of sight. At that time there was none but the old man about the houses, the rest being abroad, and not to return till night, which was usual with them. Therefore, being sure that they could not arrive in time to pursue me, I went on till night, when I stopped to rest a little, and to eat some of the provisions I had secured; but I speedily set forward again, and traveled seven days, avoiding those places which seemed to be inhabited, and lived for the most part upon coconuts, which served me both for meat and drink. On the eighth day I came near the sea, and saw some white people, like myself, gathering pepper, of which there was great plenty in that place. This I took to be a good omen, and went to them without any scruple.

The people who gathered pepper came to meet me as soon as they saw me, and asked me in Arabic who I was and whence I came. I was overjoyed to hear them speak in my own language, and I satisfied their curiosity by giving them an account of my shipwreck, and how I fell into the hands of the negroes.

"Those negroes," replied they, "eat men; and by what miracle did you escape their cruelty?" I related to them the circumstances I have just mentioned, at which they were wonderfully surprised.

I stayed with them till they had gathered their quantity of pepper, and then sailed with them to the island from whence they had come. They presented me to their king, who was a good prince. He had the patience to hear the relation of my adventures, which surprised him; and he afterward gave me clothes, and commanded care to be taken of me.

The island was very well peopled, plentiful in everything, and the capital a place of great trade. This agreeable retreat was very comfortable to me after my misfortunes, and the kindness of this generous prince completed my satisfaction. In a word, there was not a person more in favor with him than myself, and consequently every man in court and city sought to oblige me; so that in a very little time I was looked upon rather as a native than a stranger.

I observed one thing, which to me appeared very extraordinary. All the people, the king himself not excepted, rode their horses without bridle or stirrups. I went one day to a workman, and gave him a model for making the stock of a saddle. When that was done, I covered it myself with velvet and leather, and embroidered it with gold. I afterward went to a smith, who made me a bit, according to the pattern I showed him, and also some stirrups. When I had all things completed, I presented them to the king, and put them upon one of his horses. His majesty mounted immediately, and was so pleased with them that he testified his satisfaction by large presents. I made several others for the ministers and principal officers of his household, which gained me great reputation and regard.

As I paid my court very constantly to the king, he said to me one day, "Sindbad, I love thee. I have one thing to demand of thee, which thou must grant. I have a mind thou shouldst marry, that so thou mayst stay in my dominions, and think no more of thy own country."

I durst not resist the prince's will, and he gave me one of the ladies of his court, noble, beautiful, and rich. The ceremonies of marriage being over, I went and dwelt with my wife, and for some time we lived together in perfect harmony. I was not, however, satisfied with my banishment.

Therefore I designed to make my escape at the first opportunity, and to return to Bagdad, which my present settlement, how advantageous soever, could not make me forget.

At this time the wife of one of my neighbors, with whom I had contracted a very strict friendship, fell sick and died. I went to see and comfort him in his affliction, and finding him absorbed in sorrow, I said to him, as soon as I saw him, "God preserve you, and grant you a long life."

"Alas!" replied he, "how do you think I should obtain the favor you wish me? I have not above an hour to live, for I must be buried this day with my wife. This is a law on this island. The living husband is interred with the dead wife, and the living wife with the dead husband."

While he was giving me an account of this barbarous custom, the very relation of which chilled my blood, his kindred, friends, and neighbors came to assist at the funeral. They dressed the corpse of the woman in her richest apparel and all her jewels, as if it had been her wedding day; then they placed her on an open bier, and began their march to the place of burial. The husband walked first, next to the dead body. They proceeded to a high mountain, and when they had reached the place of their destination they took up a large stone which formed the mouth of a deep pit, and let down the body with all its apparel and jewels. Then the husband, embracing his kindred and friends, without resistance suffered himself to be placed on another bier, with a pot of water and seven small loaves, and was let down in the same manner. The ceremony being over, the mouth of the pit was again covered with the stone, and the company returned.

I mention this ceremony the more particularly because I was in a few weeks' time to be the principal actor on a similar occasion. Alas! my own wife fell sick and died. I made every remonstrance I could to the king not to expose me, a foreigner, to this inhuman law. I appealed in vain. The king and all his court, with the most considerable persons of the city, sought to soften my sorrow by honoring the funeral ceremony with their presence; and at the termination of the ceremony I was lowered into the pit with a vessel full of water, and seven loaves. As I approached the bottom I discovered, by the aid of the little light that came from above, the nature of this subterranean place; it seemed an endless cavern, and might be about fifty fathoms deep.

I lived for some time upon my bread and water, when, one day, just as I was on the point of exhaustion, I heard something tread, and breathing or panting as it moved. I followed the sound. The animal seemed to stop sometimes, but always fled and breathed hard as I approached. I pursued it for a considerable time, till at last I perceived a light, resembling a star; I went on, sometimes lost sight of it, but always found it again, and at last discovered that it came through a hole in the rock, which I got through, and found myself upon the seashore, at which I felt exceeding joy. I prostrated myself on the shore to thank God for this mercy, and shortly afterward I perceived a ship making for the place where I was. I made a sign with the linen of my turban, and called to the crew as loud as I could. They heard me, and sent a boat to bring me on board. It was fortunate for me that these people did not inspect the place where they found me, but without hesitation took me on board.

We passed by several islands, and among others that called the Isle of Bells, about ten days' sail from Serendib with a regular wind, and six from that of Kela, where we landed. Lead mines are found in the island; also Indian canes, and excellent camphor.

The King of the Isle of Kela is very rich and powerful, and the Isle of Bells, which is about two days' journey away, is also subject to him. The inhabitants are so barbarous that they still eat human flesh. After we had finished our traffic in that island we put to sea again, and touched at several other ports; at last I arrived happily at Bagdad. Out of gratitude to God for His mercies, I contributed liberally toward the support of several mosques and the subsistence of the poor, and enjoyed myself with my friends in festivities and amusements.

Here Sindbad made a new present of one hundred sequins to Hindbad, whom he requested to return with the rest next day at the same hour, to dine with him and hear the story of his fifth voyage.

THE FIFTH VOYAGE OF SINDBAD THE SAILOR

All the troubles and calamities I had undergone could not cure me of my inclination to make new voyages. I therefore bought goods, departed with them for the best seaport, and there, that I might not be obliged to depend upon a captain, but have a ship at my own command, I remained till one was built on purpose, at my own charge. When the ship was ready I went on board with my goods; but not having enough to load her, I agreed to take with me several merchants of different nations, with their merchandise.

We sailed with the first fair wind, and after a long navigation the first place we touched at was a desert island, where we found the egg of a roc, equal in size to that I formerly mentioned. There was a young roc in it, just ready to be hatched, and its beak had begun to break the egg.

The merchants who landed with me broke the egg with hatchets, and making a hole in it, pulled out the young roc piecemeal, and roasted it. I had in vain entreated them not to meddle with the egg.

Scarcely had they finished their repast, when there appeared in the air, at a considerable distance, two great clouds.

The captain of my ship, knowing by experience what they meant, said they were the male and female parents of the roc, and pressed us to re-embark with all speed, to prevent the misfortune which he saw would otherwise befall us.

The two rocs approached with a frightful noise, which they redoubled when they saw the egg broken, and their young one gone. They flew back in the direction they had come, and disappeared for some time, while we made all the sail we could in the endeavor to prevent that which unhappily befell us.

They soon returned, and we observed that each of them carried between its talons an enormous rock. When they came directly over my ship, they hovered, and one of them let go his rock; but by the dexterity of the steersman it missed us and fell into the sea. The other so exactly hit the middle of the ship as to split it into pieces. The mariners and passengers were all crushed to death or fell into the sea. I myself was of the number of the latter; but, as I came up again, I fortunately caught hold of a piece of the wreck, and swimming, sometimes with one hand and sometimes with the other, but always holding fast the plank, the wind and the tide favoring me, I came to an island, and got safely ashore.

I sat down upon the grass, to recover myself from my fatigue, after which I went into the island to explore it. It seemed to be a delicious garden. I found trees everywhere, some of them bearing green and others ripe fruits, and streams of fresh pure water. I ate of the fruits, which I found excellent; and drank of the water, which was very light and good.

When I was a little advanced into the island, I saw an old man, who appeared very weak and infirm. He was sitting on the bank of a stream, and at first I took him to be one who had been shipwrecked like myself. I went toward him and saluted him, but he only slightly bowed his head. I asked him why he sat so still; but instead of answering me, he made a sign for me to take him upon my back, and carry him over the brook.

I believed him really to stand in need of my assistance, took him upon my back, and having carried him over, bade him get down, and for that end stooped, that he might get off with ease; but instead of doing so (which I laugh at every time I think of it), the old man, who to me appeared quite decrepit, threw his legs nimbly about my neck. He sat astride upon my shoulders, and held my throat so tight that I thought he would have strangled me, and I fainted away.

Notwithstanding my fainting, the ill-natured old fellow still kept his seat upon my neck. When I had recovered my breath, he thrust one of his feet against my side, and struck me so rudely with the other that he forced me to rise up, against my will. Having arisen, he made me carry him under the trees, and forced me now and then to stop, that he might gather and eat fruit. He never left his seat all day; and when I lay down to rest at night he laid himself down with me, still holding fast about my neck. Every morning he pinched me to make me awake, and afterward obliged me to get up and walk, and spurred me with his feet.

One day I found several dry calabashes that had fallen from a tree. I took a large one, and after cleaning it, pressed into it some juice of grapes, which abounded in the island. Having filled the calabash, I put it by in a convenient place, and going thither again some days after, I tasted it, and found the wine so good that it gave me new vigor, and so exhilarated my spirits that I began to sing and dance as I carried my burden.

The old man, perceiving the effect which this had upon me, and that I carried him with more ease than before, made me a sign to give him some of it. I handed him the calabash, and the liquor pleasing his palate, he drank it off. There being a considerable quantity of it, he soon began to sing, and to move about from side to side in his seat upon my shoulders, and by degrees to loosen his legs from about me. Finding that he did not press me as before, I threw him upon the ground, where he lay without motion. I then took up a great stone and slew him.

I was extremely glad to be thus freed forever from this troublesome fellow. I now walked toward the beach, where I met the crew of a ship that had cast anchor, to take in water. They were surprised to see me, but more so at hearing the particulars of my adventures.

"You fell," said they, "into the hands of the old man of the sea, and are the first who ever escaped strangling by his malicious embraces. He never quitted those he had once made himself master of, till he had destroyed them, and he has made this island notorious by the number of men he has slain."

They carried me with them to the captain, who received me with great kindness. He put out again to sea, and after some days' sail we arrived at the harbor of a great city, the houses of which overhung the sea.

One of the merchants, who had taken me into his friendship, invited me to go along with him. He gave me a large sack, and having recommended me to some people of the town, who used to gather coconuts, desired them to take me with them.

"Go," said he, "follow them, and act as you see them do; but do not separate from them, otherwise you may endanger your life."

Having thus spoken, he gave me provisions for the journey, and I went with them.

We came to a thick forest of coco palms, very lofty, with trunks so smooth that it was not possible to climb to the branches that bore the fruit. When we entered the forest we saw a great number of apes of several sizes, who fled as soon as they perceived us, and climbed to the tops of the trees with amazing swiftness.

The merchants with whom I was gathered stones, and threw them at the apes on the trees. I did the same; and the apes, out of revenge, threw coconuts at us so fast, and with such gestures, as sufficiently testified their anger and resentment. We gathered up the coconuts, and from time to time threw stones to provoke the apes; so that by this stratagem we filled our bags with coconuts. I thus gradually collected as many coconuts as produced me a considerable sum.

Having laden our vessel with coconuts, we set sail, and passed by the islands where pepper grows in great plenty. From thence we went to the Isle of Comari, where the best species of wood of aloes grows. I exchanged my coconuts in those two islands for pepper and wood of aloes, and went with other merchants pearl fishing.

I hired divers, who brought me up some that were very large and pure. I embarked in a vessel that happily arrived at Bussorah; from thence I returned to Bagdad, where I realized vast sums from my pepper, wood of aloes, and pearls. I gave the tenth of my gains in alms, as I had done upon my return from my other voyages, and rested from my fatigues.

Sindbad here ordered one hundred sequins to be given to Hindbad, and requested him and the other guests to dine with him the next day, to hear the account of his sixth voyage.

THE SIXTH VOYAGE OF SINDBAD THE SAILOR

I know, my friends, that you will wish to hear how, after having been shipwrecked five times, and escaped so many dangers, I could resolve again to tempt fortune, and expose myself to new hardships. I am myself astonished at my conduct when I reflect upon it, and must certainly have been actuated by my destiny, from which none can escape. Be that as it may, after a year's rest I prepared for a sixth voyage, notwithstanding the entreaties of my kindred and friends, who did all in their power to dissuade me.

Instead of taking my way by the Persian Gulf I traveled once more through several provinces of Persia and the Indies, and arrived at a seaport. Here I embarked in a ship, the captain of which was bound on a long voyage, in which he and the pilot lost their course. Suddenly we saw the captain quit his rudder, uttering loud lamentations. He threw off his turban, pulled his beard, and beat his head like a madman. We asked him the reason; and he answered that we were in the most dangerous place in all the ocean.

"A rapid current carries the ship along with it, and we shall all perish in less than a quarter of an hour. Pray to God to deliver us from this peril. We cannot escape, if He do not take pity on us."

At these words he ordered the sails to be lowered; but all the ropes

broke, and the ship was carried by the
current to the foot of an inaccessible
mountain, where she struck and
went to pieces; yet in such a manner
that we saved our lives, our provisions,
and the best of our goods.

The mountain at the
foot of which we were
was covered with wrecks,
with a vast number of
human bones, and with
an incredible quantity
of goods and riches of
all kinds. These objects
served only to augment
our despair. In all other
places it is usual for rivers to
run from their channels into the sea;
but here a river of fresh water runs from the sea into a dark cavern,
whose entrance is very high and spacious. What is most remarkable in
this place is that the stones of the mountain are of crystal, rubies, or other
precious stones. Here is also a sort of fountain of pitch or bitumen, that
runs into the sea, which the fish swallow, and evacuate soon afterward,
turned into ambergris; and this the waves throw up on the beach in great
quantities. Trees also grow here, most of which are of wood of aloes,
equal in goodness to those of Comari.

To finish the description of this place, it is not possible for ships to get
off when once they approach within a certain distance. If they be driven
thither by a wind from the sea, the wind and the current impel them; and
if they come into it when a land wind blows, which might seem to favor
their getting out again, the height of the mountain stops the wind, and
occasions a calm, so that the force of the current carries them ashore; and

what completes the misfortune is, that there is no possibility of ascending the mountain, or of escaping by sea.

We continued upon the shore, at the foot of the mountain, in a state of despair, and expected death every day. On our first landing we had divided our provisions as equally as we could, and thus every one lived a longer or a shorter time, according to his temperance, and the use he made of his provisions.

I survived all my companions; and when I buried the last I had so little provisions remaining that I thought I could not long survive, and I dug a grave, resolving to lie down in it because there was no one left to pay me the last offices of respect. But it pleased God once more to take compassion on me, and put it in my mind to go to the bank of the river which ran into the great cavern. Considering its probable course with great attention, I said to myself, "This river, which runs thus underground, must somewhere have an issue. If I make a raft, and leave myself to the current, it will convey me to some inhabited country, or I shall perish. If I be drowned, I lose nothing, but only change one kind of death for another."

I immediately went to work upon large pieces of timber and cables, for I had a choice of them from the wrecks, and tied them together so strongly that I soon made a very solid raft. When I had finished, I loaded it with some chests of rubies, emeralds, ambergris, rock-crystal, and bales of rich stuffs.

Having balanced my cargo exactly, and fastened it well to the raft, I went on board with two oars that I had made, and leaving it to the course of the river, resigned myself to the will of God.

As soon as I entered the cavern I lost all light, and the stream carried me I knew not whither. Thus I floated on in perfect darkness, and once found the arch so low, that it very nearly touched my head, which made me cautious afterward to avoid the like danger. All this while I ate nothing but what was just necessary to support nature; yet, notwithstanding my frugality, all my provisions were spent. Then I became insensible. I

I went on board with two oars that I had made, and leaving it to the course of the river, resigned myself to the will of God.

cannot tell how long I continued so; but when I revived, I was surprised to find myself on an extensive plain on the brink of a river, where my raft was tied, amidst a great number of negroes.

I got up as soon as I saw them, and saluted them. They spoke to me, but I did not understand their language. I was so transported with joy that I knew not whether I was asleep or awake; but being persuaded that I was not asleep, I recited the following words in Arabic aloud: "Call upon the Almighty, He will help thee; thou needest not perplex thyself about anything else: shut thy eyes, and while thou art asleep, God will change thy bad fortune into good."

One of the negroes, who understood Arabic, hearing me speak thus, came toward me, and said, "Brother, be not surprised to see us; we are inhabitants of this country, and water our fields from this river, which comes out of the neighboring mountain. We saw your raft, and one of us swam into the river, and brought it hither, where we fastened it, as you see, until you should awake. Pray tell us your history. Whence did you come?"

I begged of them first to give me something to eat, and then I would satisfy their curiosity. They gave me several sorts of food, and when I had satisfied my hunger I related all that had befallen me, which they listened to with attentive surprise. As soon as I had finished, they told me, by the person who spoke Arabic and interpreted to them what I said, that I must go along with them, and tell my story to their king myself, it being too extraordinary to be related by any other than the person to whom the events had happened.

They immediately sent for a horse, and having helped me to mount, some of them walked before to show the way, while the rest took my raft and cargo and followed.

We marched till we came to the capital of Serendib, for it was on that island I had landed. The negroes presented me to their king; I approached his throne, and saluted him as I used to do the kings of the Indies; that is to say, I prostrated myself at his feet. The prince ordered me to rise, received me with an obliging air, and made me sit down near him.

I concealed nothing from the king, but related to him all that I have told you. At last my raft was brought in, and the bales opened in his presence: he admired the quantity of wood of aloes and ambergris; but, above all, the rubies and emeralds, for he had none in his treasury that equaled them.

Observing that he looked on my jewels with pleasure, and viewed the most remarkable among them, one after another, I fell prostrate at his feet, and took the liberty to say to him, "Sire, not only my person is at your majesty's service, but the cargo of the raft, and I would beg of you to dispose of it as your own."

He answered me with a smile, "Sindbad, I will take nothing of yours; far from lessening your wealth, I design to augment it, and will not let you quit my dominions without marks of my liberality."

He then charged one of his officers to take care of me, and ordered people to serve me at his own expense. The officer was very faithful in the execution of his commission, and caused all the goods to be carried to the lodgings provided for me.

I went every day at a set hour to make my court to the king, and spent the rest of my time in viewing the city, and what was most worthy of notice.

The capital of Serendib stands at the end of a fine valley, in the middle of the island, encompassed by high mountains. They are seen three days' sail off at sea. Rubies and several sorts of minerals abound. All kinds of rare plants and trees grow there, especially cedars and coconut. There is also a pearl fishery in the mouth of its principal river, and in some of its valleys are found diamonds. I made, by way of devotion, a pilgrimage to the place where Adam was confined after his banishment from Paradise, and had the curiosity to go to the top of the mountain.

When I returned to the city I prayed the king to allow me to return to my own country, and he granted me permission in the most obliging and honorable manner. He would force a rich present upon me; and at the same time he charged me with a letter for the Commander of the

Faithful, our sovereign, saying to me, "I pray you give this present from me, and this letter, to the Caliph Haroun al Raschid, and assure him of my friendship."

The letter from the King of Serendib was written on the skin of a certain animal of great value, very scarce, and of a yellowish color. The characters of this letter were of azure, and the contents as follows:

"The King of the Indies, before whom march one hundred elephants, who lives in a palace that shines with one hundred thousand rubies, and who has in his treasury twenty thousand crowns enriched with diamonds, to Caliph Haroun al Raschid.

"Though the present we send you be inconsiderable, receive it, however, as a brother and a friend, in consideration of the hearty friendship which we bear for you, and of which we are willing to give you proof. We desire the same part in your friendship, considering that we believe it to be our merit, as we are both kings. We send you this letter as from one brother to another. Farewell."

The present consisted (1) of one single ruby made into a cup, about half a foot high, an inch thick, and filled with round pearls of half a dram each. (2) The skin of a serpent, whose scales were as bright as an ordinary piece of gold, and had the virtue to preserve from sickness those who lay upon it. (3) Fifty thousand drams of the best wood of aloes, with thirty grains of camphor as big as pistachios. And (4) a female slave of great beauty, whose robe was covered with jewels.

The ship set sail, and after a very successful

navigation we landed at Bussorah, and from thence I went to the city of Bagdad, where the first thing I did was to acquit myself of my commission.

I took the King of Serendib's letter, and went to present myself at the gate of the Commander of the Faithful, and was immediately conducted to the throne of the caliph. I made my obeisance, and presented the letter and gift. When he had read what the King of Serendib wrote to him, he asked me if that prince were really so rich and potent as he represented himself in his letter. I prostrated myself a second time, and rising again, said, "Commander of the Faithful, I can assure your majesty he doth not exceed the truth. I bear him witness. Nothing is more worthy of admiration than the magnificence of his palace. When the prince appears in public, he has a throne fixed on the back of an elephant, and rides betwixt two ranks of his ministers, favorites, and other people of his court. Before him, upon the same elephant, an officer carries a golden lance in his hand; and behind him there is another, who stands with a rod of gold, on the top of which is an emerald, half a foot long and an inch thick. He is attended by a guard of one thousand men, clad in cloth of gold and silk, and mounted on elephants richly caparisoned. The officer who is before him on the same elephant, cries from time to time, with a loud voice, 'Behold the great monarch, the potent and redoubtable Sultan of the Indies, the monarch greater than Solomon, and the powerful Maharaja.' After he has pronounced those words, the officer behind the throne cries, in his turn, 'This monarch, so great and so powerful, must die, must die, must die.' And the officer before replies, 'Praise alone be to Him who liveth forever and ever.'"

The caliph was much pleased with my account, and sent me home with a rich present.

Here Sindbad commanded another hundred sequins to be paid to Hindbad, and begged his return on the morrow to hear his seventh and last voyage.

THE SEVENTH AND LAST VOYAGE OF SINDBAD THE SAILOR

On my return home from my sixth voyage I had entirely given up all thoughts of again going to sea; for, besides that my age now required rest, I was resolved no more to expose myself to such risks as I had encountered, so that I thought of nothing but to pass the rest of my days in tranquillity. One day, however, an officer of the caliph's inquired for me.

"The caliph," said he, "has sent me to tell you that he must speak with you."

I followed the officer to the palace, where, being presented to the caliph, I saluted him by prostrating myself at his feet.

"Sindbad," said he to me, "I stand in need of your service; you must carry my answer and present to the King of Serendib."

This command of the caliph was to me like a clap of thunder. "Commander of the Faithful," I replied, "I am ready to do whatever your majesty shall think fit to command; but I beseech you most humbly to consider what I have undergone. I have also made a vow never to leave Bagdad."

Perceiving that the caliph insisted upon my compliance, I submitted, and told him that I was willing to obey. He was very well pleased, and ordered me one thousand sequins for the expenses of my journey.

I prepared for my departure in a few days. As soon as the caliph's letter and present were delivered to me, I went to Bussorah, where I embarked, and had a very prosperous voyage. Having arrived at the Isle of Serendib, I was conducted to the palace with much pomp, when I prostrated myself on the ground before the king.

"Sindbad," said the king, "you are welcome. I have many times thought of you; I bless the day on which I see you once more."

I made my compliments to him, and thanked him for his kindness, and delivered the gifts from my august master.

The caliph's letter was as follows:

"Greeting, in the name of the Sovereign Guide of the Right Way, from the servant of God, Haroun al Raschid, whom God hath set in the place of vice-regent to His Prophet, after his ancestors of happy memory, to the potent and esteemed Raja of Serendib.

"We received your letter with joy, and send you this from our imperial residence, the garden of superior wits. We hope, when you look upon it, you will perceive our good intention, and be pleased with it. Farewell."

The caliph's present was a complete suit of cloth of gold, valued at one thousand sequins; fifty robes of rich stuff, a hundred of white cloth, the finest of Cairo, Suez, and Alexandria; a vessel of agate, more broad than deep, an inch thick, and half a foot wide, the bottom of which represented in bas-relief a man with one knee on the ground, who held a bow and an arrow, ready to discharge at a lion. He sent him also a rich tablet, which, according to tradition, belonged to the great Solomon.

The King of Serendib was highly gratified at the caliph's acknowledgment of his friendship. A little time after this audience I solicited leave to depart, and with much difficulty obtained it. The king, when he dismissed me, made me a very considerable present. I embarked immediately to return to Bagdad, but had not the good fortune to arrive there so speedily as I had hoped. God ordered it otherwise.

Three or four days after my departure we were attacked by pirates, who easily seized upon our ship because it was not a vessel of war. Some of the crew offered resistance, which cost them their lives. But for myself and the rest, who were not so imprudent, the pirates saved us, and carried us into a remote island, where they sold us.

I fell into the hands of a rich merchant, who, as soon as he bought me, took me to his house, treated me well, and clad me handsomely as a slave. Some days after, he asked me if I understood any trade. I answered that I was no mechanic, but a merchant, and that the pirates who sold me had robbed me of all I possessed.

"Tell me," replied he, "can you shoot with a bow?"

I answered, that the bow was one of my exercises in my youth. He gave me a bow and arrows, and taking me behind him on an elephant, carried me to a thick forest some leagues from the town. We penetrated a great way into the wood, and when he thought fit to stop, he bade me alight; then showing me a great tree, "Climb up that," said he, "and shoot at the elephants as you see them pass by, for there is a prodigious number of them in this forest, and if any of them fall come and give me notice." Having spoken thus, he left me victuals, and returned to the town, and I continued upon the tree all night.

I saw no elephant during the night, but next morning, at break of day, I perceived a great number. I shot several arrows among them; and at last one of the elephants fell, when the rest retired immediately, and left me at liberty to go and acquaint my patron with my success. When I had informed him, he commended my dexterity, and caressed me highly. We went afterward together to the forest, where we dug a hole for the elephant, my patron designing to return when it was rotten, and take his teeth to trade with.

I continued this employment for two months. One morning, as I looked for the elephants, I perceived with extreme amazement that, instead of passing by me across the forest as usual, they stopped, and came to me with a horrible noise, and in such numbers that the plain was covered and shook under them. They surrounded the tree in which I was concealed, with their trunks uplifted, and all fixed their eyes upon me. At this alarming spectacle I continued immovable, and was so much terrified that my bow and arrows fell out of my hand.

My fears were not without cause; for after the elephants had stared upon me some time, one of the largest of them put his trunk round the foot of the tree, plucked it up, and threw it on the ground. I fell with the tree, and the elephant, taking me up with his trunk, laid me on his back, where I sat more like one dead than alive, with my quiver on my shoulder. He put himself at the head of the rest, who followed him in line one after the other, carried me a considerable way, then laid me down on the ground, and retired with all his companions. After having lain some time, and seeing the elephants gone, I got up, and found I was upon a long and broad hill, almost covered with the bones and teeth of elephants. I doubted not but that this was the burial place of the elephants, and that they carried me thither on purpose to tell me that I should forbear to kill them, as now I knew where to get their teeth without inflicting injury on them. I did not stay on the hill, but turned toward the city; and after having traveled a day and a night, I came to my patron.

As soon as my patron saw me, "Ah, poor Sindbad," exclaimed he, "I was in great trouble to know what was become of you. I have been to the forest, where I found a tree newly pulled up, and your bow and arrows on the ground, and I despaired of ever seeing you more. Pray tell me what befell you."

I satisfied his curiosity, and we both of us set out next morning to the hill. We loaded the elephant which had carried us with as many teeth as he could bear; and when we were returned, my master thus addressed me: "Hear now what I shall tell you. The elephants of our forest have every year killed us a great many slaves, whom we sent to seek ivory. For all the cautions we could give them, these crafty animals destroyed them one time or other. God has delivered you from their fury, and has bestowed that favor upon you only. It is a sign that He loves you, and has

261

some use for your service in the world. You have procured me incredible wealth; and now our whole city is enriched by your means, without any more exposing the lives of our slaves. After such a discovery, I can treat you no more as a slave, but as a brother. God bless you with all happiness and prosperity. I henceforth give you your liberty; I will also give you riches."

To this I replied, "Master, God preserve you. I desire no other reward for the service I had the good fortune to do to you and your city, but leave to return to my own country."

"Very well," said he, "the monsoon will in a little time bring ships for ivory. I will then send you home."

I stayed with him while waiting for the monsoon; and during that time we made so many journeys to the hill that we filled all our warehouses with ivory. The other merchants who traded in it did the same; for my master made them partakers of his good fortune.

The ships arrived at last, and my master himself having made choice of the ship wherein I was to embark, loaded half of it with ivory on my account, laid in provisions in abundance for my passage, and besides obliged me to accept a present of some curiosities of the country of great value. After I had returned him a thousand thanks for all his favors, I went aboard.

We stopped at some islands to take in fresh provisions. Our vessel being come to a port on the mainland in the Indies, we touched there, and not being willing to venture by sea to Bussorah, I landed my portion of the ivory, resolving to proceed on my journey by land. I realized vast sums by my ivory, bought several rarities, which I intended for presents, and when my equipage was ready, set out in company with a large caravan of merchants. I was a long time on the journey, and suffered much, but was happy in thinking that I had nothing to fear from the seas, from pirates, from serpents, or from the other perils to which I had been exposed.

I at last arrived safe at Bagdad, and immediately waited upon the caliph, to give him an account of my embassy. He loaded me with honors and rich presents, and I have ever since devoted myself to my family, kindred, and friends.

Sindbad here finished the relation of his seventh and last voyage, and then addressing himself to Hindbad, "Well, friend," said he, "did you ever hear of any person that suffered so much as I have done? Is it not reasonable that, after all this, I should enjoy a quiet and pleasant life?"

As he said these words, Hindbad kissed his hand, and said, "Sir, my afflictions are not to be compared with yours. You not only deserve a quiet life but are worthy of all the riches you possess, since you make so good a use of them. May you live happily for a long time."

Sindbad ordered him to be paid another hundred sequins, and told him to give up carrying burdens as a porter, and to eat henceforth at his table, for he wished that he should all his life have reason to remember that he henceforth had a friend in Sindbad the sailor.

THE CONCLUSION OF THE STORY OF
THE SULTAN AND HIS VOW

The Sultan of the Indies could not help admiring the prodigious and inexhaustible memory of the sultana, his wife, who had entertained him for a thousand and one nights with such a variety of interesting stories. His temper was softened and his prejudices removed. He was not only convinced of the merit and great wisdom of the sultana, but he remembered with what courage she had offered to be his wife, regardless of the death to which she knew she exposed herself, and which so many preceding sultanas had suffered.

These considerations and her many other good qualities induced him at last to say to her: "I confess, lovely Sheherazade, that you have appeased my anger. I freely renounce the oath I had imposed on myself, and I will no more sacrifice any damsels to my unjust resentment."

The sultana cast herself at his feet and tenderly embraced them to show her gratitude; and the sultan then went to announce his decision to the grand vizier. Heralds soon made the news known throughout the city and couriers were dispatched to proclaim the tidings in the other portions of the realm, even to the remotest towns and provinces. Everywhere there was rejoicing, and the sultan and his beautiful consort gained the universal applause and blessings of all the people of the extensive empire of the Indies.